THE PRIDE OF FARROWLINE

BOOK FOUR: THE PACK OF FARROWLINE SERIES

A catalogue record for this work is available from the National Library of Australia

https://www.nla.gov.au/collections

Title:	The Pride of Farrowline
Series:	The Pack of Farrowline Series
Volume:	Book IV
Author:	Rojo, A L
ISBNs:	9780648869016 (paperback)
	9780648869023 (ebook – epub)
	9780648869030 (ebook – Kindle)
Subjects:	FICTION: Romance/Paranormal/Shifters; Fantasy/Romance; Romance/Fantasy; Fantasy/General

Cover concept by A L Rojo
Cover design and layout by Ally Mosher at allymosher.com
Cover images used under licence from Adobe Stock and Envato Elements
Interior Formatting by Katelyn at Design by Kage

THE PRIDE OF FARROWLINE

BOOK FOUR: THE PACK OF FARROWLINE SERIES

A L ROJO

ALSO BY A L ROJO

The Heart of Farrowline

The Power of Farrowline

The Strength of Farrowline

The Pride of Farrowline

Author Note

The Pride of Farrowline contains themes of substance abuse, murder, violence, depression and adult content.

Please head to www.alrojo.com.au for all content warnings and information.

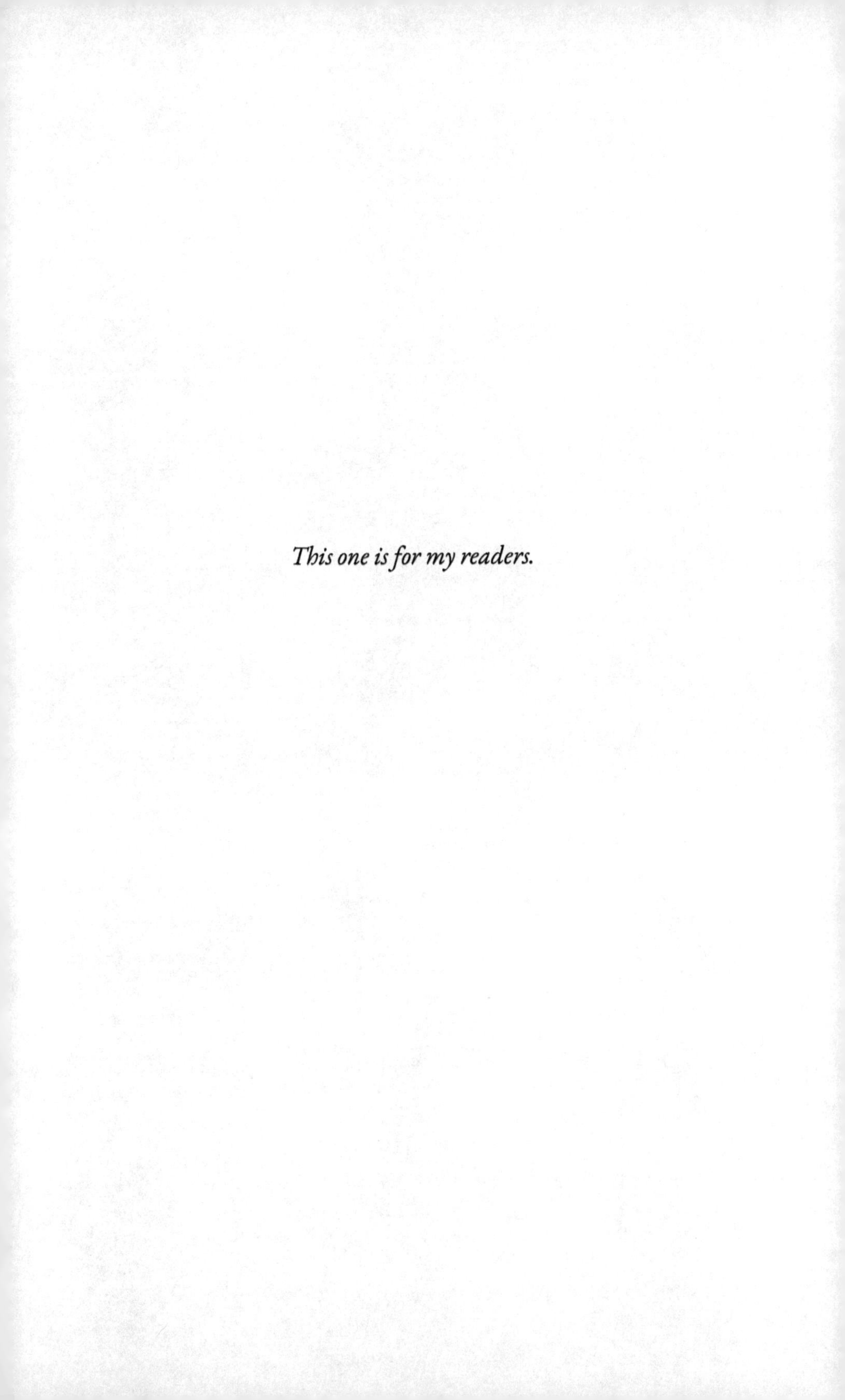

This one is for my readers.

A Tracker is born, not made.

Chapter One

Chest heaving, heart pounding, I slip through the trees on silent paws. Controlling my breathing is effortless. It's a skill that I was born with. A skill honed over the years as my wolf has grown into her ability. An ability that I worked out at a young age not many wolf shifters have.

Frankly, I haven't met another like me. Which is hard and only made worse with the frightening changes I've been experiencing lately.

But I push all my fears and worries aside as I stop and draw in the scents around me. The forest is eerily quiet. The dark adding to the thrill of the hunt. I have a job right now and my beast loves it.

As the smells of Farrowline fill my senses, I quickly process each individual strand. The ones I expect out here in deep territory to the new ones that let my wolf know what kinds of animals are out here in the wilderness of the forest. It takes me only a heartbeat to pick up the one I'm looking for. Lips peeling back, my wolf growls and bounds forward.

Running, I dodge debris littering the forest floor and jump over a fallen tree trunk. Chuckling in my mind, I veer left, finding it amusing that they have tried to outwit me. That they believe they can hide from a shifter like me.

The forest blurs by and I know exactly where the male is. Not stopping, I jump over the large boulder soundlessly and slam into the body trying to hide. The male howls and rolls, taking me with him. We spin through the forest and down a short hill. Teeth snapping, legs kicking we both try to get the upper hand.

A deep grunt comes from him as we land heavily. I bare my teeth as I look down at the large blonde wolf who I know has let me win and be on top so that I didn't get hurt. We are all tangled limbs and muddled fur, but it's exhilarating and I can see the humour in his blue eyes. Tapping me with his muzzle, I draw in the scent of sandalwood, citrus and malt and relax as the mighty male finds his feet and stands over me. He does a quick check that I'm okay, which I allow as I lie happily on the forest floor being looked after by such a dominant male.

Stepping away when he's satisfied, I jump up and shake out my limbs. My fur shifts as I pull on the human side of my soul and stand on two legs and watch as Oliver does the same thing.

Everyone says that Oliver Tyler looks like a Norse warrior with his blue eyes and those long, lush locks of his. He ties it up like he's a Viking and I love teasing him about it especially because he uses more product than I do. I love him, full stop. He's just solid strength. Oliver was always that male that I would make sure I sat next to, always asked for his advice. The first time I felt my wolf, I found Oliver and shared my fear and joy. When he was an adolescent and I was a younger pup, I'd annoy him constantly by showing up wherever he was, just so that some of his 'coolness' could rub off on me. I think I've been following him around my entire life. He's probably the quietest out of the Circle wolves of Farrowline, the leaders of our Pack, if any of them can be called quiet. But there's no denying that he's the most protective, especially of the females. He can be really annoying in his rules, but he'd die for you. His love is endless.

The big, hunky male runs his hands through his unbound hair that's now covered in dirt.

Glaring at the smile on my face, Oliver doesn't seem too impressed that I'm here. Which just adds to my growing grin.

'Jax is dead,' he grumbles and I can't hold in the burst of laughter. It fills the forest and has me forget for a moment about the growing lump of anxiety that has grown and has now settled against my chest for months now.

Growling a very unimpressed sound, Oliver starts to stomp back in the direction of inner territory. He isn't really angry, mostly he's just annoyed that he lost. I know because he stills looks behind his shoulder to make sure I'm following as we move through the trees and stops to offer his hand when the ground becomes tricky despite the fact that I'm perfectly capable.

I take it, loving his attention, and knowing he can't help himself.

He's a dominant male.

Oliver keeps uttering nonsense under his breath as we powerwalk toward where Jax is. The group in the clearing reserved for the dominants of Farrowline are all lounging around on the plush grass which just makes Oliver grow in size.

Chest puffed out, he storms from the tree line to the six wolf shifters in the clearing. This space of territory is covered in rich, soft grass. There's a building to the right that has all the amenities and rooms that any of the dominants who patrol and protect our lands can use. It's very extravagant, but that's Tobias and the Circle for you. No expense is ever too much for the Pack.

Pack is Pack after all.

I follow slowly behind and bask in the cheering that erupts amongst the 'blue' team as they see me with the leader of the 'red' team. There are many shouts of 'Go Gilly' and 'Gilly is a Queen', before Oliver growls deeply, shutting everyone up instantly.

Well, all except Jax.

Jax's response is to just laugh louder. Stirring up the serious male now huffing down at him.

Jaxon Layland is a monster of a male. He is our Gamma, the largest and strongest after the Alpha and Beta. In a fight, he'll always win, but it's not his ability to protect Pack that makes him one of the most loved members of Farrowline. No, he's loved because he gives us everything. He's kind and caring and selfless and funny and brilliant.

Hands on hips, Oliver unleashes his anger. The two younger wolf shifters behind Jax shuffle back to be closer to his body and I cover my giggle with my hand.

'We had one rule Jax! One!'

'Did we?' Jax innocently exclaims, rubbing his chin as if trying to remember the rule we all heard at the Pack barbeque last night when this silly training game was created between Jax and Oliver.

'Yes! Using Gilly is cheating!' Oliver points in my direction and Jax's gaze follows, he winks one of his golden eyes at me behind Oliver's back.

Biting my bottom lip, I clear my throat to get control over myself.

'Your entire team is here. Sitting on their arses while mine are out in the forest trying to find you all.'

Putting his hands up, Jax shrugs. 'Hey, all I heard was that the winning team is the one that finds the leader first.' Waving in Oliver's direction, Jax looks mighty smug with himself as he lounges back in the grass. 'And we found you. The leader. We win. So pay up.'

Mouth falling open, Oliver goes to rebut his statement, stops, frowns, growls loudly, and says, 'shit! Fucking hell, Jax. You're such an arsehole.' Digging into his back pocket, Oliver pulls out a wad of cash and throws it beside where the arrogant Gamma sits like the king of the fucking grass patch.

Shaking my head, I move toward the group of intimidated youngsters who've just watched the exchange in awe and a little fear and step over Jax's legs. He's too busy still arguing with Oliver who is now telling him that from this day forth, he will be the one to give instructions to any training events. I'm a little shocked that Oliver didn't realise Jax was playing him last night. We all knew it. Not that we knew what his plan actually was and frankly I forgot that they had set this training game up. Getting dressed in my room only about an hour ago, the oversized male stormed into my parent's den, scaring my mum half to death, kissed her endlessly in apology and begged and pleaded for me to help. It didn't take me long to see his end game and then agreed instantly.

Sweeping up the money that is more than the hundred I was promised for being part of this scheme, I start to move away thinking I'm going to get away with it. Until a hand snakes around my ankle, locking me in place. The two are still going at it and I look over my shoulder at my Gamma who flicks those yellow eyes to my face. Narrowing his gaze, Jax asks, 'You going with the others to the nightclub tonight for Rita's birthday?'

Nodding, because talking about what I'm doing tonight might make me rethink my decision to go out with everyone. I wait to see what he's going to do and if he'll let me take the money. It's not that I don't want to go. It's just not so much fun anymore.

A shiver runs through my body at the thought of being in the crowded nightclub, Underworld, with so many bodies.

Releasing me, Jax says, 'have a good time. Buy a drink for everyone from me.'

Smiling wide, I promise I will and stop before running back to den to finish getting dressed when Oliver steps towards me. Still mumbling that now he has to go find the young adolescent wolves in his team, he hands me a few more hundred-dollar bills and tells me to have a good night and to call if we need anything. My heart swells and I can just imagine how everyone is going to react to our night being financed now by the two very rich leaders of Pack.

'I will,' I promise and rise up on my toes to kiss his cheek and feeling bad for my part in this, I say, 'two of your wolves are about a few hundred meters that way.' I point in the direction I can smell them. 'And the other four are near the river.' I indicate to the spot they're hiding, deep in the forest. I sigh inwardly at the scrutinising look Oliver throws me before he covers it up and thanks me with a kiss on the forehead.

Even Jax stopped laughing when I just told them that I can pinpoint others even from this distance. I can almost hear their thoughts of how I'm good but I shouldn't be that good.

Ignoring it, because frankly it is fucking weird that I can smell the wolves hiding that far in the forest, I hurry off trying to keep my panic at bay.

Knowing when I'm out of earshot, I lean up against one of the large trees and allow myself a moment to fall apart.

Chapter Two

Gripping my chest, I try to take deep breaths. Head resting on the hard, rough surface of the living trunk, I close my eyes and try to not fall into a pit of anxiety.

Like all wolves, I can smell and hear and sense things. But for someone like me – for a tracker— I take that one step...no, a bloody leap forward in what I can pick up with the simple power of my nose.

I hate it.

I've been told it's a gift from the moment my Pack realised what I could do. Even before my wolf came of age and I shifted for the first time, I was able to pick up on smells and the tiniest of scents. That was accelerated tenfold by the wolf in my blood the moment she could take control and I haven't told anyone this secret, mostly in fear of how hard it's making my life, but since exchanging the blood ritual with Ridley and Tobias—my Alpha's, and becoming a Circle wolf of Farrowline, it has gotten so much stronger. And so much harder to manage.

I don't see it as a gift, despite being told repeatedly that it is. All it does is make it impossible for me to be around others for too long now. Drinking is one of the things that I have found that helps 'dampen' my senses. I know it's not healthy and it is why I keep making bad choices.

I haven't really done much with my 'gift' anyway. Growing up it was patrols and finding missing packmates, mostly other adolescents who would find themselves lost in the need to give into the wolf and run for days without realising where they're going. It happens to most of us. Never me though, the few times my wolf took control and I stayed wolf for days I always knew where I was and how to get back to Pack.

With Farrowline's recent issues with loners—Packless nomads who've banded together under a makeshift 'alpha' Cade Fletton— I've been pushing my abilities further than I ever have in my life. There have been a few intruders testing boundaries since the last attack that saw the loners lose miserably, thanks to one of our newest packmates.

Dad told me recently that he thinks I'll have more to learn about my tracker abilities. They don't realise that I can barely sit in a closed room with others without wanting to rip my nose from my face. I've always been able to distract myself by doing the things that I love. Partying and hanging out with my friends is one.

Until recently that is.

I'm fully aware that everyone thinks my recent behaviour is because of what Jay did to me, which in part it is, but I let them believe it is because I'm afraid that something might be wrong.

I don't want to be different. I don't want to be what I am.

I keep getting told that time will heal my broken heart like what Jay Houston did is a small crack. They don't see that he tore out the organ, stomped on it with a simple text message and shattered it into the universe. It's been months and it still fucking hurts. And it doesn't help that I can't escape him or his mate. Having them stay with Farrowline sucks. They're everywhere I look. Holding hands, kissing, loving each other and all the while I have to pretend that I'm over it. That I didn't lose one of my best friends and my heart at the same time.

I scent Kurt and Gene, my two best friends in the distance and get control over myself. Plastering a smile on my face just as they come from the forest demanding to know what I'm doing, I pretend that I'm ready to go partying.

With each thundering beat of the bass filling my body, I grind up against the muscular thigh between my legs and throw back the burning liquid from the glass bottle in my hand. I have no idea who the cheetah is that's groping me not so subtly on the dance floor and frankly I couldn't give a shit. The world has that blissful hazy fog that comes with being absolutely wasted and I no longer have that bitchy inner voice in my head commentating my life and highlighting everything I've been doing wrong lately.

She sucks! But lucky for me, alcohol works to shut her the fuck up. It also makes it bearable for me to be in this disgustingly, overpowering environment. My nostrils burn with the odours in the air. So I drink.

Not that alcohol works as well for a shifter as it does for a human, which is a bummer, but hey, means I just have to drink more—and there's nothing wrong with that.

I take another mouthful of liquor and force myself to swallow it down.

After pushing away the fuzzy face of the male who tries to slam his lips on mine again, I shrug and turn away when he growls some rude comment about me being a 'tease slut'—which makes no sense even in my drunk state— and leaves to find what he's looking for.

With the absence of the solid body, I blink away the fog and sober up too quickly. The dancefloor is littered with partygoers. The flashing lights coming from the DJ stand illuminates the crowd and the sweaty exchange of body fluids happening around me. I have to swallow the bile building in my throat at the stench of it. It's repulsive. There are times when my extra-sensitive, tracker nose shits me.

Pouring the last few drops of bourbon down my throat, I stare miserably at the empty bottle in my hand and sigh. Having scented the shifter who bumps into my back before he even started making his way towards me, I nod at Gene when the very drunk male informs me that we're leaving. I have no idea why he's laughing so much and frankly I don't care. I can smell the booze and the other male on his skin. Shaking my head to expel the lust now up my nose, I watch the others move through the crowd toward the exit of the nightclub.

I shrug and take Gene's hand when he becomes distracted by a very pretty random female twirling her neon skirt round and round. I don't question what the fuck she is doing, having clearly picked up on the smell of the drug permeating from her sweat and pull Gene through the nightclub and out to the busy street. Not shocked to see the long line of partygoers still trying to get into the club despite the early morning, I all but throw the now semi-unconscious male into the back of the limousine and hop in.

The fun doesn't stop and I take the flute of champagne handed to me and down it before the happy birthday cheers even begin. I forget who we are celebrating and I just take the bottle when Kurt starts on a very funny story of the last event we all partied. I know I should feel bad for not caring. They're my family. My Pack. But I just can't get out of my own head.

CHAPTER THREE

'Gilly, sweetheart, you need to get up, dear.'

Groaning, I roll over and get pushed rather forcefully back onto my side. Which just gets me sworn at by the other male in my bed.

'Gilly,' my mum sings in her too bright and too cheerful for this time-of-day voice.

'Mum,' I manage to grumble through my very dry throat, 'please, what time is it?' It has to be super early in the morning because I only felt like I just closed my eyes.

'It's nine o'clock. You have to meet the Circle in half an hour and look at this mess.' The noises of shuffling and rummaging has me crack one eye open. I glare at the female fussing around sorting through the dirty laundry on the floor of my bedroom. Unable to keep my burning eye open, I try desperately to ignore the muttering female and go back to sleep. But when Tasha Sommers gets on a topic, there is nowhere to hide.

'Mummy Tasha, please,' Kurt pleads from beside me, his face is half in the pillow and I know he's in just as much pain as I am. 'It's too early.'

'It is not early...' The lectures begins. On and on she goes about our behaviour and how much she has already done while we were sleeping.

Fuck me.

Covering my ears as my mother's voices hitches up a notch when she begins to tell us that we are too old for this nonsense, I shove Kurt who should know better than to poke my mum. That's when Gene practically pushes me from under the sheets with a growl to listen to my elder and also, 'get the fuck up so she'll leave us to sleep.'

Hitting the ground with a thump, I roll over and blink up at the white ceiling and raise my arm when my mother ends her sermon of how a daughter should behave. 'Please, I hear you Mum.'

I cover my chuckle with a fake cough when Kurt mumbles into the pillow that, 'the entire fucking Pack did,' and cop a very impressive scowl from the female who owns my soul through and through. Gripping the shoe now in her hand, Tasha pegs the now missile expertly and whacks Kurt in the head. The sound it makes is hilarious and when the shit-stirring male raises his head slowly and gifts my mum one of his famous grins, she shakes her head and chuckles.

'Love you, Mummy Tasha,' Kurt utters before falling back to sleep. Gene shuffles to be closer to the now snoring male with a simple, 'love you mummy.'

'You're all banned from my den,' Tasha demands while calling us all kinds of nonsense words under her breath. With her arms full of our laundry, she leaves the room. The smirk on her face lessens the threat and if anyone had spoken to my mum the way Kurt just did I'd rip their fucking throats out with my teeth, but I know my best friends love my mum as much as I do. They joke around with each other but whenever she needs a helping hand, Kurt and Gene are the first ones here to assist. And my mum knows it and it is why I hear the fridge being opened in the kitchen down the hall, the pots being clanked around and then after a few minutes, the smell of frying bacon wafting through our den.

Pushing myself up off the floor, I fumble around to find some pants and stumble out of the room before I'm late for my Circle meeting.

Blinking up at the clear bright blue sky, I stay focused on what's happening around me and not the overwhelming scents in the air. Laying on the scratchy grass in the middle of the circle of bodies feels comfortable—stinky, but comfortable. With two mugs of coffee in my system thanks to Jax who took one look at me when I stumbled into his den, huffed, and handed me the hot brew and a bacon and egg muffin and barked at me to eat.

I'm now wide awake and way too sober.

Easton is presenting something that I probably should be listening to.

'We have to be aware of how much change the Pack has been through and how much the past year has impacted everyone. There's a great deal of anxiety around the Pack.'

Easton Silas, the sexy male, with his lean, muscular body and that manicured hot as hell, short beard, is our Pack Enforcer for a reason. He's newly mated and I swear looks like he's on top of the world. Unlike the others, Easton came to Farrowline when I was around fourteen years old. His presence caused quite a stir with us younger ones. Mostly because he's hot. As is the human female he's happily mated to. Adalee is such a blessing and not just because she can cook. And I mean— C.O.O.K. She has only been in Pack for a few weeks and is already an integral part of our everyday lives. I love just going to her den and sitting on the barstool and chatting to her. She's sweet and caring and while she has so much going on personally, she always has time to listen.

Lounging on the single wicker seat, Easton's gaze flicks to us all as he gives his report before landing on our Alpha. Tobias Farrow. The centre of our Pack.

He is larger than life and to me, he's a superstar. It never matters what time of day it is, if I need him, he's there. He protects and cares for us all no matter what. It helps also that he's super gorgeous, and honestly his muscles have muscles, not that I see him in that way, I have eyes obviously, but he's my Alpha. He is my heart.

'I know,' Tobias states simply. His arm is draped over the small female beside him who is curled up on the long outdoor lounge eating through a bag of crisps with Oliver. He sits patiently beside the female picking the best pieces out of the bag he's now holding. Ridley looks so tiny and vulnerable between the two mighty males and I have no control over the small smile that forms on my lips because the Luna of Farrowline is anything but. She is the light in my darkness of uncertainty. With her dark red hair, athletic build and her foul mouth, she keeps me grounded just with her presence, she is one of the things that has changed around here. When Tobias and Ridley mated, it altered Farrowline in a fundamental way. The entire Pack felt it. It was like we have all become more grounded and secure together. Tobias's happiness has been infectious and we have probably the largest group of pregnant females in the Pack in years, despite the issues we're having with loners.

Loners, the thought of them makes me cringe. They're the pack-less nomads who continue to test our boundaries. We've recently learnt that there are packs out there who may be using them as paid muscle.

Only one pack comes to mind though.

Silasline.

Chapter Four

Easton is right, the Pack has been through a lot lately, but Farrowline has gained so much with the new females who have joined us.

One of those females appears from the trees in that moment and I turn my head to see the shifter as she greets everyone with a nod that screams at all of us to stop looking at her. That's until her eyes lock on the male sitting on the chair to my left. That's when her entire body seems to relax. I marvel at the look that creeps over her face and turn to look at my Beta.

Dominic Knox is magnificent, in every sense of the word. He is over-protective and can be a real grump, but he is magic in the way he looks after everyone and feeling the love radiating off him as he stares at his mate is beautiful and heart shattering at the same time. Envy is not in my nature but fuck, I envy their love and happiness.

Delfina steps one of her short, toned legs over me but she falters for a moment and I look up and smile at the way she is beaming down at me. Her eyes are identical to Easton, they're siblings after all, and her colourful hair falls around her shoulders and tickles my face as she bends to practically sit on my stomach. She plants a quick, firm kiss on my forehead. Delfina smells like fire and hazelnuts and something else that tells me enough about what her and Dominic got up to this morning, which is totally gross, but makes me extra happy for them. Scents change if you are strong enough to pick them up. Most of the Circle would be able to. Everyone has certain distinct scent signatures with ones that come and go depending on what they have been doing or what they are feeling.

Surrounded by the warmth and power of a wolf shifter like Delfina Knox makes the beast under my skin roll around in glee. She doesn't say a word and rises on those powerful legs to step over me and fall into the male who has opened his arms for her.

Her simple touch and affection released the tension in my shoulders and I relax into the hard ground further. There are moments when my tracker senses calm, certain smells help as they fill my soul and calm my beast. Delfina surprisingly is one of them. Oliver is too.

'We just need to continue doing what we can. It's all our responsibility to make sure that everyone have rests, especially our dominants. When do we expect to hear back from Asher Silas?' Jax asks, breaking my train of thought.

Sharing the same long seat as Dom, Jax watches as Delfina gets comfortable on our Beta's lap with a funny look on his face. He randomly grabs at Delfina's leg and brings it up to his lap. She winces and I watch as Jax keeps talking about the last time the loners tested us and failed miserably, thanks to Delfina, and removes her black boot. Dominic throws the large male a look of thanks as Jax begins to massage and roll Delfina's ankle. She hurt herself yesterday training some of the adolescents on patrol. Her eyes roll back in pleasure.

'I haven't spoken to him since our conversation a few weeks back when we decided not to meet up with them and you all went to Port Foldon to be with Adalee instead. Asher Silas made it clear that Silasline had nothing to do with the attacks on Adalee. Loners are just loners. Maybe we were wrong about thinking Silasline had anything to do with the way they have been targeting Farrowline,' Liam Weston declares, he's the 'father' of the Pack, or so Kurt and Gene like to call him—sometimes to his face. Mostly when Liam has finished on one of his dad-talks about behaviour. Not that it seems to bother the very serious male.

Liam has recently found out that he'll be a father for the second time. Mated to Tobias's youngest sister, Sara, Liam is the calm voice of reason on most of our decisions and whilst he can come across as a bit harsh, he'll do anything for you and he has for me on so many occasions over my life.

'I still have my concerns,' Oliver states and pours the crumbs of his chip packet into Ridley's waiting hand. 'For now, why don't we keep the dominants on extra patrols but change the rotations schedule. I'm sure it's not going to last. Farrowline is strong. We can get through anything together. Adalee is doing very well in Pack too. She is settled, right, Easton?'

'Yeah, she's doing well. It'll take her a while to find the confidence to go to classes at the university again on her own after the loner attack but I won't let her out of my sight.' The memory of how Adalee was attacked and threatened on the campus of Sylo University where she is a student of literature makes me so mad. She was fine, Delfina saved the day, which is kinda her thing, but it still gets my blood boiling.

'He would've been dealt with if you all let me hunt him. I had his scent.' I don't mean to sound petulant. Can't help it really. I wanted to rip that fuckers head off but Oliver and Jax refused to let me hunt the loner that touched Adalee.

'Gilly, not helping,' Tobias says firmly and I shut my mouth and huff like an adolescent. My wolf grumbles under her breath. It was almost painful the days after the attack to not follow the scent and my instinct to hunt.

'If you or Adalee need any help, brother. You only have to ask,' Jax reassures Easton, changing the focus.

I instantly calm. I don't envy Easton all that he has to think about, it was his mate that was targeted. It's safe to say that since coming back from her hometown of Port Foldon for the memorial for her brother, Adalee has been different. It was emotional and difficult but she smells happy now. Which makes us all happy.

'Asher told us that he had no idea as to why Julian stood us up at the Meet we called in Hiltumbler after the attack on Ridley and Delfina. He claimed to not have any knowledge of loners being used as paid muscle for their own agenda.'

'He *also* said that he would investigate and get back to us.'

The mention of Easton and Delfina's birth pack gets a communal rumble of annoyance from the males around the circle. We have a suspicion that our issues with loners may be caused by Silasline. We even tried to call a Meet a few months ago that they didn't show up for. It's been really messy. We were actually supposed to meet with their alpha recently to discuss the growing tension between our pack and theirs. However, we chose to support Adalee at her brother's memorial and not show up. It's an understatement to say that Farrowline is on edge.

The memory of those two days with the males of the Circle in the small town of Hiltumbler has me internally cringe. It was a tense and dramatic few days while we waited for Silasline to show and when we got the call that the loners had attacked Ridley and Delfina, Tobias and Dom were a nightmare to manage. But it was the conversation I had with Tobias on our first night away that still replays in a continual loop in my mind that has me shudder at the memory. No one wants their Alpha to tell them they have a time limit on how long they can continue to work out their shit. I was given only a few months to fix myself up and stop the drinking and self-destructive behaviour before he promised me that my position in the Circle will be threatened. I should've told him the truth about what has been happening since the blood exchange and my tracker abilities, but I didn't and I don't know why. I'm scared to tell them all that I freakily smell everything now.

Like *everything*.

I know that the mated males around me right now had sex within the last two hours. I know what Easton had for breakfast because there's a small spot on his loose, off-white trousers where he spilt his yogurt. I'm fully aware that Ridley is exhausted and that Delfina will get her cycle sometime today. I can pinpoint every wolf working around the clearing and further into the trees we are sitting in.

It's too much, its nearly painful. My head constantly hurts. My nose is always irritated and there is nowhere for me to escape.

'Let's just hope loners stay away for a little longer,' Liam states and everyone seems to deflate at the thought of the beasts that have caused us too many issues.

Rubbing his face, Tobias throws Ridley a sweet, loved-up smile when she extends an arm to grip his hand. 'Let's be thankful for the respite. Keep our guard up, but let's put on a big Pack barbeque this weekend. If Asher calls any of you, you let us all know instantly.'

Chapter Five

'You know you don't have to do this kind of stuff anymore?'

I shrug and continue to pull the bio-degradable containers from the takeout bag. 'Why? Because I'm in the Circle now?' I throw the male behind the table a scolding look. I don't see how being a leader means that I get to sit on my arse while everyone does my old job here at Farrow Group. I've been working at this company since high school. Mum and Dad thought getting me a job with the Alpha and the Circle would help me to stay on track during my studies. I was a bit of a rebel. Hated classes. Hated doing anything but hanging with my packmates and Jay. I started out helping at reception with paperwork filing and odd jobs for the Alpha.

Oliver raises a single eyebrow. 'Or you could let the new human interns do it, seeing as how it's their job.' He chuckles and I shrug. I like buying food for everyone. 'And maybe because you are in the Circle now, Gil. You know Jax and I want you to take on a more prominent role here in Farrow Group. It will help to establish your new standing in Pack.'

My heart sinks a little at that. I know he is in no way implying that I need help in asserting a bit more dominance and a higher standing in the Pack but I can't help the way I take it. Adjusting to the new position has been rough. Throw in the fact that I used an entire tube of oil in the last three days because of my damn nose and I'm a pile of anxious nerves.

'Ridley's job hasn't changed,' I mumble, collecting the still heavy bag to take to Jax.

Those crystal eyes don't leave my face and I bite the inside of my check to keep from saying something I shouldn't, like— I wish I never did the blood exchange with Ridley or that I'm afraid that I shouldn't have done it and that no one wanted me in the Circle. I'm young. I'm not as dominant and I'm really messed up. Rejection hurts so bad.

'Now, that's not true.' He watches me as I shrug once more and then huff and sit when he tells me to. Not asks me to sit but *tells* me. That's Oliver, always bossy and assertive. A true leader. While I have to ask three times for the older packmates to follow my instructions and that's after they look to one of the males for confirmation. I know what everyone in Farrowline is thinking. I know what they see when they look at me—what Oliver sees in me— I'm an adolescent, heart-broken, irresponsible, drunk who would rather party than lead a pack of wolf shifters.

'You going to tell me what that look on your face is about?' Oliver asks, opening up the three containers of food. He pulls out the cutlery set, spears a fork into the mound of fried rice in one container and pushes it towards me. He gets to work finding a spare fork in his top draw.

'I still have to get these to Jax,' I tell him, lifting the bag still in my hand. Oliver doesn't acknowledge what I said and leans over his massive table and presses a button on the phone base. Seconds later, Betty from the intern team pokes her smiling face in the doorway. The bright and bubbly human was so excited to get this job and there is a part of me that feels we would've been great friends if I wasn't so broken. Our interactions since she started have been minimal and professional.

'Yes, Mr Tyler?' I almost laugh out loud at the way she's looking at Oliver, all doe eyed and in awe of his looks and energy. I look up from the rice container to Oliver glaring at me like he knows what I'm thinking. I bite my lip to keep my humour in check.

Blue eyes pull from me to the young lady. 'Betty, could you take Mr Layland his lunch please?' Oliver is polite but professional and I hand the bag over when Betty exclaims how much she would love to assist. She closes the door softly behind her and I realise with a sigh that I have no choice but to sit here and eat all of Oliver's lunch. *Oh well, I guess if I must.* I grab the fork and begin to shovel rice in my mouth so that Oliver can eat.

'Here, have some of these as well.' Oliver bends over the table, piling spring rolls on top of the rice and then a few pieces of chicken from one of the other containers. He doesn't stop until I tell him that it's enough and then go about spooning some rice for him and ignoring his protests to eat my lunch. Damn wolf shifter males and their instinct to feed us. I push a small lid full of rice his way and tell him to take it or I don't eat. He does with a hardness around his mouth that has me smile again.

'You didn't answer my question. What's wrong?'

'Nothing is wrong,' is my automatic reply.

Oliver grunts a very distinct sound that tells me he doesn't believe the lie. 'I have known you since you were born, Gilly. I know it's been a little rough around Pack and that you feel like we've been leashing your wolf lately.'

I don't respond because I'm worried I'll get too angry. They *have* been leashing my wolf. After the incident with the loner approaching Adalee, I could have found the arsehole. I had his scent from where he touched her, but Oliver told me to drop it and shadowed me for days after so that I wouldn't start a hunt.

I shove food in my mouth and indicate to it so that I don't have to tell him what is wrong. He frowns and I watch that perfect face darken a little. I know he is worried about me. I am too.

Chapter Six

I'm busy with Pack duties all day and enter the fourth den that I've been invited to. I swallow the bile in my throat and fight to find enough oxygen in the air to fill my lungs. My nostrils burn at the excess scents in the air and my breathing becomes shallow. I love Ridley with all my heart, but she's such a human in the way she thinks that the candles she burns makes her den more inviting.

The mass of females sitting around gossiping and helping the Luna with her wedding details don't seem that concerned with the smells, mostly because a great number of them are less dominant, meaning their senses are nothing compared to mine.

Adalee is cooking with Mama, Maree and a few of the others who have only just recovered from influenza. Mama still smells a little off to me which I'm making a mental note to keep track of. There was a terrible sickness going around the pack a few weeks ago that hit some of the older wolves including Mama. I can scent the sickness in every breath she takes. I spoke to Kieran, our pack healer the other day and he assured me that he's monitoring her.

My mum is one of the females cooking and she greets me with a warm hello. Falling into her embrace, I make sure to kiss everyone who is making me lunch, mostly because you'd be stupid to not hug the ones that feed you and also because it's my job. I feel their joy at seeing me all the way to my heart and my wolf laps up the attention.

Adalee just grins when I smack a kiss on her cheek. I don't know if everyone working in the kitchen realises that our newest member is slowly turning into the leader of them all. She's constantly asked to try food and about her thoughts on what should be made. Even Mama seems to be leaning towards her more and more and to be honest she seems perfectly happy to let Adalee take the reins with the responsibility to feed everyone.

Mama wraps a comforting arm around my shoulders and pulls me closer to her side as I stand beside her and pick at the platter she's creating. I smile and agree to visit three more families tomorrow when I'm asked to help with finding a few of the adolescents' dresses for a formal school event they all have coming up in a few weeks. The young females in question look up when I agree and beam at me. Their thanks is infectious and I nod absently when Mama whispers how lucky the pack is to have a leader like me.

To be honest, I can't really focus on much with all the candles and I look up the moment the powerful energy that is Delfina comes through the open bifold doors of the Alpha's den.

I don't know if she realises how much of an impact her energy has. Everyone smiles at her appearance, including Ridley. Waiting to see if she's as disturbed as much as I am with the smells permeating the air, I smile when our gazes collide. Locked with the dominant female who takes a few steps into the room, stops and scrunch up her nose, I bite my laugh at the look of disgust that floods her face.

Moving through the space, I grab my packmate and chuckle at her low growl of disgust. I want to rip my nose from my body, it's all scratchy and sore from the odour.

'We'll get the grill started,' I declare loudly to no one in particular and whisper, 'come, it's safer out here.'

Throwing me a look of utter thanks, Delfina grips me back and lets me lead her out while she replies to the many demands that come our way about what to turn on and what needs to be added to the fire.

Now safely outside in the breeze, we both take a deep breath and then stare at each other and laugh. 'Thanks, that was...a lot.'

Delfina has only been around for a few months but has become so important to me that it's crazy to think she wasn't in my life six months ago.

'You're welcome.' I chuckle and we move over to the large outdoor grill, frown and stare blankly at the complicated cooker. 'How do you turn this thing on?'

Shrugging, Delfina just frowns along with me as I begin to turn and pull at the different nobs with no success.

'You going to the outing Gene and Kurt are planning tonight? I think they're going to some new club in Sylo Central.'

'Not my kind of scene,' Delfina replies casually. 'I offered to be on patrol with Dom tonight so that Tobias and Ridley can have a quiet night together. Adalee is watching Noah. That pup is constantly at her den anyway because of his obsession with Atticus,' she mentions Adalee's little dog and I can't help but grin. It was super weird at the beginning having a dog around Pack and it took everyone some time to get used to the yappy little animal, but he is actually pretty cute. 'What about you?'

Shuddering at the idea of being around that many smelly bodies after managing the same thing last night, I shake my head in reply. I hate that I can't have fun freely anymore. The old Gilly would've been the one organising the shenanigan's.

Maybe I'll try. Like last night at Underworld. Shrugging, I tell her, 'I'm not sure,' and leave it at that.

We are both focused on our task of starting the grill until Delfina pulls on something, gasps and looks up at me with a tube in her hand. We both freeze. Hazel eyes jump to me and then we both stare at the connection that we both know shouldn't be dis-connected. After a heartbeat of worried silence, a cackle of laughter escapes my lips and we both throw our heads back and howl in a fit of amusement.

'Shit,' she mumbles and then gets to work trying to fix what she has done. 'Jax is going to kill me if I break this. We're doing nothing to show that we're independent, strong females right now.'

'Come on, I think you could break this thing in half and still be seen as an independent female after what you did to save Ridley, Chase and Darrow against the loners and that douchebag fake alpha, Cade. Then, the way you handled that loner who approached Adalee, you kicked arse, babe.'

For twenty minutes we fail at starting the damn barbeque and are both crying with laughter at our useless attempts when I feel every muscle in my body tense. Delfina sobers instantly which I'm guessing is because of the change in my energy and turns. I don't need to. I know that Jay's mate, Katrina, is walking up the steps with Jay's mother and sister. Only just able to pick up her scent as she has used some kind of overpowering perfume on her clothes, I still know Katrina is there. I can smell Jay's mother, Zelda and her famous fried rice she promised to show me how to make only a week before Jay left to Lilongranline for work and found his mate. Meaning that she never taught me.

That hurt too.

Even Jay's sister, Paula stopped talking to me once Katrina came along. She's behind me too. I still don't know why they both cut me out so harshly.

'Hi there,' Zelda sings and I know that I'm being rude by pretending like the barbeque has my full attention and I'm distracted but I...can't. I already got in trouble with Easton a few weeks back for the way I was apparently behaving towards her. Which I still have no idea what I did.

Delfina flicks those stunning eyes to me and I watch in my peripherals while she runs that intimidating gaze over the three females before landing on the small, quiet one in the middle. I know it's wrong that I feel happy that she's on my side when it comes to this situation and I have no idea how the three lesser dominants are dealing with the attention of someone like Delfina. I hear the shuffled feet, the small intake of air, before Delfina clears her throat and offers a small smile. I'm not even sure if the predator beside me knows what she's doing. She is just pure power.

'Hey,' she casually waves, 'can I help you carry anything?' she offers like most dominants would. The question has me turn around.

I have no control over the way my focus falls on the female whose presence changed so much in my life. Katrina is mid-height, curvy, as most less dominants can be, with long, fuzzy brown hair, brown eyes and soft features. The complete opposite of me, and I can't help but be affected by that. I'm a typical dominant in build, but I have a slightly wider bottom half and large boobs compared to say someone like Delfina. Mostly because I'm not as dominant as her and technically if it wasn't for my tracker nose, would probably be an average wolf sent on the occasional patrol but mostly stay within Pack and focus on den-making. But I don't have the same energy as a shifter like Katrina, she is more like Mama and my mum. So I guess I don't really fit anywhere fully.

Paula averts her eyes as I look to her and it cuts deep. Even Zelda nods tightly toward me and I know that all three are uncomfortable.

Katrina's the one to quietly answer Delfina, 'no thank you Delfina.' She has a genuine smile and holds up the heavy looking book in her hand, 'I thought the Luna might want to look through the scrapbook I made for her with mating stuff. Jay and I only had a small blood ceremony with family but I still...' Tension fills the air and with deep brown wide eyes, Katrina looks to me with a look of regret.

The female who steps from the bifold doors takes over the situation instantly. 'That is very kind of you Katrina, I think Ridley would love for you to show her. Come on through.' Stern, motherly eyes fall to me in reprimand as Jay's family follows the instructions with relief. Mama throws Delfi and I one last look of reproach before saying, 'I need that barbeque on in the next two minutes, hurry along you two,' she demands before striding back into the kitchen.

'She loves us,' I tell Delfina who grins wide as we turn back to the damn barbeque.

Chapter Seven

Later that afternoon, I'm knee deep in three different tasks for Mum, Mama and the other Pack females when Emma, one of our Pack healers, comes shouting from the tree line.

Confused and a little unsure what exactly she is saying, I cradle the bags I grabbed from the boot of Mum's car and turn as she gets closer.

'Gilly, thank goodness,' she huffs through each word. I try to calm her down and work out what the problem is but it's just one big word, 'Jenny has lost control and no one can find her we need you...' Sucking in a deep breath, Emma grips her knees and begins to try and tell me that she has to get out of the hospital more. As one of our Pack healers, Emma is a valuable member of Farrowline, but she only goes wolf when she has to.

Shifters are not wolf or human alone. And a healthy wolf shifter is when there's a balance between the two sides of our soul. The more dominant the wolf, the harder it can be to keep the balance. The lesser the wolf, the more 'human' a wolf shifter can be. Emma falls into that category. While I need to shift every three days or else my wolf becomes unbearable and it starts to physically hurt, a shifter like Emma can go a week, sometimes more and be happy still.

Since the blood exchange and the change in my tracker abilities, I've felt the time between needing to shift has lessened. The only other time I felt so shaken in my own body was going through the hard adolescent years. Once again, the more dominant the wolf, the harder it is when your beast awakens and they can start taking control. Which just adds to my deep anxiety that something is wrong with me.

But there is no time for self-doubt. Jenny isn't a dominant but she has been going through a hard time with the other adolescents lately and if she has gone wolf and left territory, she must be having a really hard day.

'Shit,' I growl and hand over the bags to Emma and hurry towards where she points. This stuff happens, but with the constant threat of loners, Jenny could get into trouble if she is out of territory lines.

Giving myself over to the beast under my skin, I shake my fur out and allow the smells and sounds around me to fill my senses.

Running at full speed, the forest blurs past and I collect all the scents in the air as I go. There are thousands of trails to work through.

Sorting through each one that hits my tracker nose, I pick up on the floral tones that are Jenny. I follow her path. I keep my head high, absorbing the clues that tell me where her wolf went. My wolf growls when she realises it's out of territory.

Jumping over rocks and boulders, I hurry past a group of wolves who whip their heads around when I appear. I run my gaze over them to make sure everyone is all right and keep moving. I know I don't imagine the look of relief on Jenny's dads face or the fact that Darrow is pacing territory line, which is impressive, but I know for a fact that the leash on his wolf will snap soon.

Jenny and Darrow are hot and cold and I don't really know if it's on or off at the moment. Jenny's brother is not too far behind him which could mean disaster if Jenny isn't found soon.

Which just makes me push faster. I have Jenny locked down. I can smell her wolf and know that she's near the river deep in the forest up ahead. It's far but not too far.

Despite the situation, I feel exhilarated and calm. My wolf has purpose and a job as she hurries towards the scent of a packmate who just needs help to manage the emotions that come with being an adolescent wolf shifter, and a female one at that.

Breaking a line of trees, the sound of running water fills the forest. I find the small wolf lying amongst the long grass. Her eyes are downcast as she whimpers. I'm fully aware of our surroundings as I make my way slowly towards her.

I'm ready to pull her back and help her to find her balance.

'You did good today.'

 Raising my beer in a salute, I continue to look out into the forest. I feel flat and drained. It took me hours to get Jenny to shift back to human. Her wolf even tried to bite me once and I hated going all dominant on her and forcing her to comply, but I had to. It wasn't nice what my wolf did to hers but it was necessary. However, she is now safe and sleeping in her bed under the watchful eye of her dad and brother.

Oliver takes a seat beside me and I instantly feel calmer. His presence always grounds me. His shoulder brushes mine as he bends to grab a bottle from the esky on the deck.

Cracking open the lid, we both drink in silence.

'How's Darrow? He was pretty shaken by Jenny going rogue.'

Oliver swallows his mouthful before telling me that Easton has sent him to shadow Delfina on her patrol to let off some steam. Apparently, Jenny and Darrow got into another one of their fights before Jenny lost it. Easton, as our Pack Enforcer, has the job of dealing out these sorts of punishments and ensure harmony amongst our packmates.

'Delf would be loving that,' I say and smile at Oliver's deep chuckle. Easton probably did it on purpose to piss off his sister. Delfina is much happier patrolling on her own.

'She wasn't too impressed when Easton suggested it.'

We don't speak for another few heartbeats. We're sitting at the back of my parent's den. It's where I go to 'hide'. If one can actually hide in this place.

'I feel like you're keeping something from me.'

Watching the soft breeze move through the trees, I shrug and nod when Oliver says, 'I know what Jay did was horrible and I'm truly sorry, Gil. Your heart will heal.'

I want to yell and shout that he has no idea. I want to ask if he knows what it's like to get his heart smashed or have your life change and your wolf feel different under your skin after so many years. Or that being around others is hard and hurts my head but stop myself. He wouldn't understand. Instead I go for humour. It's easy. 'You sound like an old wise male. *My youthful heart will heal,*' I mock.

'I am an old wise male,' he states so finally that I tsk and shake my head.

'Jeez, you are like eight years older than me, relax.' I wave off his comment. 'Old males don't look like you.' I indicate to the magnificent body he was blessed with. And the hair. I need to go and steal his shampoo again, maybe Kurt will help me.

'And what do I look like?' I snap my attention from the beer in my hand to his face, unsure what his tone means. Those crystal eyes, set within a handcrafted face with his chiselled jawline, study me intensely. My senses seem to shut down.

He grins slowly until I see the perfect rows of his teeth. Wanker was teasing me. 'You're a loser,' I huff and push into his shoulder. He doesn't budge. He is solid muscle.

'And you are...'

I turn and point at him. 'Don't you finish that. I was having a peaceful time here reflecting and processing what happened today. I don't need you coming here with your male arrogance calling me names.'

A large hand comes up and grips my wrist. I'm pulled forward a little, my body now closer to the shit-stirrer. 'And when have I ever called you a name?'

I struggle to come up with an example and snatch my hand back, and only because he lets me, when he chuckles lightly.

I get all awkward for no real reason as my wrist burns from his touch. Shaking off the odd feeling. I place my beer down and plaster on a smile that I know doesn't reach my eyes. 'I told Kurt and Gene I'd go out with them tonight.' *I didn't but I don't want to be here. I want booze and distraction.* I stand and stretch. Looking over my shoulder, I watch as Oliver stares with those knowing eyes that have always disarmed me. Oliver has always been able to read me and right now I can't be around him. I feel like I'm going to explode.

The imposing male nods, his thick arms resting on his knees. 'Have a good time and call me if you need me.'

Nodding, I swallow the weird feeling that begins to form in my throat at the sight of him watching my every move. 'Will do.' I walk away on shaking legs, unsure what just happened.

Chapter Eight

'Gil, maybe we should slow it down a little?'

Laughing myself to tears at what Kurt has just said, I grab the small bottle on the table and chuck the burning liquid down my throat. I have no idea what everyone's problem is. We are having a great night. The club is new and fresh and the music is fucking unreal. Everyone was laughing together and drinking a few hours ago and now they are all being weird and bossy. I have on my best black dress and I need to drown out the world for a night.

'Um Gil, I think I want to go home,' Glenda says. Her pink tipped hair matches Gene's tonight. She isn't looking at me but at the row of glasses I have in front of me on the table. I follow her gaze and laugh loudly again.

'Then go home,' I sing, taking another drink. There is a distant part of my mind that tries to tell me something important but I shut it up with more alcohol.

I'm only half aware of the way the group look at each other.

'I don't like the look of the cheetahs that just entered Gil, I think we should go,' she says again, a hint of hurt in her voice that I wave off.

Gene is the only one at the table who seems to be on my side. 'We're here to party!' Gene slurs and falls into my lap. I hug him close and suck on the pipe he places at my lips. 'Let's dance.'

I drink and dance and drink and dance and feel my body detach from my damn overbearing thoughts for the first time in days.

The lights around me lull me into the oblivion I crave. My nose no longer works and I have no idea who is touching me and my neck feels wet and warm. I'm absently aware of being surrounded by heat and a hard male body against mine. Then all of a sudden the weight is gone and my wolf tugs deep in my soul, clearly unhappy with my drinking. I blink trying to get the face now glaring down at me into focus. All I see is a striking blue colour and I smile.

'Oliver,' I sing and throw my arms around his neck, sway my hips to the beat.

'What the fuck, Gilly,' he growls and I laugh at how mad he sounds. Drawing in his scent, I love that I can't really use my nose properly. 'That cheetah was sucking on your neck.' It's an accusation and I frown and touch my neck. It's wet and I laugh again. I don't even remember dancing with a cheetah. Big, grumpy cheetah bastards are hot but a little handsy for me typically.

My hands are firmly around Oliver's neck and I rest my head against his solid chest, feeling like I'm flying.

'Do you even know where you are right now or that your packmates called me to come and get you all. This place is crawling with predators, Gil!'

I smile at his cranky tone and lift my hand to tip more alcohol down my throat and protest colourfully when the bottle disappears. 'Hey!'

'We are leaving!' he growls aggressively and pulling my arms from his neck, he grips my hand and drags me off the dancefloor. I try to not stumble over my feet and see Jax at the exit with Glenda and the others. They all look like a row of adolescents in trouble with the teacher.

I ugly snort and laugh so hard that I get a headache. Jax's yellow eyes narrow in my direction and I see his teeth when he turns and ushers our group from the club. I'm still being dragged and I stumble a little and am pulled into Oliver's side with a grumble just as we step out into the night. The bite of the cold air seems to lift some of the cloud fogging my mind. I shiver.

There is a line of Farrowline cars along the curb, parking in what I'm sure is a no parking zone. Easton is leaning against one of his more sensible cars, his hazel eyes narrowed in my direction and I know that he is pissed. Liam is standing next to the large van we use to transport a number of the pack around and with a mighty shake of his head at me, he opens the back door and demands everyone gets in. Head hanging, Kurt, carrying a drunk Gene, hops into the back with one last look in my direction.

'What is everyone's problem?' I bark and try to wrestle my wrist from Oliver's death grip. He just ignores me and pulls me towards Easton. I look over at the van and the rest of the group and wonder why I'm the one that has to go with the cranky Circle. Jax swings the passenger door open and Oliver pushes me towards the back of Easton's car with a firm hand after letting me go.

'Fucking hell, calm down,' I snap when I almost trip.

'Just get in the damn car Gilly,' Oliver demands and I'm powerless to the command even though we are both leaders of the same Pack. I guess that is the problem, I will never be a match for these males. How can I lead when

I don't have a voice amongst them? My feet move of their own accord and just before I begin to climb in the back, I feel the bile rising in the back of my throat. Bending over, I expel the contents of my stomach and hear the three males curse loudly.

'For fuck's sake.' Oliver is there at my side in an instant pulling my hair from my face. He collects it in a ball at the back of my nape while his hand rubs calming circles between my shoulders. No matter how mad he is, his instinct is to look after a female of his pack. It makes me want to cry and in my drunk mind I don't know if it's the fact that I'm vomiting or if it is something else that has tears streaming down my face.

Finished, I wipe my face and take the opened bottle that Jax hands over the other side of the door. I rise slowly and down half the bottle before Oliver tells me to take it easy. Looking over my shoulder, I study the deep emotions on Oliver's face and hate that I'm the one that made those handsome features so harsh.

The moment my butt hits the seat and I'm surrounded by the scent of my packmates as they pile into the car, I pass out.

Chapter Nine

I wake slowly and painfully. Groaning, I blink my dry eyes open knowing through my nose that I'm not in my room or even in my parents den. Oliver's sandalwood and citrus scent fills my lungs. Everything is fuzzy and I turn slowly to stare at the floor to ceiling glass doors that take up the entire side of Oliver's den. The forest of Farrowline is thick in this section of the territory where Oliver built his den. It's too bright and I groan. Spying the note with my name on the low table to my left, I roll over and see the tall glass of water and the bottle of aspirin with a firm note that tells me to take two and get my butt to breakfast. Smiling despite the unclear memories that come back, I sigh loudly and do what I'm told. Laying back down, I know that I fucked up last night despite not really knowing to what extent or what I actually did.

Not wanting to rush to what I'm sure will be an arse kicking when I find the rest of the Circle, I look around Oliver's bedroom and the luxury of the place. I've never woken up here and wonder why he didn't take me to one of the many spare rooms in his den. A fuzzy memory of Kieran coming over and touching my head comes to the forefront. I'm not sure if I imagined

Oliver watching over me all night as I fell in and out of consciousness but the idea makes me cringe. I've made an absolute fool out of myself.

Thick curtains have been pulled back to reveal the gorgeous view of the trees and I just stare out into the forest to find the courage to get out of bed. I've always loved Oliver's den. There's a deck just outside with a single chair for Oliver to sit in the mornings and drink his gross black coffee and contemplate life. He loves to do that.

The rest of the room is a mixture of greens and browns. The bed is pillowy soft and larger than any bed I've ever seen and I hope I'm not in too much trouble that I can't get him to let me use the monster, pool-like bathtub he has in his ensuite. It too has one-way glass in the corner so when bathing you feel like you're outside. It's deep enough to fit most of my body and big enough that Kurt, Gene and I can sit comfortably inside with our bathers and eat our cheese platter. Not that I have done that in ages.

Getting reluctantly out of bed, I look down at the male shirt I'm wearing and groan. Fuck, I was so plastered that Oliver had to change my clothes and the taste in my mouth reminds me that I threw up in front of Jax and Easton too. Hating myself, I head to the bathroom, look longingly at the bath and find the tube of toothpaste and quickly use it to clean my mouth a little.

Staring at myself in the oval mirror, I take in the mass of tangled brunette hair, the dark blue eyes that look like deep water compared to Oliver's crystal, pale ones and the roundness of my face. Taking a few deep breathes, I ready myself for what I know is coming and head towards the scent of my Alpha.

I stop at the edge of the hallway. Oliver's room is the only door on this side of the den. The open, spacious kitchen/dining/living area sits in the centre of the den and the rest of the bedrooms, bathrooms, laundry and second and third loungeroom are on the opposite side through a large archway. Oliver's kitchen takes up the entire wall to my left. The glass runs the length of the den along the right.

I hesitate at the sight of the Circle and steel my spine when Jax looks up from his half eaten plate and stares before wordlessly going back to his food. He takes a deep breath and releases it through his nose, the noise telling me enough about his mood with me right now. He is sitting to the left of Liam with a single vacant one between the pair.

Dom and Oliver are in the kitchen making coffees and their conversation falters as they stare my way. Oliver's eyes skim the shirt of his I still have on and averts his eyes with a shake of his head. Dom just keeps staring until I have to look away. I hang my head, feeling young and stupid.

The tension is thick in my mouth. It tastes like my regret and their anger. Liam doesn't bother to look at me and it hurts because he's doing the 'dad' thing and making me feel guilty for going out and getting wasted. I want to scream at him like I *am* an adolescent and tell him that I know I fucked up. I keep my mouth shut because the Alpha's shoulders are tense. His back is to me as he sits at the head of the long, wood table that cuts the kitchen and lounge room. I can smell his emotions. All their emotions are sickening on my tongue.

Fuck.

'Sit Gilly,' Tobias states and I fiddle with the sleeves of the button up shirt before obeying. The light blue fabric falls to just on my knees. I take the seat between Jax and Liam. I keep my eyes on the table. Everyone is silent while Tobias fills a plate for me. They have already started but that is because I was passed out in the bedroom or they would've waited, it's clear they all stopped when they heard me waking up.

The plate is placed in my line of vision. 'Eat,' Tobias growls and I quickly pop a few bits of pancake into my mouth to satisfy the males so they can go back to their breakfast. I can feel that I will need food in my stomach to withstand the shitstorm that is coming my way.

Chapter Ten

The tension is killing me and after five small bites of my breakfast, I wait to be scolded and end up saying, 'Tobias, I didn't mean…'

His forest green eyes snap to me, holding me captive, until I have to look away. His power is choking. He's a force of nature to my left.

I shut my mouth.

'You didn't mean to what?' he asks, his voice deep and full of the wolf. I clamp my lips together, throwing quick glances at the males in the den watching the exchange. Not one of them is going to help me I realise. I made my bed and I'm about to sleep in it. 'Do you mean that you didn't mean to…get so drunk that you put your packmates in a situation that was not only reckless but dangerous?' My heart sinks. 'That you didn't mean to not act like a leader of this pack and ignore a packmate who told you she was worried and wanted to go back to Farrowline or that you didn't mean to tell her that she could go if she wanted. Instead of being a Circle wolf and getting her out of that damn club and putting her needs above your own!'

I flinch. *Fuck.* I did say that to Glenda. I feel the colour drain from my face.

He isn't finished with me and I hang my head and take what I deserve. Tobias doesn't shout. He doesn't raise his voice. He doesn't need to. He has anger lacing each word. His wolf growling and communicating to mine between each sentence that I really messed up. 'Or that you were so *drunk* that you didn't realise that you were in the presence of multiple loners.'

My jaw hits my lap. I had no idea.

'Don't even get me started on the cheetah that was all over you and you didn't even realise!'

I shuffle in my chair. My wolf wants to run.

'I messed up,' I mumble and close my eyes when Dom tells me that messed up is an understatement. 'I'm sorry,' I apologise and look up to quickly look at Tobias and then down at my lap again.

The Alpha of Farrowline makes a deep noise that tells me that he hates doing this. I know I deserve it. I deserve to get my arse kicked.

'Gilly, you did mess up and I have to say that I don't know where this leaves us.'

My bottom lip wobbles but I catch it between my teeth and bite down hard. Tobias sighs and runs a hand through his hair as he sits back in his chair.

'You gave a blood oath to Ridley and me. Your wolf knows her worth but you clearly do not.' I don't know where this speech is heading but my skin prickles and I look up and stare at the Alpha. 'I need some time to figure out how we move forward from this. Farrowline doesn't need to see their Circle crumbling. Not when we have multiple threats at the moment. Our Pack is amidst great change and we have to show strength and power. We have to show that every wolf is part of our heart. And at the moment, Gil, you are being reckless and doing none of that.'

It's like I've been slapped. The pain of his words hit me hard. If I was a packmate and not a Circle member, I'd get a slap on the wrist and told to hydrate and get some rest but now that I'm a leader of this Pack, I am being held at a different standard. In that moment I regret ever offering the blood oath to Ridley and curse my wolf for thinking this was a good idea. Who gives a fuck that I'm a tracker…

I sit silently while everyone begins to eat their breakfast. My heart pounding as I try to work through my next move and what will happen now. I'm wallowing until a howl from the forest draws all of our attention instantly. I move before my mind can catch up with the fact that our territory has been breached.

I hate loners.

As I dodge and kick and jump back behind the Alpha as he roars and leaps from the trees, I watch in awe as the mighty male takes out two beasts in a single heartbeat. Having avoided a set of claws to my side, I roll away from the bear loner who barges from the trees ready to remove my head from my shoulders.

The Alpha is busy taking out another set of intruders, so I use my smaller size to bite and scratch while staying well clear from the larger animal who isn't having as easy a time like he thought when challenging me.

I can sense what he is about to do by the simple change in his scent. When he favours his right foot as he is about to spring forward, I can smell the dirt under his giant paws being disturbed. The information useable as I predict his every move. Which means I am never caught. I know that I can't take him out on my own but I don't need to because I know who is coming from the trees behind me and when she is close, I lay flat on my stomach, my wolf working in unison with my human logic and watch as the female wolf comes flying from the trees.

Delfina is next level amazing. Her howl shakes the world as she collides with the male, spins him, and rips out his throat before he has time to register what has happened.

Turning that aggressive elongated face, now dripping with blood to where I lay, I see her assess the situation in a heartbeat. Her eyes are dark and deadly as they take me and the two injured packmates I'm protecting before she throws herself into the battle our Alpha is in.

The others hurry onto the scene from their own battles and take control.

There are two injured Farrowline wolves behind me and I whirl around to face my Alpha when he barks a command meant for me alone. Hunt, his wolf tells me. Our issues earlier are now pushed aside, it's my job to detect if we missed any. Our beasts understand each other perfectly and as my packmates eliminate the last loner who threatens our territory, I close my eyes, knowing I am safe as three males appear at my side.

I can hear the injured being looked after by Oliver who is now on two legs and I block out all the noise as I draw in a deep, steady breath under the watchful eyes of my Alpha and Jax, our Gamma. Our Third.

Pulling apart the scents in the air as they fill my tracker nose, I identify the ones I'd expect out here in Farrowline. I smell the forest, my fellow packmates, the few small animals hiding in the distance, the grass, the dirt. The shifters that came by here over the last few weeks that have left markers around this section of forest. All this happens instantly. My brain working through the scents efficiently and meticulously.

However I keep my senses from going out too far. I can't manage it when there is too much to work through and then I pick it up.

Intruders.

Eyes flying open, I growl deep and the three males beside me spring into action as I indicate south toward where the two intruders are hiding within our territory.

Chapter Eleven

'How are they?'

'Wade is good. Eliza is a concern. She lost a great deal of blood but she will recover. Kieran has everything under control,' Oliver explains how the two injured wolves are going as he sits down beside me on Ridley's long lounge. I stayed with the Luna, Adalee and Delfina while we waited to hear how the wounded were. It's been a few hours since the attack and everyone is only just starting to calm down. It helps that I've eaten my body weight in Adalee's pasta.

'And the cheetah that slipped away, what happened with him?'

You can tell Delfina is still unimpressed with the idea that we lost the cat that was on our territory. Cats are fast and they can climb and the son of a bitch got away from Jax and the Alpha. The pair have been huffing around in a state of male annoyance at being bested. It would be funny if I wasn't so bloody tired and bruised from the verbal bashing this morning. The cheetah was one of the males I smelt after the fight, the one that slipped into territory. They got the bear who was with him though.

'The cheetah isn't in Farrowline,' I reassure them all for the hundredth time. I've only just come in from scouring the forest making sure that it was safe. Tobias locked the Estate down but I am confident that the loner left. I tracked him all the way to territory lines before I threw up everywhere, much to Dom's horror. It was just a response to using my nose for such an intense, short amount of time. It happens. It has been happening a great deal more since my tracker nose has gone berserk. I feared that he thought I was still hung over.

'Well, there isn't much that we can do about it now,' Oliver declares, grabbing me by the hand to pull me from the couch. 'You need to rest,' he tells me pointedly and I let him pull me out of the Alpha's den. We walk in silence through the streets towards my parents den.

Last night was shit and while I can't remember everything, I remember enough.

'I fucked up, bad.' I want to run away and disappear. If I wasn't bone-tired I would.

'Yeah, you did,' is his response and I don't know why that hurts me more than having the Alpha reprimand me in front of everyone.

'What can I say to make it better?'

'I honestly have no idea.'

That makes me so mad. 'That's unfair! None of you have any idea what I am dealing with.'

Oliver turns around quickly to glare down at me. 'No we don't, because you shut yourself off from everyone and drink yourself to blacking out instead of letting anyone help you. Let me help you!'

He is furious and too bad because so am I. 'You can't help me!' I shout, seeing the disappointment on his face. 'No one can help me!' I storm away, very aware that Oliver trails behind, making sure that I get back to den safe.

For a week Farrowline has a calm energy that reminds me of pre-loner times. We've had three Pack barbecues and everyone seems happy, except maybe me. I've been avoiding everyone, especially my friends whom I apologised to for my actions at the club. They accepted and moved on while I've been moody and quiet.

Roaring and chasing the mass of pups running round the large open spaced area behind the row of dens on the north side of Farrowline Estate, I pick up the small pup who bares his little teeth at me and twirl him around. There are a few parents and less dominants working and chatting as the young ones play. It's my happy place. The sun is setting and I know I'm late for a Circle meeting the Alpha called this morning while I was at work, but nothing will keep me from the Pack pups. We have a Pack barbeque planned for later tonight and Adalee and Mama are busy preparing the meal.

Having only gotten home a half hour ago, I'm still in my work clothes.

'You want to fight me?' I play shout and laugh at the way the small pup squeals and giggles in my arms, the sound is matched by the horde of would-be predators now trying to tackle me to the ground. My wolf basks in the joy and energy and draws in the soft scent that all little ones have.

Tickling and roughing his hair when I place the pup in my arms down, they all run off screeching which makes me unbelievably happy and content.

Today was a hard day at Farrow Group. I barely managed to get through the amount of work I buried myself under. It didn't help that there was a massive meeting that had the meeting room packed full of smelly humans wearing ridiculous colognes, I have a sore head and a sore stomach.

I actually ran out of the meeting room and ended up throwing up in the bathroom. My actions didn't go down well. Jax was particularly pissed and while I wasn't too offended when he smelt me to ensure I wasn't drunk, it did sting a little. Some days I can cope. Other days I find it hard to get through the day. I still haven't told the others about the struggles I'm having with my out-of-control tracker abilities. It's never the right time. My entire life feels off-kilter and I have no idea how to right it back on its axis.

Chapter Twelve

I'm late for the meeting and wave at the small pack of pups now looking for their next prey. That's when I scent him approaching. Cursing softly, I hurriedly pick up the bags of clothes Ridley asked me to grab on the way home from work and try to hurry away without being too obvious.

My heart pounds in my chest as adrenaline courses through my veins in a mixture of emotions. Praying that he doesn't see me or just ignores me like he usually does, I put my head down and begin moving towards the Alpha's den. I don't get too far before Jay calls my name and I don't know how to feel because he hasn't acknowledged me in so long.

'Gilly, wait up.'

Groaning internally, I grip the bags and try to quickly work out an excuse to ignore the male I can smell coming up behind me. Looking around and spotting Gene and Kurt working on something under a tree and a few of the other dominants scattered around enjoying the sun, I take a breath and force myself to be friendly. I don't need to create any more drama. I'm already in enough shit.

Spinning, I have no control over how my eyes skim over the approaching male. Jay is lean and tall with mousey short hair and muddy brown eyes. I don't want to see him as attractive, but I do. I still get the butterflies and the longing despite him breaking my heart. He was my best friend for such a long time, it's been really difficult not having him around. Yes, I'm craving some skin-on-skin contact, but it's not really the thing I miss the most. It's the waking up to someone in my bed who smiles and kisses me with a 'good morning'. Or curling up and watching a movie together in each other's arms. Granted, I do all those things with my fellow packmates, used to anyway, it's just…not the same.

Jay's a dominant with the same kind of energy I used to have. He's not in the same league as the male who catches my attention from the other side of the space. Liam's piercing stare shoots to me the moment my attention slips from Jay. I see the question in his hard eyes, his wolf asking if I need him. Despite how badly I've been screwing up, he would save me from the situation in a heartbeat.

Shaking my head slightly, I focus back on the male standing before me. The one who hasn't spoken to me properly in a really long time.

Clearing my throat, I ask, 'what can I do for you, Jay?' I try really fucking hard to keep my voice light but am also fully aware that this male knows me better than anyone else in my life and knows it's all fake.

His emotions are all over the place and I frown at the one that scents the air. Jay smells off and I'm too busy trying to work out what's going on that I miss the anger in his tone when he says, 'look, I'm sorry for how everything went down between us, but Katrina and my family haven't done anything to you, Gil.' Watching him run his hand through his short hair distracts me from responding and honestly I don't think I truly understand what he's saying and why after all this time he thinks it's okay to come up to me with such rage in his energy.

Reeling and a little confused at what's going on, I frown and mumble, 'what?'

Growling a sound deep in his throat that I'd never have imagined could come out of Jay's throat, I take a small step back like I've been slapped. We've barely interacted since he sent that message ending our long-term relationship and he is...*growling at me?*

I just stand, lost for words.

'You're making it really hard for Katrina to feel accepted in Farrowline, Gilly. I've spoken to Easton a number of times about this problem. Only a few weeks ago I asked him to speak to you, Gene, Kurt and Delfina about how you all acted at one of the barbeques. Now, I had to go to him again about the way you and Delfina acted with my family when the females got together for Ridley's wedding planning afternoon last week.'

I remember the 'talking to' I got from Easton. Apparently we all made Katrina feel uncomfortable at a Pack barbeque a while ago. All four of us had no idea what we had done wrong which is saying something because if Gene and Kurt want to give someone a hard time, they know it, and would own up to it.

'I rang Easton this morning as I think this is affecting Pack and he advised me to speak with you myself. Everyone loves you Gilly and they see how you're behaving towards my mate and it's causing problems for her.'

Mouth hitting the grass, I'm shocked by his words, 'you spoke to Easton about me again?' I try to remember the situation he is talking about. I know it was awkward between his family and I the other day when Delfina and I broke the barbecue.

I can't have Tobias hearing about this. My position in the Circle is under scrutiny enough as it is.

'Yes,' Jay grumbles. 'He's the Pack Enforcer. I thought you were better than this. I thought with you being a Circle member now it'd mean that you'd grow up, because I have. One day you'll realise that the partying and the drinking and the bitchiness is just so...immature. So, stop. You're affecting how everyone interacts with Katrina and it's not fair. When you find your mate, you'll understand. So just stop,' he repeats and then walks away.

I stand stuck to the spot having no idea what has just happened.

Turning, I unconsciously start to move. My feet take me through the estate and right into the den full of large predators laughing and chatting away while they prepare the meats for this evenings Pack barbeque. The Alpha called everyone together at his den to go through some important news he's been given and I dump the bag in my hand down on the long hall table at the door before making my way to the kitchen. My brain hasn't caught up with what just went down.

Watching as Oliver starts to howl in joy at whatever Jax has just told him, I take a deep breath and draw in the combinations of scents in the air. Scents that seem to stabilise me in this moment.

My wolf recognises Pack.

I haven't seen Oliver since our moment in the forest where I shouted at him. He has kept his distance and I fucking hate it. To be honest, I haven't tried either.

Ridley and Delfina are chatting away at the long dining table while Noah plays with Atticus. I look over at the Alpha and Beta who sit side by side on the lounge that should fit four but is barely enough room for the two males.

I move without thought. Drawn to them.

The pair don't look up at my approach. They keep chatting while I draw in their individual markers that mark them to my wolf as Pack. They both shuffle back a little to make room for me and without a word and in desperate need of comfort, I crawl into the space they've created. The lounge is super soft and I curl up by tucking my legs under my body and lean into the hard, warmth of my Alpha.

Taking a deep breath, I close my eyes and try to forget everything that has happened. My wolf pushes up against the hand the Alpha begins to run up and down my arm. Tobias's large, powerful arm comes down over my shoulder and draws me closer to his side. It doesn't matter how mad he is at me, he is my Alpha and while I hate everything I've done, I know he always has me.

Easton walks into the den and I can't help but track his movements. Liam is beside him. His hazel eyes lock on me when he breezes through the space but I don't see any reprimand in them.

Crouching down in front of me, Easton rests his hands on my knees, 'Gilly, we can't keep doing this.'

Nodding, I feel a wave of nausea and shame. 'I know. I didn't...I don't...I know,' I repeat with a sigh of defeat.

'Gilly did nothing wrong!' is the demand from the table and I look up and over at the female glaring at her brother. Easton just sighs and ignores Delfina. 'It happened over a week ago, if it was such a big deal, why didn't Jay call you sooner?'

'I never said she did anything wrong. And you can stop too, Delfina. I heard how you behaved with Katrina and the other females outside of Mama's while you were breaking the barbeque. Jay rang me this morning after trying to work this out on his own,' he throws back over his shoulder and I quickly jump in because the powerful female's eyes have just gone dark. No one needs their arguing tonight.

'I didn't break the barbecue,' Delfina's words come out as a deep growl. Dom's body vibrates beside me as he holds in a chuckle.

We did break the barbecue.

'Please, don't fight,' I interject. 'I understand what you're saying, Easton. I'll check my behaviour.' I feel Tobias's disapproval but he doesn't stop comforting me.

I have no control over how I look up and over at Oliver. I'm unsure what the look on his face means as he studies me from across the room.

Chapter Thirteen

'Come on Gil, is this about Jay *Beige Sex* Houston, again?'

Growling, I turn my back and try to find some clean clothes in the mess that is my small walk-in wardrobe. 'No! I just don't want to go to an underground rave tonight.'

After the shit day at work, the encounter with Jay and what I've just heard about Silasline in the meeting with the Circle, I'm tired and even unsure how I'm going to survive a massive Pack barbeque. It's hard to control the tracker wolf under my skin when I'm tired. Everything is heightened and it makes socialising hard. So, I'm definitely not in the mood to be squashed between smelly, sexed up bodies at the elusive, invitation-only, high-stakes party that Gene, Kurt and the others want to go to tonight. After what happened, I don't think I will ever go out again.

Gene's hair is hot pink today and the tall, thin shifter is making a solid mess of my makeup as he applies eyeshadow before my vanity mirror. Kurt is laying on my bed doing his nails.

'I'm just going to go to the barbecue and come back to den.' I volunteered to be out on territory lines tonight but the Alpha told me that it would be good for everyone to see the Circle relaxing and having some *fun*.

'You need to get over Jay *Only Had Missionary Sex* Houston by getting under someone else before you turn into a boring, responsible Circle member.'

'Well, it doesn't help when Glenda and the others call the fucking Circle when I'm out drinking with you all. I'm never going out with them again. I got my arse handed to me.'

'We know,' he replies solemnly. I ignore the fake sorrowful look on his face.

I feel my soul shudder at the thought of letting any male close to me again anyway. Until I hear the mating words, I have vowed to not put myself back in the same situation where I give my heart to someone to have them deny me when they find their mate.

I will not fall in love.

Sex sounds good but I don't think I really know what love is anymore. Jay and I, we partied and we had fun. Like crying in laughter kind of fun. We were friends first. Best friends. We grew up together and explored life together.

'Kurty darling,' Gene sings from the mirror, 'you know that Gilly doesn't like when you speak badly about Jay *Vanilla Sex* Houston.'

'Hey,' Kurt is sickly sweet with fake innocence. 'I love Jay *Starfish* Houston, he's my packmate. But I think Gilly *Needs to Get Pounded By A Sexy Dominant Male Hard* Sommers has to move on from this and the only way to do that is to *cum* out tonight,' Kurt states so casually that I shake my head and cover my smile.

'I hear you lovely Kurt. I hear you,' Gene sighs dramatically. 'Jay *Doesn't Know Where To Find It* Houston is my littermate. But Gilly *Never Had Mind-Blowing Sex Before* Sommers needs time to get over her heartbreak in her own way.'

'You two aren't funny,' I grumble and get a few reassuring comments that it must be my lack of understanding of great sex that's the reason for my lack of humour.

'Our sex life wasn't boring,' I state half-heartedly and get two pairs of sympathetic eyes blinking at me like I'm some kind of charity case. Even I know that it's probably a lie. Sex with Jay was never bad. We were comfortable with each other. We knew what we liked and it worked...most times.

'Come on you two let's go, I'm hungry and the Alpha will be pissed if I'm late.'

Only slightly tipsy, having left the bottle of untouched gin under Oliver's seat outside, I cradle the beer in my hand and listen to everyone chatting around me. Alcohol really does help in these situations.

Ridley and Noah are having a blast playing with the Pack pups in the brand-new play equipment that was recently installed at Mama's den and I sit amongst the Circle trying to be polite when all I want to do is rip my nose from my face and disappear into the trees. The smell of the barbeque is making me slightly queasy and I know she has no idea but the perfume that the Luna is wearing is so strong that I push off the chair and make my way further into the den.

Mama and the others are busy in the kitchen mostly chatting and laughing away as they do whatever it is they all do in here and I head to the female on the long table sitting before her laptop.

Nicolette Farrow, with her mane of dark, black, curly hair that shapes her face and hauntingly green eyes flick above her device the closer I get. Raising an eyebrow at whatever she sees on my face, she kicks the chair beside her out without a word. I flow into the hard seat with a sigh. Nicolette has only just recently come back from a trip to Mama's birth Pack, Rhiattline. We all know why Mama sent the stunningly beautiful and successful female away. Everyone has always gossiped about Nicolette and her 'ways' for as long as I can remember. She is strong enough to be a Circle member, has as much authority within Pack as a leader even without the title, and yet, she would much rather be at her desk in the high-rise building in South Sylo than managing Pack business. Which to the elders of Farrowline is a complete conundrum that they try desperately to understand. Questions like – 'why wouldn't she want a mate and to be consumed by the inner politics of Pack?' Or, 'doesn't every female want that?'

Frankly, I think everyone should leave her alone.

Nicolette has always acted older, even when I was an adolescent. The age gap felt larger than what it truly is. It was made worse when our previous Alpha, Caleb Farrow, her father, was murdered by another Pack. I still have no idea why the battle between Farrowline and Vestraline happened. It's been just over six years since we lost Alpha Caleb and most of his Circle. It changed Farrowline and the holes in the Pack's soul have only just started healing since Ridley has come along. But I don't think Nicolette has ever dealt with the trauma of losing her dad and despite how hard she is trying to hide it, she has changed since coming home from her trip to Rhiattline. Everyone can see it. The others she went with are being very tight lipped about their trip and I caught a few of them throw concerned side looks at Nicolette since they got back.

'What's wrong?' Nicolette asks straight up, her eyes on her laptop screen as she types away. The female is a machine and is richer than Tobias. Yes, she is a head boss at Farrow Group, but she has so many side-hustles and projects that if you saw her without a device attached to her hand you probably wouldn't recognise her. 'You look like shit, Gilly.'

'Thanks,' I chuckle and finish my beer to manage my overactive senses. Fiddling with the label, I look over at the burning, scented candle someone lit down the table and fight my gag reflex.

Fucking lavender is the worst scent in the world.

Pulling the small tube of eucalyptus oil from my jean pocket, I dab a very small drop on my finger and then under my nose. The sharp and pungent aroma hits me and I breathe in the subtle minty and citrus hints buried under the overpowering fragrance. It's one of my favourites because it wipes my palate clean so that I can have a break from being a tracker for a moment.

Throwing me another quick glance, Nicolette stays quiet. That's why I love seeking her out when I'm not in the mood, especially when she has that serious look on her face. No one comes too close to Nicolette when she looks like she's ready to throw her laptop across the room. Nicolette Farrow is a dominant female through and through. My wolf always feels at ease beside her like she knows that she can relax. A dominant wolf always sits on edge, ready to protect and fight for Pack. I'm very aware that I'm not the most dominant of dominants. It's who I am. I'm not in the same league as the other members of the Circle or with a shifter like Nicolette, and it's okay. It's not my job. I am a tracker...*whatever the fuck that is worth.*

'I messed up a lot lately and I'm just waiting for Tobias to decide what he wants to do with me. To punish me,' I say to the bottle, the label now destroyed in my hand.

Making a small sound in the back of her throat that makes me smile, Nicolette speaks to her busy fingers as they fly over her keyboard. 'Gilly, you've been miserable for months and yes, you fucked up the other night at the club. I don't think Tobias is punishing you. He doesn't have to, you are doing a good enough job of that yourself.'

Damn, that stings. 'I know,' I agree with a sigh. 'But I can't stop feeling like giving the blood oath with Ridley was the wrong thing to do.' I want to scream that doing it screwed me up and that my tracker's nose is now broken and I think I'm going mad but bite my tongue hard enough to taste blood.

'Gilly, did you feel the pull?'

Referring to the deep stirring feeling that formed in my soul when I stood watching a very injured, pale Ridley sitting before the Pack as one by one the Circle wolves declared their love and loyalty to her as our new Luna, I nod slowly remembering that moment. 'I did feel it.'

We're taught as wolves that when an Alpha and a dominant have a connection that will benefit the Pack, they feel a pull to bind themselves to each other. Tobias speaks of it often and Ridley and Delfina couldn't stop discussing the way they knew they needed to 'keep each other' as Ridley would say when it happened for them recently. My biggest issue is that I felt the need to offer the blood exchange and bind myself to Ridley and Tobias first when normally it is the Alpha that does. Watching the others with Ridley, I had an out of body experience and before I knew what I was doing, I was kneeling before her, speaking the words that would make me a leader of Farrowline and promising to serve her and Tobias until my dying day.

That part I don't regret.

However, I don't fit the mould of a typical Circle wolf. I'm not as dominant, I'm not that aggressive and deep down, I really just feel broken and self-conscious.

Everything is different now though.

'The only thing standing in your way, is you, Gil,' Nicolette continues and I'm now the centre of her attention. The impact makes my wolf stand to attention and listen. She is a Farrow through and through because when those eyes find you, you listen. 'Stop it.'

Chapter Fourteen

Feeling lighter after confessing some of my concerns with Nicolette, I throw my head back and laugh at the very inappropriate story Jax is telling everyone. The sun paints the sky in deep orange and reds and the fire drums scattered amongst the drinking and happy Pack are slowly lit. It's still early and should be a great night with Pack.

We all needed this and the energy around the backyard is light and comfortable. The food is cooking and I lay back on the large male beside me on the outdoor lounge in need of some contact. As if picking up on my desires, Oliver curls his arm around me and tucks me in close. He smells like sandalwood and citrus splashed with a tinge of malt. The strength of the scent tells me that he was just running around on four legs. It's intoxicating.

Ridley cradles Noah against her chest as the young pup slowly drifts to sleep. Delfina is laughing hysterically at the dumb Jax story while Dom sits beside her chuckling in that sexy male way with his focus on his mate. He has a dopey look of love on his face.

Easton scowls then jumps in to defend himself when he appears in Jax's story. His gaze is set on the giggling female tucked into his side. Adalee seems very content. Sara is nursing Gianna while Liam feeds her a snack trying not to laugh at the way Jax and Easton start to argue. Her little bump is only just now showing. I can smell the subtle sweetness that all pregnant females have. The further a pregnant females gets, the stronger the scent. I can't describe how that smell fills your soul and makes you smile.

The laughter builds as does my spirit. I have no desire to grab for the bottle of gin under the chair. I love that no matter how tense it has been between Oliver and I, the moment I sat next to him, he pulled me close.

Too focused on Oliver as he massages my shoulders while we discuss a potential holiday we've all been talking about that we know isn't going to happen until the myriad of issues Farrowline have to face are resolved, I barely register the two newcomers until it's too late to run. When the male speaks, my muscles clench in reaction and I blink up at Oliver who throws me a sympathetic look before squeezing my shoulder in reassurance.

'Jay. Katrina. How are you both this evening?' Tobias asks.

'We are well, thank you Alpha,' Jay replies, his voice shaking slightly which draws my attention to him. Katrina is nervously shuffling on her feet and I put it down to being in front of all of the massive, intimidating males. What he said to me plays in my mind and I have to literally shake my head to rid myself of the memory of our last day as a couple. He had already left for Lilongranline and I was sitting around waiting for his call to say he had gotten to the small town safely, which never came. I was worried sick and even had the Alpha call and check to make sure he and the other packmates that went with him were okay. I didn't think anything was wrong when Tobias reassured me they were fine and that Jay was too busy to speak to me.

I was so stupid.

Katrina still seems a little lost amongst Pack and I contemplate if Jay was right in that I've made it harder for her through my actions.

Jay is very animated as he interacts with everyone and I stay silent, waiting for him to include me in the conversation, which doesn't happen. Not that I expected it really.

I take the time with their backs to me to really study the pair. They seem 'off' and my wolf stirs slightly under my skin as I become fixated on Katrina's narrow waist. Jay is laughing too loudly at whatever Ridley has just said and Delfina and I catch eyes for a moment and I see that she is thinking that this is an odd interaction too.

Shrugging slightly, I start to put it down to the pair just being awkward and am about to lean back against Oliver when I sense it.

My back stiffens and my blood chills in my veins as I register what I've just scented. It's like the world slows down and my poor, useless brain needs a solid minute to understand this new information. An involuntary gasp escapes my lips and when Jay turns around to lock those familiar eyes I used to get lost in, I see the moment he realises that I know.

Oliver tenses beside me and I avert my gaze and try to work out how to function.

'Is everything all right?' Tobias asks and I can't help but think that he knows what's going on which wouldn't surprise me, the senses of an Alpha trump anything that I possess.

Jay pulls his attention from me and draws Katrina to his side. 'Well, Alpha we just wanted to let everyone know that we are...' the dramatic long pause does nothing to help me and I fear for a moment that I can't draw enough air into my lungs. I'm frozen, unable to move. The pair share a look and the energy around the Circle changes instantly and I want to cover my nose to block out the sweetness. The last piece of my heart is shattered when Jay finishes, 'pregnant.'

The cheering and back slapping fills the backyard and it doesn't take long for the rest of the Pack to pick up on what's going on. Everyone takes a turn in congratulating the mated pair and while I feel many eyes on me, I can't find the words.

Sitting on the lounge, staring into space, I silently break. Every stupid self-doubting word comes to mind as I quickly reach for the bottle under the seat and slink away. My feet can't carry me fast enough as I pretend like I'm super happy for the couple while I die inside.

Finding it hard to draw in enough air, I hurry into the trees and the moment I'm out of sight, I run.

I run and run, afraid that there's nowhere in this world where I can escape.

Chapter Fifteen

I'm miserable and grumpy and ready to bite someone so I stay wolf and patrol one of the south sections of territory that's deep in the forest of Farrowline. It's dark now and I'm not technically on duty because of the barbeque and I should have a second packmate with me, but out here I can relax and I don't have to control my senses.

It was supposed to be me.

I was supposed to have Jay's pups and make a den with him and grow old together. It was my dream. I believed it would be me.

I never got any closure. I never got the anger or the months before a breakup where you begin to protect your heart before you finally leave. No, I was in full blown love with him. I was 'walking on sunshine,' as they say. Then in a single, out of the blue moment, everything changed and I was dumped for someone else.

I'm too busy wallowing in self-pity when I hear the rumble of thunder in the distance. Rain belts down only moments after and I stand thinking that this is a clear representation of my life right now. Soaking wet in the middle of the dark forest on my own, I roll my eyes and settle in for a long night.

Back against a smooth trunk, I'm not too far from the territory line that divides Farrowline to the city neutral zone at the very far side of our Pack lands.

I can't help feeling like this is somehow a metaphor for my life right now. I'm drenched, depressed and on my own. The only good thing is that I finally have a moment to myself without having to control my overbearing nose. Out here, in the wilderness, I'm free.

In a half state of rest and alertness, I frown deeply when my skin erupts in shivers.

Sitting straighter, I search the forest. A growl builds in my chest and I have no idea why. My wolf is unsettled and it confuses me as I watch the lightning streak through the sky, illuminating the darkness.

Rolling thunder shakes the trees and I have an overwhelming and uncharacteristic need to act.

The pull on my wolf is impossible to control. Like an adolescent, I have no power when she decides to hunt and I shift.

Hunt.

It is a command. A force driving me to act. There's no logic in it. No *human* in it.

Running through the dark and dense forest, I can barely feel the weight of the water as it hits my fur and slides off. The thick drops smash my eyes, get up my nose and into my ears. My tracker senses are not affected though. There's a tug in my soul. A force driving me forward as I run toward the brink of territory lines.

Lightning brightens the sky and the rain intensifies. It's pouring and my paws sink into the now soaked soil.

Jumping rocks and dodging trees, I follow the pull and grind to a halt at the invisible barrier keeping me safe in Pack.

Staring out into the forest of Sylo, I know there's something out there. Something that requires my attention.

Looking in the direction that my wolf desperately wants to continue towards and then back to inner territory, I battle between what to do. The torrential rain isn't helping and catching a very faint scent on the air only because of the power of my tracker abilities, my hackles rise and totally under the control of the beast, we take off into the trees.

I'm far from Farrowline territory and breaking countless rules when I come to a halt, my paws covered in mud, and growl.

Scanning the trees, I know there's a beast up ahead and every muscle in my back tenses when the cheetah finally steps into view.

Despite the weather, I can see perfectly.

My nose is strong and I pick up a subtle identifier that lets me know that the loner is the one who came onto our territory. That he was one of the ones who hurt my packmates.

I bare my teeth in warning and rage.

This is what my wolf was hunting. I'm all animal. She has completely taken over.

The loner stands still, his head bent as he assess me. We are separated by large rocks and a fallen tree but I'm fully aware that it means nothing in a battle. My stupid human logic starts to work and I realise that I shouldn't pick a fight with a predator on my own this far from den. I have no idea what I was thinking. I stand my ground contemplating my choices. It was my wolf who led me out here, pulled by something I can't understand.

Silence fills the world as I stare into bright yellow eyes. My attention is locked on the cheetah when the ground vibrates with the next rumble of thunder. It's distracting and I turn to quickly look at what has caused the cheetah to no longer be focused on me.

Stepping out from the forest to my right, one of the largest wolfs I've ever seen slowly emerges.

Chapter Sixteen

My stomach drops and I feel adrenaline rush my veins at the sight of the stranger. I almost lose control of my wolf as fear takes over and I manage to not shift. I need to be on four legs. I need my teeth and animal instincts.

The new shifter is completely calm as if he knows that he's the biggest and scariest predator in the forest right now. And frankly, he is.

There's a part of me that wants to lower to my belly and submit and another that weirdly wants to go to him and stand beside him. I take in the jet-black fur with the strip of brown that runs down his chest. His black eyes clash with mine and I take a small step back.

For too long, I stand completely still, my eyes dancing between the cheetah and the wolf. I have no idea what is about to happen but I do know that I'm fucked. Against the cheetah and with my anger, I had a chance. But if I have to fight this male, I'm screwed.

Calling to Farrowline is not an option.

The tension in the air is volatile and is only made worse when two more male wolves come from the trees. One is a deep blonde, the other similar in colour to the jet black one eyeing off the cheetah but with a strip of white running down his chest.

I don't move a muscle. The situation is so confronting and confusing that I have no idea what I should do. With a bit of luck the males will start fighting each other and I can get the fuck out of here. However with the way my life has been going lately, it's unlikely I will get out of this unscathed.

The two new males stay back as if uninterested in what is going on. It's the predator close to me that I keep an eye on.

The feline looks between me and the massive wolf clearly trying to work out if we are on the same side and frankly, I'm not naïve enough to believe that just because we are both wolf shifters that he'll help me.

Our world doesn't work like that.

He is not Pack.

The wolf just seems bored, his energy is calm like coming across this sort of situation happens regularly for him and it makes me want to bite him for some reason.

However, I find my focus locked on the loner that hurt my family and not the one who could kill me with a single flick of his paw. The others are keeping their distance which I pray they continue to do.

Male ego always wins and it is no surprise that the cheetah seems to make a decision and turns to face me. No matter what, we are here for a fight and he smells like a male who wouldn't back down.

With limited choice and with the energy coming off the wolf telling me that he isn't really here to start anything, I keep him in my peripherals and turn to find myself back in a staring match with the feline.

My muscles tense as I ready myself for the fight that's about to happen and curse the damn beast under my skin for the hundredth time for getting me into this situation.

Standing firm, I pray that this isn't my last night on earth.

The cheetah shows me his intimidating fangs before taking a step in my direction and then stops in his tracks when the male wolf mimics his actions. Moving closer toward the space dividing me and the loner, the energy around the new wolf changes.

Wide eyed, I try not to take my focus from the cheetah but it's impossible. Male wolf's eyes are clear and almost glowing as he watches the feline.

My jaw almost hits the floor at what he is doing. The cheetah tries his luck and steps again in my direction to stop once more when the male steps with him.

Getting angry at the way the cheetah is behaving, like he knows he can take me out and can do this slowly, I shuffle on my feet, bare my teeth and am about to match the walking game that is happening—but stop dead.

The male wolf whips his head in my direction and growls a sound that liquifies my insides. I understand the warning. I can't believe the nerve of him. Like I'm Pack and he's my superior, he has just told me to stay.

It lights a fire under my rage but before I can respond, the two males go back to sizing each other up. Having clearly realised that he's no match to the wolf, the cheetah gives us one last hiss of hate before he slides back into the trees.

I'm now alone with the deadly predator.

Running those black eyes over me one last time, I watch in awe as the unknown wolf shifts to human.

I gape at the tall, bulky and incredibly captivating male now standing before me uncaring about the thick rain. I guess he's in his early thirties. He has wavy black hair that falls to his shoulders, a wide jaw, thick eyebrows that shape his masculine features and he radiates aggressive, unwavering energy which is emphasised by the hard-as-nails look on his face. With his fair skin, I begin to try and piece together where he could be from. He's wearing loose hiking pants, a black, long sleeve breathable shirt and brown mountain boots, and a look that makes me want to show him my canines and warn him to back off.

Chapter Seventeen

'You are Farrowline.'

I shiver at the tone of his deep, gravelly voice. I don't know if he has just asked me a question or stating a fact. Without showing any kind of emotion or concern about having my teeth bared or that we are both dripping wet, he turns his back.

Like actually turns his back.

It's an insult.

The growl that vibrates through my body is involuntary.

The arrogant ass makes a sound and the two males, who are lounging in the rain like they are on holiday, rise reluctantly and come over to us. I dig my claws into the wet, soggy ground and watch, hyper focused as the pair shift to become just as equally attractive males.

My core clenches.

The one with blonde, shoulder length hair, a perfectly straight nose set on a face so flawless, I swear he stepped off a runway, has me almost swallow my tongue. He smells like birchwood and molasses and something very subtle I can't put my finger on. It's sweet and intoxicating. A complete and utter contrast to the larger, douche-ie first male.

The younger of the two walks over to stand beside the arrogant male—*it's like his face is stuck on that look*— and grins at me. I nearly fall to the floor. I know that he and Stuck-Face are brothers. All blood family have a strand of scent that connects them as related but they couldn't be any more different. The young one has a boyish charm. Light, brown hair that falls around his face, covering honey-coloured eyes. He is beautiful with full lips and long, *I'd die for them*, lashes.

Blonde Hot Male steps up, his smile wide and his blue eyes gleaming. Similar in age to Stuck-Face, he emits an alluring energy that has me stop baring my teeth in warning. Which seems to make him grin wider, like he has won some kind of prize.

'Forgive us, female of Farrowline. We mean you no harm.'

This one is obviously the leader and he holds his hand out to Young Male who hands him a scrunched, yellowish envelop in a clear sleeve that he grabs from his back pocket.

I pick up the subtle tell-tale strand that informs me that the trio are related. Two brothers and a cousin—I guess.

Well, I know. I just doubt my ability.

Holding the envelope in the air towards me, I become fixated on the way the thick muscle in his arms bunch and stretch before he snaps me back to what he is saying when he declares, 'I have a message for the Alpha of Farrowline. My name is Elliot Colton of the Pack of Coltonline. My packmates, Banner St. Cloud,' Elliot indicates to Stuck-Face who just keeps that stuck, emotionless look on his face like he's too cool to be here.

'And Logan St. Cloud.' Young Ones salutes. They all have on the same butt-hugging jeans that you see in those human cowboy movies. The trio give off that rough-it on the land, vibes.

'I request a Meet with your Alpha and his Circle to discuss urgent matters.'

The statement pulls me from my thoughts and I once again bare my teeth. The request is formal and hard to ignore. Coltonline is a remote Pack in the deep south of the country. You don't hear their name often. I have to really shuffle through all I've ever learnt about them over the years and even then all I can come up with is the possibility that they may be the ones that live at the bottom of the country in the harsh forests of Jenolan.

If I'm correct, the forest of the south is typically covered in snow and is notorious for being dangerous. The shifters down there are rough and live a very different Pack structure than Farrowline. Much smaller family units within sections of the wider territory are responsible for their own assigned parts and patrolling their little territory.

Catching the hints of aromas coming from the envelope, I can practically taste the snow and the intoxicating smell of snow gum trees.

A little stunned and uncertain, I only shift to human because I can't communicate effectively on four legs. But I keep my distance. Which doesn't seem to bother them. They all look at me with varying degrees of appraisal and I force my feet to not shuffle as they all run their eyes over my body.

'We will not harm you, female,' Stuck-Face, or rather the one Elliot introduced as Banner, states.

Brow rising, I can't help but clap a hand on my hip and give him what I hope is a killing glare. Water gets into my mouth as I talk, 'you could try, Banner St. Cloud of the Pack of Coltonline.' I get a great deal of satisfaction by making those thick eyebrows rise. 'You're a long way from home,' I declare, my eyes back on Elliot. I don't know much about their Pack but with the last name Colton, I assume he is related to their Alpha.

Young One, Logan, smiles wide at how I've spoken to his brother.

'We are. And I request a Meet,' Elliot informs me.

I wonder at the power dynamic between the trio when Stuck-Face interjects, reminding me that, 'honour requires you to take us to your Alpha or a leading member of your Pack.'

What a douchebag.

He moves to take something from his back pocket and I brace myself, my wolf ready as we watch what he's going to do. Slowing down his movement, with his focus fixed on me, I watch in stunned awe as Banner pulls out a small hunting knife and slices his palm quickly. The metallic tang of blood hits me and my nose wiggles involuntarily at the impact.

'I come with no hate in my heart and swear to not harm a member of Farrowline or yourself, unless in self-defence or the laws of the Meet are broken. My packmates will honour my oath.'

Grunting a noise at my silence, which I only interpret as indifference, Banner seems to be waiting for something from me, which he can continue to do as I work through my options.

Young One doesn't speak, just cuts his palm with a knife from his own pocket. Elliot doesn't seem in much of a hurry to declare a blood oath but he eventually does.

This is the worst time for something like this.

Farrowline doesn't need any more drama and we have a bad history with the outsiders coming to our territory and using those words. That's how we lost our old Alpha and half of his Circle. I'm torn between the trauma of the past and my honour as a leader of Farrowline.

I spin around and let my senses flare when I feel a change in the energy around us. It dawns on me how far out of territory I am and that I'll be missed soon.

Making a decision I can't help but feel will have a profound impact on my life somehow, I motion for them to follow and start running just before I shift and feel the mighty males do the same close behind me.

Chapter Eighteen

The storm is relentless and loud enough to hurt my ears.

My brain hurts.

I shake off my fur and stand on two legs and stretch out.

'Shouldn't you call someone, female?'

I don't reply and continue to lead them to Farrowline territory. I know where to take them that'll ensure my pack's safety. I plan to read the note Elliot showed me, assess the situation and then call Tobias.

I'm hungry and drained so I just ignore Banner who *tells* me, 'you must call your Alpha or Pack leaders. Only they can give permission for outsiders to enter their territory.'

I don't feel the need to let him know that *I am* a Farrowline leader. Letting the males know that they can stay or follow, that it makes no difference to me, I feel the moment my feet step back onto Farrowline.

It's home.

My wolf relaxes and I feel safe and secure, even with the potential threats behind me. I don't falter but continue to head in the direction of the cabin. I'm fully aware of the males who stop at the invisible line.

Having scented the two Farrowline dominants before they come from the trees, their wolves large and imposing, I turn and signal the three behind me to stop.

A little nervous, I indicate for Gregor and Molly to shift when they come stalking from the forest. Gregor's grey eyes assess the situation instantly and I hold out my arms when he and Molly growl. I feel the energy behind me change as Banner, Elliot and Logan tense. They stay quiet though.

Eventually responding to my command to change, Molly and Gregor, two of our senior predators, stand tall.

'What's going on Gilly?' Gregor asks and I try to remind myself that I'm a Circle wolf and that I hold authority now.

'I need you to go and get Alpha Tobias and the others quickly,' even I can hear the hesitation in my own voice and I curse myself. I'm not used to holding power and frankly I don't feel like I do.

Frowning deeply, Gregor hasn't taken his eyes off the males behind me. He hasn't moved or listened to my instructions. Molly hesitates as if unsure what to do. Instead of following my instructions, she asks what's happening. The pair look on edge, like they could wolf-out at any minute.

Turning toward the three newcomers, I know I have to stay calm or risk some kind of breaking of Meet laws. Wolf shifters are bound by Pack laws as well as rules set down by our society. Alpha's from around the country meet annually and we all ensure the safety of our community. Laws and rules around a Meet are sacred and why Farrowline didn't get into a great deal of trouble with the other pack alphas after the incident that claimed the lives of our previous Alpha, Caleb Farrow, and the majority of his Circle. The Pack that broke the laws of our shifter society, Vestraline, were wiped out after that. A decision made by not only Tobias, Dom and the other Circle, but by a number of Packs in the country.

'I have everything under control. The laws of a Meet stand. Please go and get the Alpha. We will be at the cabin,' I implore, praying that they listen. I don't know if I should be telling them more than that. A year ago they were my superiors.

The newcomers don't speak and I'm grateful.

The pair share a look that I can't decipher before telling me to be careful just before they both shift and head into the trees.

A little anxious and uncertain, I lead our group quickly through the trees to the cabin nestled deep in this far section of Farrowline.

Entering the studio style den, I try to ignore the smells that wash over me when I'm met with Delfina and Dom's scents. The pair have been using this place for months and despite Delfina living with Dominic now, they use this space regularly, much to everyone's amusement.

Flicking on the lights, I leave the door open for the trio to follow. The wooden cabin is old and tucked amongst the thick forest of this side of Farrowline. Gene, Kurt and I used to come here when we were adolescents to sneak booze and fool around with Gene's stupid Ouija board and scare the shit out of each other.

Nothing much has changed with the furniture. There is still the same dark wood bedhead and bedside table along one wall. The kitchenette against the back and the door to the small bathroom is to the left. The loungeroom has the same ancient television but the couch has been updated and I don't really want to know what Dom and Delfina did to the last one to require a new lounge.

'Take a seat,' I inform the males as they step cautiously through the door. Banner is in the lead and I take note of the position they have placed Elliot. Young One is at the back, with the other Coltonline male in the middle. It tells me a great deal and I wonder for the billionth time why they're here.

I put on the kettle and begin to look to see if there is anything to eat in the white fridge I swear used to belong to my great grandmother.

Chapter Nineteen

I'm starving. Even with my back turned to the rest of the cabin and the males in it, I'm fully aware of them moving around. Elliot takes the seat I offered at the chipped ancient dining table.

'I'm uncomfortable that you have not gained permission for us being here. We have urgent matters to discuss with your Alpha,' Banner states like a broken record.

Turning, I flick the fridge closed and watch the male pace the cabin like he's a trapped wild animal. Young One has claimed a position leaning against the door and if I wasn't in such a state, I'd be wiping up my drool from the floor if I had time to truly admire the sight. I can't wait to describe him to Gene and Kurt.

Banner is the only one moving around.

'Why do you assume that I don't have the power to grant you permission myself?' My temper is snapping and my body is still a little high on adrenaline from the almost fight I just had out in the forest.

The side-look I get is enough to have me see red, but I bite my tongue. He just continues like he can't pick up on my energy. Which is ridiculous because he is dripping with dominance.

'Probably has something to do with the fact that you were out of your territory lines picking a fight with a male loner three times your size. A leader wouldn't do that, or at least not in my Pack or family unit. Also, your packmates didn't seem to jump into action at your words.'

My jaw hits the floor. 'Excuse me?' I huff, I can almost feel the heat of my rage. 'You don't know—'

'What?' he cuts me off. 'I don't know that you were doing the wrong thing before?' Banner asks the table beside the bed that he's inspecting like he's getting the lay of the land in case he needs to protect himself. It's a very male thing to do which makes me even grumpier. It's offensive that he thinks I would put a wolf shifter who has formally asked for a Meet into a situation that would endanger his life.

'It was very dangerous, what you did. You are lucky you don't belong to me.'

I open my mouth to tell him to go fuck himself but am cut short by the attractive male at the table.

'Banner, don't pick fights with the locals, and especially not a female one at that. Knowing your luck, her mate will walk in and rip you to shreds and what would I tell my dear mother? That her beloved eldest nephew was mauled by a Farrowline wolf because he couldn't keep his comments to himself?'

'I can just see the headstone now,' Young One, Logan, adds and his tone makes me smile despite my rage. There's something about the way his eyes twinkle as he winks at me that has my stomach flutter. 'Beloved brother and Pack leader. Died because of his mouth.' The two share a good laugh while Banner ignores them completely.

Banner makes a point of saying, 'she doesn't have a mate.'

Which has my teeth elongate. They retract the minute he flicks those dark eyes over his broad shoulder. They scream at me to never do what I did out in the forest again.

The audacity.

'Fucking hell, Banner, shut up,' Elliot groans and draws my attention from the arsehole. Logan just looks like he is having the best time watching the exchange. 'Gilly, I apologise for my cousin. We have travelled a long distance and have barely stopped.'

'He's *hangry*,' Logan mumbles which I don't understand because he could whisper and we would all still hear him. Banner growls at him and I smile because I know a number of males who act just like this when they are hungry and angry. Logan seems to read my mind because I get a wink that melts my anger a little.

'What does your letter say?' I bark out instead of telling Banner to go to hell.

Banner doesn't even flinch at being reprimanded by his cousin, he continues to move around the space and he stops at the end of the bed and touches the folded blanket.

He's different to the males of Farrowline, they all are.

A little like Delfina, I can feel their wolves on the surface as if they wear their beasts more than their human, which should make every alarm go off in my head. However, I don't feel threatened.

'It's for the eyes of Tobias Farrow or a leader of Farrowline, Gilly,' Elliot says as a way of apology. I think I'm also a little hangry because I have to fight with my wolf to stay calm as she brushes against my skin, ready to get loose.

'You're safe with us,' he states unexpectedly, having clearly misunderstood my energy. 'We are only here to speak to your Alpha and leaders.'

'I'm not afraid of you,' I whisper and get a grip over myself and stand tall.

I busy myself getting towels for us and throwing them over so that they can dry off. Which they each catch effortlessly.

Silence descends in the cabin and I keep Banner in the corner of my eye as he continues to pace, having sensed that he's probably the biggest threat.

Getting to work boiling the kettle and organising mugs to make some coffee, I spin around when the wolf stops and all three males come to attention. Logan pushes off the wall. His eyes darting to Banner and Elliot. Banner steps into the middle of the room and I'm not sure who he is guarding as his body is more angled to be in front of me than Elliot.

The arrogant arse gets bigger as he stands tall and goes to move to the door.

I stop him with a quick, blunt growl that has him pause and look eerily slowly back at me as if to tell me that he's in charge now—not me.

Wanker.

Chapter Twenty

I *feel* Tobias, Oliver and Jax before they come striding through the door. Wind rushes through the cabin bringing with it the scents of Farrowline. We are deep in the forest. The only light coming from the relentless lightning streaking the sky just before the world shakes with thunder.

Tobias is all Alpha as he steps into the cabin looking toward me instantly as if to ensure I'm okay before those forest green, intimidating eyes fall onto the newcomers.

Banner to his credit stands tall in all his dark glory and looks our Alpha in the eye before bowing his head slightly in respect. Jax and Oliver are walls of pure muscle behind Tobias.

Elliot jumps off his seat instantly and moves to Banner's side and I can't help but think he's trying to tame the solid predator. 'Alpha Tobias, I apologise for our unannounced appearance close to Farrowline territory. My name is Elliot Colton of the Pack of Coltonline. Eldest nephew to the Alpha of Coltonline. These are my cousins, Banner St. Cloud and Logan St. Cloud, the sons of the Beta of Coltonline.'

My heart summersaults and flutters staring at the backs of the three large, very attractive, very intimidating and intriguing males.

Well, all except Banner. I know males like him and frankly, it's not my cup of bourbon. No, my eyes go to the blonde supermodel. Elliot is hot even from behind.

'We found your female...' Elliot begins and I'm pulled out of my daydreaming.

Banner looks over his shoulder at me and I feel my face heat.

Shit!

I try my best to control my now pounding heart so that the males standing around the cabin don't hear it. A muscle twitches under my eye as I force my face to not react to the adrenaline pumping through my veins.

Double shit!

Tobias and the others will kill me if they find out that I left territory. I think I technically broke about five Pack rules today. Banner and I find ourselves in a weird staring match and I pray to the heavens that he can see the warning, or let's be honest, I think my eyes are now pleading with the male to stop Elliot from giving me away. I'm already in the bad books with Tobias. The way I've been acting and the threat of my position in the Circle being made clear, I can't have this.

I don't think I take a breath until I see those dark very man-ly eyebrows furrow slightly as if he can hear the voice in my head shouting at him to keep his plump- *I wonder what they taste like if he wasn't such a dick-* bloody lips closed.

Banner turns back around and I watch in pained anticipation as the male touches Elliot subtly on the side of his arm.

Totally confused and unsure if I'm seeing things, I almost miss the end of Elliot's sentence.

'She found us,' Elliot concludes much to my surprise and continues with his back to me. 'I have requested this Meet as I have urgent matters to discuss.' 'Your female assured us that coming here was approved,' Banner interjects.

Eyes now narrowing at the newcomer who has just saved my bacon but still doesn't believe that I have authority, I wait to see what Tobias will do. Oliver and Jax share a look that makes me smirk.

Tobias shows no emotion as he says, 'you've been approved to enter Farrowline by one of my Circle.'

I smirk at the way Banner's back tenses slightly at hearing that I'm a leader of this Pack. I want to shout, 'take that', like an adolescent, but keep my mouth shut.

Even I can feel my own gloating in the way I stand taller.

Banner gives me the side eye and I swear I can see the annoyance in his gaze. I have an overwhelming need to flip him off.

Logan looks over at me and I smile like a youngster with a crush when he winks again.

Elliot laughs out loud and seems to find the entire thing funny.

Tobias watches everything closely as he continues, 'you're all welcome here as a guest for now, Elliot of the Pack of Coltonline.'

Tobias indicates for Elliot to sit at the round table close to where I'm now standing. They all size each other up and I bite the inside of my mouth to keep from making a noise in humour when Ridley's voice whispers in my head about predatory shifter males and their ape-ish-like chest beating behaviour.

Logan moves to the far wall and Oliver positions himself strategically close to me. Banner walks close to Elliot's back, keeping his body between my Alpha and his obvious leader.

Jax stays by the door.

Elliot says nothing as he hands Tobias the envelope from his pocket and we all stare as the Alpha of Farrowline takes it. Watching Tobias reading the letter, I'm hyper-focused on his face, looking for any reaction.

Tobias declares finally, 'several pack members of Coltonline have gone missing.'

Stunned, my wolf grumbles along with Oliver and Jax's beasts at the odd and confusing news. My eyes stay locked on our guests. The three haven't moved their gaze off my Alpha.

There is no emotion. Nothing. Each one hard and cold.

Nodding, Elliot finally speaks. 'Yes. My Alpha and uncle, the Alpha of Coltonline, Balthazar Colton and his only daughter, Sasha Colton, went missing two weeks ago.'

Chapter Twenty One

My heart sinks at what I've just heard and there's a moment of deep silence in the den that chills me to the core. The fact that an Alpha and a future Alpha are missing is incomprehensible. The impact that would have on a pack is huge. Their Alpha is not just their heart but the essence of their strength and power.

'And you know for a fact they haven't just left?' Tobias questions sceptically. I can hear the underlining concern in his tone and only because I know him.

Elliot speaks, his rough tone is deep and full of something that I can't quite name. Gone is the smile that has been on his face since I met him. 'We lost three young adolescents a little over a month ago. The trio went missing a few weeks prior to the disappearance of our Alpha and his daughter. We found two of the young ones a week after their parents sounded the alarm. Both dead. No older than seventeen. We were unable to name what killed them. We're yet to find the missing female.'

There isn't a single sound in the cabin as we absorb this information.

'We're not a large pack and every effort to find our Alpha family unit has been fruitless. We're currently without an Alpha. Our Beta is doing his best to step in, but we're on the verge of a massive shift in power.' My gaze quickly jumps to Banner who gives nothing away before landing on Logan. The poor male isn't as good at hiding his emotions. His eyes scream sadness and I can only guess the strain and pressure his father must be undertaking caring for a pack on his own. A Beta is second, Dom could do everything Tobias can, but he isn't Alpha. Even Oliver seems to relax his guard near the younger male in sympathy.

'We've heard of the loners who test your boundaries, Alpha Tobias. At the moment we've kept them at bay the four times they've tested our borders. But I'm not naïve to think that it will last. None of us are. They will see that we are weakened and one day they'll win. There *will* be major ripples for every Pack in this country if Coltonline falls. We need answers in order for our Pack to heal and look to our future.'

Again, no one speaks or reacts. The males around the room tense and I instinctively do too. I know I still have a great deal to learn about the skills and knowledge needed as a Circle member and leader, but we all know that every pack and territory in our country is important to the overall safety of our society. There aren't just loners we have to be concerned about, but other shifters and alphas. The battle for territory is the ultimate prize. Other packs keep us safe. Our alliances keep Farrowline secure despite us being the most powerful in this country. We still need to play the political game. Tobias, like his father before him, has worked on our relationships with all predatory and non-predatory shifters in the country. An entire pack collapsing would mean families needing shelter and the power of that land being given to whomever challenges Coltonline for it. Farrowline will be impacted.

I can see Tobias working through what is being said. Calculating each possibility.

'And you're asking for what?' Jax asks eventually.

'Assistance,' Banner is the one to answer and I cannot tell by the tone of Banner's voice who his anger is directed at. The mysterious male seems to be in pain. Clearly he's not happy about asking for help.

'What does your Beta and pack believe Farrowline can offer you in your search that will assist you?' Tobias asks casually, sitting back in his chair. He crosses his muscular arms over his broad chest and I bite my tongue to stay silent as a strange feeling grips my chest.

Running his gaze over the mass of shifters focused on him, Elliot gives off no emotion despite the situation he's in, 'it's no secret that you have a shifter in your Pack that has the power to help, Alpha. We've heard the rumours about the wolf who surpasses any tracker alive today or any we have seen in our collective history.'

Holy shit!

My brain short circuits at what he has just said.

There's a heavy silence, all eyes now on Tobias. His face doesn't give anything away. It takes my mind a ridiculous amount of time to work out that he could be referring to me. Which is confusing and a little intimidating.

Mind racing, I try to stay in the conversation. *How would anyone outside of Farrowline know of me? Or is it just a coincidence?* There are other gifted packmates in Farrowline, some that can track very well.

'You want us to send a wolf to help Coltonline? Send *our* tracker with you?' Elliot nods in response to Oliver's question. His crystal eyes stay locked on the newcomer in an assessing way. Not one of my packmates look to me.

'Who's going to guarantee the protection of any of ours on your territory?' Jax asks.

What happens next shocks me to my core.

Banner steps forward slightly. 'I am,' he growls. He seems to grow in size as he stares Jax down. 'I'll personally see to the protection of any wolf of Farrowline who is sent into our territory to assist in the recovery of our Alpha.' The passion and ferocity in the way Banner speaks has the room of shifters step closer in readiness for his attack. The male just stands, pulls out that same hunting blade from his belt, and cuts his palm again. He looks each and every one of us in the eye and I gasp silently at what he's doing. My chest tightens further and I find it hard to breath as I watch the blood drip from his palm to the wooden table. The scent hits me hard and I take an involuntary step back, feeling as I've just been punched. There's a pull in my body to answer his declaration, the same one that drew me out of Farrowline to hunt.

My wolf pushes against my skin, demanding to be released which just adds to my unease. She has never done this until today. We've always worked together but for the first time in my life I have no idea what she wants.

'As am I,' Logan supports his claim by mimicking his brothers actions. Elliot doesn't move.

'Your tracker will be under the protection of the family unit of St. Cloud. Me and mine will protect him with our lives,' Banner announces as if answering my question as to why Elliot hasn't spoken a declaration.

I almost chuckle at the 'him'.

I look to Jax and Oliver who make a point of not giving away anything as they meet my gaze. They definitely don't look impressed. Frankly, Oliver looks about ready to rip someone to shreds. He is hiding it well but I know him, I've known him my entire life.

Chapter Twenty Two

Unmoving, Tobias finally says calmly, 'this is a very unusual scenario.' I see his mind ticking in the way his jaw tenses.

I go to open my mouth and shut it as I don't know what I want to stay. My wolf scrapes against my skin, wanting out...wanting something.

'I understand, but we're in a dire situation, Alpha. Farrowline is our only hope,' Elliot replies coolly as if this isn't an intimidating meeting for him, its odd that he's so calm. 'Coltonline is barely hanging on. We need to find our Alpha, Alpha Tobias. We need to protect our pack. My cousins and I have swallowed our pride, travelled for days to get here and have given you our oath in order to do just that.'

'You do not know what you ask,' Oliver growls.

'No,' Elliot frowns. 'But you'd all do the same thing in our situation.'

Jax and Oliver share another look.

Biting my tongue to keep control, I shuffle on my feet. Pain shoots up my back and over my body as I fight to stay on two legs. Mind racing, I close my eyes to keep calm. The call for help has stirred something in me. Something deep and ingrained into my very soul. My wolf knows it, my human side takes a minute to understand what it is.

Before I can fully process my thoughts, Tobias speaks. 'I'd never deny a tracker a call to help. It's their nature to hunt and I wouldn't be worthy of my title as Alpha if I didn't let them decide. You have my permission to ask for assistance of our packmate and the best tracker you'll ever find. It will be up to the tracker to decide to hear your call of aid and the call Coltonline has sent.'

I don't think I'm breathing. I listen to Tobias speak with a lump in my throat as I realise what has my wolf so ready to react. I need to hunt. I'm compelled to answer this call. To let my wolf do what she was born to do. For the first time in my life, I feel like I know where I need to be and for the first time in my life it's not in Farrowline.

'I thank you, Alpha. The rumours of your leadership are correct,' Elliot sounds like he has won, that smile from before on his face again. He's a very attractive male.

'You can ask my tracker to hear your call for aide, Elliot Colton. It would be their decision.'

My stomach drops to my feet. *Am I doing this? Can I do this? Do I have the ability to find two shifters who've been missing for two weeks?*

Again, Banner is the one to speak, 'please, lead me to him and I shall offer a life debt for his service. He will be an honoured guest in my family unit and in my den. I have a family who are prepared to care and protect him in our territory.'

Looking across the room, I lock eyes with Oliver whose face has broken out in a grin and I'm sure it's in response to what I assume is the look on my face. Trust this arrogant ass to believe it would be a male he is looking for.

'Well, after that speech,' Tobias states, humour surrounding his words, 'ask our tracker.'

Brow furrowing slightly, Banner seems to consider what Tobias has just said. His gaze runs over Oliver and Jax quickly before landing back on our Alpha. 'Present him to me and I will.'

Tobias makes a deep sound in his throat. 'She's right here.'

I thank every god who may be listening that I kept my focus on Banner because the frown that forms on his face is priceless. Dark features now locked on my face, Banner's dark eyes are on mine. I need to move my gaze so I look about the room.

Oliver and Jax are staring. Tobias is just watching Banner and I think Logan and Elliot have now realised that I'm the tracker they have travelled all this way to find.

Logan laughs a sound that has me jump. It fills the cabin with humour, breaking up the tension in my body. Elliot claps his hands like this is the best news he has ever heard.

'You?' Banner asks and I have an overwhelming need to bare my teeth.

'Yes me,' I grumble.

'You're the tracker I've heard whispers about?' Doubt, it drips from every word Banner speaks.

That's it.

My growl rips from my throat and I let my wolf slip into my eyes. Oliver and Jax react similarly but not one of the males of Farrowline step in to defend me. They wouldn't disrespect me like that to show an outsider that I need one of them to back me. I can do this. I might not match the dominance of the males in the room but I am a leader of Farrowline.

'Yes, I am,' I bite back. 'And if you want my help, you can stop insulting me.'

'Oh cousin, for the second time, shut up.' Elliot jumps from his seat, forcing Banner to move aside. He's so unbelievably handsome, that I feel myself blush. My wolf hasn't reacted like this to a male in such a long time.

With a sweetness and yet, assertive and humble, Elliot bows. 'My Pack is in need, Tracker of Farrowline. We need your wolf. Coltonline needs you.' His eyes sparkle as they slowly rise to my face. Elliot stands tall and I forget how to speak for a moment.

Pulling my gaze from his is hard and I look to Tobias, seeking guidance from him to give me an order. I stand unsure what to say because how can I leave my Pack? It is all I know.

'But there's so much going on here, Tobias,' I whisper to my Alpha.

Nodding as if reading my mind and the struggle I'm in, Tobias doesn't get up having sensed that I need space to think. 'I know, but I know that you need to make the decision on what you feel is right. On what your wolf is saying. Do not feel that following your instinct is wrong or that you're doing something against Farrowline by saying yes. We will help Coltonline because that is who we are, Gilly. It is who *you* are.'

The males stay quiet as I process what Tobias has just said.

Tobias is an energy like no other. He stands and draws every eye to him. Filling the space with his Alpha presence, he states calmly, 'I think this is a decision that must be slept on. We have to discuss this with my Beta and other Circle wolves present. Elliot, you and your cousins are welcome here in Farrowline. It is almost morning. We have a small den close to inner territory for guests where you can rejuvenate from your journey which you can use while Gilly makes her decision.' Tobias has moved to the door, expecting everyone to start following.

'We cannot wait too long. I have to return to my territory,' Banner interrupts and he receives the full force of the Alpha of Farrowline who turns scarily slowly, his green eyes too dark as he stares unimpressed at the male a few steps from me.

'It's not a decision that can be rushed. Either you wait Banner St. Cloud of Coltonline or you remove yourself from my territory and find assistance elsewhere.'

Elliot springs into action, gripping his cousin's arm, I watch as his fingers dig into Banner's jacket and states with that perfect smile on his face, 'please Alpha Tobias, take the time you need.'

Banner makes a deep noise, that has me smirk but he keeps his eyes averted. He doesn't look impressed at all.

We all watch expectantly, waiting for Tobias's reaction. Nodding once after a tense pause, Tobias motions for me to come and I do instantly, hand on my back he leads me out into the waking day.

Chapter Twenty Three

I haven't said a word to anyone. Not when the Circle got together after I managed a few hours of sleep. Not when the Coltonline males were introduced to Dominic and Delfina who practically try to eat the trio, they were so protective and now I sit in the corner on Mama's patio watching as the pack hosts an evening barbeque for our guests while waiting for me to make a decision. Which I can't do with all these bodies around, invading my senses, so I'm hiding with a friendly bottle of bourbon.

Watching the three newcomers like a stalker, I stay in the shadows of the den away from everyone. Elliot, Logan and Banner moved to a table at the furthest point of the party and have been sitting and chatting with each other for an hour. No one has gone over to speak to them which is odd because Elliot oozes confidence and charm. I've been observing the way he interreacted with the members of my Pack, and it's effortless. Like a magnet he draws people to him, makes them feel at ease and has them eating from his hand. The only ones immune seem to be the Circle. I assume no one approaches their table because of the stone-faced one radiating 'don't speak to me' vibes.

Kurt and Gene both had the exact reaction to Logan as I thought they would. They are on the other side of the backyard with Ridley, Emma and Sara all giggling and chatting and throwing little looks at the group of new males.

Shaking my head, I can only imagine what the look Kurt and Gene share with each other means when their eyes drift from the newcomers to each other before they crack up laughing. The stupid voice in my head who whispers that I'm going to miss my two best friends has me sober up instantly.

I am going to miss them.

Heart in my throat, I try to swallow it down and end up choking on my emotions. I have never left Pack. I was born and raised in this forest. With these shifters. However, while it scares the shit out of me, I know I have to go. My wolf is being loud under my skin. She hasn't stopped pushing against my body wanting out. Wanting something that I'm petrified of giving her. I have no idea if I'm as talented as everyone says or if I truly believe that I'm capable of finding two shifters that I've never met before in a brand-new environment that sounds absolutely horrible.

Oliver sat me down after the tense, horrible meeting between the Coltonline males and the Circle and gave me the run-down of what it's like in Janolan. To sum it up—fucking freezing and dangerous. He wasn't happy. With that conversation playing around in my head, I put down the half-drunk bottle of liquor and make a decision.

'I'm going to go,' I tell Tobias later that night who looks up from his work laptop and stares at me. It's past midnight, Ridley and Noah are sleeping in the large room down the long hallway. I can hear their breathing. I can smell them easily despite the distance.

Tobias's face falls slightly and I stand to attention in the middle of his loungeroom trying to keep my conviction. There's a voice in my head screaming at me that I'm a freakin' moron, but there is another voice, a voice that I believe is controlled by the beast under my skin that is telling me that I *have* to do this.

That this is my calling.

'No,' is the simple yet firm declaration from behind me. My eyes stay fixed on my Alpha. I'm afraid that if I look behind me at the Beta of Farrowline and the other Circle members who have just entered the Alpha's den as if they knew what I was doing when I headed over here, that I'd agree to stay here and ignore my instincts.

'Dom,' Delfina reprimands forcefully. 'You can't tell her no.' I want to kiss the fierce, small female but I can't look away from Tobias in fear of losing my nerve.

'Yes, he can,' Easton adds and I close my eyes and wait for the argument to happen between the siblings.

Jax quickly steps in with his thoughts by adding, 'Gilly will be unprotected in a Pack so deep in the south, that not many shifters have ever been down there. It's days away. We won't be able to get to her in an emergency.'

My lip wobbles and breathing is now a mission but I stare into the forest green depths that haven't left my face. Tobias sits, listening to his advisors while I hold his gaze. I don't know what he sees when he looks at me. I know my position in Pack. I know my role and I know that I have no idea who I am anymore. That I have lost myself and going back to who I used to be is impossible. The blood exchanged between Ridley and myself triggered something within me that I can't ignore any more. The partying and the goofing around, that it's all in the past. Jay broke me and Ridley put me back together, but there are pieces missing now which are gone for good.

'Jax, Gilly cannot ignore who she is,' Delfina states simply and I wonder why she's so supportive of me when only hours earlier she was the one Dom and Jax had to control when Elliot, Banner and Logan introduced themselves. Delfina doesn't play nice with others very well and frankly, we're lucky she's on our side. I still find it odd that she thinks that this is a good idea because right about now, I think it's fucking dumb. And I'm regretting even opening my mouth.

Tobias hasn't broken our stare and for some nameless reason I haven't either. It's like I'm trying to draw strength and get confirmation that he's okay with this.

Brow furrowing when I realise that I don't think I could stay even if my Alpha told me to, I frown deeply. I have no idea what this means.

Tobias's face changes instantly and I see the moment he understands that there is no way to stop this. As if he has read my mind, he nods once and I feel the single tear fall down my left cheek.

'We can't protect her. We cannot allow this,' Liam demands in his 'dad' voice.

'We have to let her,' Oliver sounds defeated and I finally look away from the male who is my entire heart and at the other male who has been a rock in my life from the moment I was born. I hate the worry and the sadness etched on Oliver's face.

His Viking hair is out and flows down his shoulders and despite the seriousness of this moment, I smile and tease, 'I need to start using your shampoo to get my hair to look that shiny.'

Holding my gaze, Oliver steps over and cups my left cheek. Wiping the tear with his thumb, he smiles without it touching his eyes, 'you can't afford it,' he replies seriously.

The laughter boils up through my chest and with it some of the energy in my body releases. The others chuckle and I go from laughing to holding back tears in less than a minute.

Oliver pulls me into his body and wraps me in his strength. The entire Circle step over so that I can feel them. It is because of them that I'll find the courage to do what I'm about to do. To test myself in a way I never imagined I would be tested.

Tobias doesn't wait for the sun to come up. Without a word, he leads our entire group out into the forest and to the dwelling assigned to visitors. Its location is extremely defendable and far enough away from inner territory that it's safe for our most vulnerable packmates.

Gregor and a few of the wolves are patrolling the area and they watch us as we follow the path that leads us up the steps of the small but fully equipped den.

Tobias knocks because he is respectful not because he has to. This is his territory.

Banner is the one to open the door moments later. Logan is not far behind him and Elliot stands towards the back wall with a cautious look on his face.

I don't know how I found myself in the middle of the group of large Farrowline males, but I am.

Looking up at the imposing, emotionless predator taking up the space in the doorframe who seems ready for a fight, I don't catch the unimpressed look he throws me before stepping aside for us to come in.

Oliver and Jax haven't left my side and Tobias doesn't beat around the bush when he announces, 'Farrowline will answer your call for help. We will send our tracker to help you in your search for your Alpha.'

Tobias Farrow is scary when he is in Alpha mode. There is nothing of the sadness from before. No, standing in the middle of the room is Tobias Farrow, the Alpha of Farrowline.

'But hear me, Banner St. Cloud of Coltonline,' our Alpha continues, 'I will be sending one of my own with you and I'll be holding you to your blood oath. If my tracker is harmed in any way, and I will state again, in *any* way. Mark my words...'

My stomach drops, the hairs on my body stand on end as Tobias's eyes roam over the group of new males in the room.

Banner to his credit looks as stone-faced as ever.

'Your life will be forfeit,' Tobias finishes. Chills. His voice gives me chills.

The Alpha's promise hangs in the air and I hold my breath waiting to see what the hard-to-read male will do. I think everyone does as I slowly find myself pushed further behind Oliver, but Banner just nods. A single arrogant nod. His eyes never leaving my Alpha.

Chapter Twenty Four

I wake in a mood and roll out of bed. I follow my nose to the aromas of bacon and eggs and everything breakfast. I'm half asleep, my bed shirt comes to the top of my knees and I'm all blurry eyed and focused on food.

Scratching my head and rubbing at my face as I head down the hallway towards the kitchen and open living space, I sigh at the smell. 'Mum, I need coffee.' I'm not really paying attention to anything but my basic need for food and caffeine.

'The kettle is on the stove, honey,' is my mum's sweet reply.

Yawning wide and rubbing my eyes, I stretch and then stop dead when my nose seems to wake up.

Coffee. Pastries. Bacon. Eggs and *fucking males.* And not the ones I would expect in my den at this time of the morning.

Standing, with my hand in my messy, bed hair, my bed shirt now high enough to show things that really shouldn't be shown, I stare at the three oversized males at my mum's round, white table. Each one openly staring at me. Each one with a completely different look.

One with a small, very male, very masculine, grin.

One with eyes that scream humour.

And another with nothing but stone.

Elliot's smile widens when I scowl at the trio. My lips purse tightly and Logan's humour seems to grow with my growl. Banner and his expression-less face makes me want to flash my boobs or something to try and see if I he's actually alive.

Instead, I roll my eyes, try to find some dignity and head to the kettle without fiddling too much with the hem of my bed shirt.

'I was just getting to know these fine males that you'll be going with, sweetheart,' Mum sings when I throw her a glare. Mum seems totally unfazed that she has put me in this situation. To be honest she looks very content sitting amongst the newcomers and blushes when Logan leans forward and pours more tea from the teapot on the table that mum only brings out when the alpha or the Circle come over. She actually blushes and I look to the heavens for guidance. Dad had an early appointment this morning but my now working nose tells me that he was here only moments before so he was very aware who was in his den. Not that my mum would ever do anything. She and my dad are mates and have been since they were eighteen.

'How were you allowed into this den?' I ask no one in particular as I make myself a fresh coffee.

'Gilly love, we got approval to be in Farrowline by your Alpha this morning. Banner has given a blood oath. You, my dear, are now under the protection of Coltonline and your Alpha knows it,' Elliot finishes the end of his sentence speaking to his food.

I lean against the kitchen counter and let what he has just said sink in. Banner is quiet as he eats and I get the feeling, once again, that he's not impressed with this entire situation and that is exactly what I ask him. His reply is to lift those obsidian eyes to me in the most assessing and judgy way.

'Just wasn't expecting to be saddled with the runt of Farrowline when we came all the way here asking for help.'

Juice goes everywhere as Logan spits out the mouthful he has just chugged back.

Elliot chokes on the toast in his mouth and for some unknown reason my mum fucking chuckles.

Slamming my untouched mug down on the counter, I storm from the den and out into the small sitting area behind the building. I'm angry. No— I'm furious. I'm offended. I'm...shitting myself that I haven't left my pack *ever* and this'll be the first time.

Slumping down on one of the chairs up the side of the den, I grumble my annoyance. Growling at the male who comes around the corner, I only keep my teeth in my mouth because he places my coffee mug on the small table in front of me.

Turning my back so that I'm looking out onto the forest and not at the very intoxicatingly attractive predator, I ignore the way he asks if he can join me but then does so anyway.

'I apologise for my brother, Gilly. He's one of the best males I know,' Logan says as he sips his coffee. He is genuine and laughs when I tell him that he clearly needs to leave the south more and meet some people if Banner is the best male he knows.

'That's fair. Can I explain a little of our world to you? Just to help you understand,' he clarifies and smiles appreciatively when I nod.

'While my brother was out of line, we're all very appreciative of you agreeing to help us. The weight for us to come back with you was great and our father has put an immense amount of pressure on Banner to be successful here. Our pack is falling apart Gilly, and while my brother's social skills are lacking, we are all truly grateful to you. Banner especially. Our parents are influential shifters in Pack, my siblings and I live in a separate section of territory that was assigned to Banner when he came of age and became a ranked member of Coltonline. We are not like Farrowline. We're given our part of territory and it's our job to keep it safe and secure. When that happens we leave our parents and our family units to make our own ones. There are six of us siblings. Banner is the eldest, I'm second and we have two younger sisters, Grace and Maddy, and two younger brothers, Jesse and Freddy. Jesse and Freddy are twins and they will be nineteen in a few weeks. Grace is seventeen and Maddy is fifteen going on thirty-five and is partly the reason why Banner is eager to get back to our den. He is our guardian. He has been since he was thirteen really.'

Processing everything that I'm hearing, I feel a sliver of sympathy for Banner. *But only a sliver.*

Fifteen is a hard age for an adolescent female shifter. I think of all the issues we're having with our pack youngsters. I wonder if Maddy has shifted yet and instantly feel sorry for her, and for her siblings.

Moving so that I can see him better, I study the young male. His shoulder-length mousey blonde hair, his blue eyes and impressive size are one thing, but the energy that surrounds Logan St. Cloud communicates that he has a beautiful heart. He makes me comfortable and I hang on to every word that he says.

Wrapping my hands around the mug, I know Logan is watching my every move. 'Why do you live with Banner and not your parents?'

That's a great deal of responsibility to take on.

Shrugging, Logan studies me and for a moment, I feel instantly connected to him and I know he feels the same because he smiles warmly before answering.

'My dad is the Beta of Coltonline. My mum is a senior lieutenant. They both have their own territories to protect, and while my parents are supportive, they are also self-centred and self-absorbed. It was clear that pups were just a product of their love rather than something that they both planned for and frankly wanted in their lives. They're both extremely busy with Pack and as I look around Farrowline I realise it's the structure of Coltonline with how we distribute responsibility that has cultivated the culture of our Pack. But it's the only way it works in a large and harsh territory like ours. My parents never treated us badly. However, when we got the flu and chickenpox and fevers, it was Banner who would sit up with us through the night, nursing us to health. When we'd come home with a project for school and a hole in our clothes, it was my brother who glued and cut up paper and sewed our pants and everything else we needed. So, when he was told that he has territory to protect when he was nineteen, it was just natural that we all went with him. My parents didn't put up a fight and we were given a den and territory lines and left alone mostly.'

I don't know what to say. I feel like saying sorry for what I'm hearing but Logan isn't talking with hatred or resentment but love for his brother and his siblings. I have about a thousand question but instead I ask, 'so I'll be with you and your siblings in your den. Will they mind?'

Laughing loudly, Logan lights up. 'No, I think they'll be excited to have a new face around and I believe my sisters will be happy to have an adult female to put us males in line.'

Giggling, I bite my lip, contemplating what he's saying. It's so different and new. I have no idea what to expect which causes more anxiety over what I have decided to do.

'And Elliot?'

Giving me a knowing look, Logan shakes his head as if he knows why I'd ask. 'Elliot lives with my uncle and aunt a few territory lines away from ours. We are related through our mothers. His father is the brother of our missing Alpha and the family have taken the disappearance very hard.'

The fact that two Coltonline adolescents went missing and were found dead is unsettling but what I can't shake is the oddness of the third missing female that they didn't find. I wonder if Logan and the others understand that I may not be able to find their Alpha and his daughter alive. I've been contemplating this entire situation I'm putting myself in. This is so far removed from everything I'm used to. Taking a deep breath, I draw in the scents of my home and raise my head to the clear blue sky. It's set to be an amazing day in Farrowline.

My last day.

Chapter Twenty Five

Curled up in the corner of the patio outside Mama's den, I watch my Pack while wondering if I can do this. Wondering how my life has taken so many turns from what I expected that I no longer know which way is up and which way is down.

After the fucking news that was dropped at the barbeque, I feel like I have only really started to register it now as I watch Jay and Katrina across the open backyard. She is sitting on his lap and they are surrounded by shifters who Jay and I grew up with, 'our' friends and family. Now, they sit with the new couple. All of them happily chatting about genders and birth plans, while I sit on my own in a corner trying to not fall apart.

Not that I think I have any more emotions to give my heartache. Recently I feel more numb than hurt.

'You're new protectors told me you were over here.' Mum chuckles at my eye roll and sits down beside me. 'What's wrong my sweet girl?'

Resting my head on her shoulder and trying to stop my nose from picking up the damn over-powering clothes wash she has been using lately, I sigh. 'Just thinking about what I'm going to do in Coltonline.'

Patting my knee, 'you will find those shifters and then you'll come home,' she tells me with utter confidence.

Biting the inside of my mouth, my focus on Jay and Katrina, I whisper, 'what if I don't want to come home, Mum? Will you hate me forever if I leave and find somewhere else to be? A place that doesn't hurt this much. It was supposed to be me, Mum. I wanted it to be me.' My lip wobbles as I try to keep as quiet as possible. I don't have to explain what I'm referring to, Mum knows.

I taste her emotions as she registers and thinks through what I've just said. She knows what I'm talking about. 'Gilly, you're my daughter. Your father and I love you beyond words. This Pack, they love you. I told you. I told you so many times that what you were doing with Jay was not going to end well.'

Sitting up, I rest my head on the wall and close my eyes, I have heard this so many times. 'I know, Mum. I loved him. I fucked up. I've been fucking up a lot lately. I thought we'd hear the mating words.'

Tsking loudly, Mum shakes her head. 'Yes, you both did and I have to sit here and watch him be happy with his mate and watch you try and mend your broken heart. It's hard for a mother, Gilly. I know what you're going through. I know that you'll leave and there is a chance you won't come back. And, honey, I don't know if I'd blame you. Just look at them,' she changes the conversation so quickly that I have to catch up. I follow her gaze and groan. We both stare at the three very attractive, very masculine males who walk side by side from the trees. All three look up at me instantly and I shiver at the intensity of their predatory gazes. The Coltonline males are a sight for sore eyes for sure.

'I don't think you will be bored, honey. Not with males like those protecting you.'

Giggling, I throw my arms around my mum and hold her tight. 'Thanks Mum. I love you.'

Rubbing my back, I can feel her sadness and nerves to let me go. 'Oh sweetheart, I love you too. Go and heal. Go and find yourself.'

We break our embrace when my new 'protectors', as mum has just called them, make their way over to us.

Practically bowing at my mum, Elliot winks at me, completely ignoring the way I wipe the water from my cheeks quickly so they don't see.

Banner leans against the banister and follows my gaze when I look between the males to the one I can feel watching me now in the distance. Jay frowns deeply at me and shakes his head before looking away. My gaze drifts to the darked eyed male who gives away nothing of what has just transpired between me and my ex before I look over and nod when Logan asks if I want to show him around Farrowline.

The last twenty-four hours have been absolutely crazy.

I've been talked at. I've been pushed and pulled around the Pack as everyone tried to give me advice. I've been instructed on what to do and how to respond to any situation which seems to end with me calling Farrowline and wait for them to rescue me. Now I'm waiting with everyone, unsure if I've made the right decision.

Dom has organised for all my things to be sent down to Jenolan. I learnt that we're travelling south on four legs.

I don't think that I truly considered what the trio said about their long journey but it's kinda impressive that they came all the way up here with nothing more than the small bags on their backs that our shifter *'magic'* can change with. Me on the other hand, I'm now regretting saying yes to going. Stupid self-doubt has been playing in my mind and while I don't believe I can do what they think I'll be able to, I know I have to try.

Logan and I have spent the entire day together and have become fast friends. He came with me on patrol while Banner and Elliot organised our departure. And now I stand before my Pack leaders, about to leave everything behind.

There's an eery silence while I stand before my Alpha and the Circle getting instructions from Tobias.

'What if loners come on territory and I'm not here to help?' is my twentieth question for the morning as I try give myself excuses to not leave Pack. To not venture out on my own.

'We'll work it out,' Tobias states, but his focus is on throwing the heavy jacket Jax took from someone's den over my shoulders. Tobias helps me put on the heavy garment. It's a little too warm for Sylo but where I'm going it probably won't be enough to fight the cold of the south, even with my wolf running at such a high temperature.

'Your stuff should be there when you arrive. Dom has already sent it,' my Alpha instructs.

'Someone watch over Gene and Kurt for me. They were super angry at me for leaving them. I think they're arguing with each other,' I say to no one in particular as my heart beats from my chest.

'I will. I promise,' Oliver replies. He is now standing over me, studying my face.

I just blink up at him, unsure what to do and what to say. 'I don't know if I can do this,' I whisper, not wanting anyone to hear which is stupid because they all can.

Oliver shakes his head with a small smile. I have no idea why he finds my pain so amusing. 'You can do anything, Gilly Sommers.'

My heart swells and I jump a little and throw my arms around his neck. My fear and trepidation disappearing when he returns my embrace in an unwavering hold that tells me that no matter what, he will always have me.

Pulling away, I catch the pain that flashes over his face before I'm swooped into another hug. Crashed against Jax's thick body, I breath him in. My Pack grounds me in this moment of uncertainty.

Jax places me back on my feet and I look over my shoulder and frown at the sight of the three tall males in the trees waiting for me. When I look back at the Farrowline males watching me like they know something I don't know, I bite my lower lip when Tobias cups my face.

Holding my stare, my Alpha reassures me with touch that I'm protected and loved. I nod as those forest green eyes darken with his wolf because I know what he's communicating. That I am his.

No matter what.

'I know you've been struggling Gil. I'm fully aware that a great deal has happened and I know that your wolf is growing and learning what it is to be a Tracker.'

I'm shocked. I thought I hid my tracker struggles. I thought so much was going on and I was fucking up so bad that Tobias and the others were too busy or over me to notice my issues with my abilities.

Jaw dropping, I stutter, 'how do you know?' I shouldn't be surprised.

Gifting me a small smile that barely reaches his eyes, Tobias seems sad. He doesn't answer, just grips my face tighter. There is a part of me that feels like this is a goodbye. That he is saying farewell to this version of me. I feel that I will leave and when I return I'll not be the same Gilly Sommers of

Farrowline. That I'll be different. And I know in my soul that Tobias feels the same.

Dom comes up beside me and I turn from Tobias when he lets me go to feel my Beta's warmth. He hugs me close. 'You be safe now, Gilly. You go and do what you were born to do and then you come back to us. And if you need me. If you need Farrowline. You call. No matter what.' Dom breaks my heart and yet fills it with his words.

Biting my lip, I nod.

Delfina said goodbye to me earlier before going on patrol with Easton. She has already given me a similar speech. Ridley refused to say goodbye and made me promise that I'd call her every few days or she'd come down to Jenolan and 'kick my arse'. Adalee has packed me a range of sweets for the trip and promised to call me every day.

Jax is the next to tell me to call if I need him, 'no matter what,' and I stare into his golden eyes and continue to nod.

'You come back to us. Or I'll come and get you myself,' Oliver adds, making me giggle. He smiles wide even though he's serious and I nod again to his promise because that is what it is. A promise. My Pack will always be my Pack.

That my heart belongs in Farrowline.

Tobias steps up again and grips my shoulders. 'A tracker is born to hunt. It's who you are. We haven't let you stretch your legs and discover your true self, Gilly. And I *am* sorry for that. I thought your position in the Circle would be enough but I see the energy that you need to release. I know you have to do this. So go and hunt! You find the Alpha of Coltonline and his daughter and then you come back to Pack and you find your place here. You carve it out and you find your happiness.'

Falling against his chest just to feel his warmth as I absorb his words, I grip onto my Alpha afraid to let go.

Afraid of the changes waiting for me in the trees.

Chapter Twenty Six

It takes four days for the weather to start changing from mild and lovely to then freezing *fucking* cold.

We've kept wolf for the majority of the time as we move through the forest, travelling at a steady pace that meant I was mostly toward the back with Stuck-Face the majority of the time. We ate what we caught as wolves. The males always waited for me to be fed first before the catch was divided and any kind of bathing meant dunking yourself in the closest freezing cold body of water found along the way, again as wolves.

Keeping close to the river that runs through the country, we're never far from water too long and honestly, I'm at that point where I'd actually kill someone for a shower and a decent meal enjoyed as a human.

I don't mind eating as a wolf but it's always best to stay in your beast form for a few hours after so that it can digest the raw meal. If you switch too fast to human, it means a belly ache and all sorts of trouble. My wolf and I don't like when we stay in one form more than the other.

The Coltonline males seem fine with the situation, but not me. I'm proud of the balance that lives in my soul.

It also means that communication has been minimal. As animals, there is no need for excessive interactions. It is clear that Banner is in the lead on our journey which made me re-evaluate what I thought was the power dynamic in the group.

The one thing I did get right though is Logan St Cloud is a hunky, sweet and lovable character that I have instantly formed a friendship with. My wolf gravitates towards him constantly as she watches Elliot. Stone Face is always behind me being all grumpy and constantly on high alert which is fine by me.

Nose high in the air, I'm instantly concerned with the upcoming weather. I've never experienced a blizzard or any kind of snowstorm before but what I smell can only be described as pure ice.

It's why I shift the moment Banner calls a stop to today's travels. He always seems to be annoyed when we go human, there's a secret part of me that loves poking the perpetual grouch.

We're on the outskirts of a small town and I look longingly over at the pub and hotel building in the distance. The forest is extremely dense around here and I can't help but be a little unnerved by it all. This is the furthest I've been from Pack on my own. The trip to Hiltumbler was with Tobias and the others which meant I felt safe and secure. Now, I'm on my own with three males who barely talk or interact with each other.

'I'd kill for a steak,' Logan declares as he appears next to me on two legs. He stretches out his bulky arms and then winks as he catches me staring. Smiling wide, I giggle at the eye roll he gives Banner behind his back when the larger male states that we need to move on. He's obviously concerned about something because he starts pacing closer to the trees. His gaze is fixed on the thick forest we've been traveling in for days. My wolf is settled. She can't pick up on anything, so I don't get too concerned.

'This storm is going to hit hard soon, Banner,' Elliot states as he catches up. He took off a little while ago. The phone in his hand is still open so I can only assume that he was on a call but kept his distance for privacy. I didn't get that luxury on my last call with Ridley. Banner was so bloody close I could feel his fur on my back.

Banner grunts in response.

'That's a yes,' Logan translates 'Banner talk' for me and gets the reaction he wants when I giggle again.

Elliot, as if realising that I'm still here, looks in my direction and gifts me a charming, *I know I'm beautiful,* male smile.

'Gilly love, you're hungry.' He makes a big show of stating the obvious when I think this entire region can hear my stomach growling. Banner growls that he knows I'm hungry.

Shrugging is the extent of the conversation I want to have right now. My wolf and I are uneasy. We want to go home. The last time I spoke to anyone in Farrowline was two days ago before the damn phone died and we haven't been anywhere near electricity or plumbed water in days. We have covered countless miles, following Banner's instructions as he keeps us clear of territories and other shifters lands.

Elliot and Logan have a word-less conversation over my head. Their eyes dart to the pub in the distance before Logan nods and I watch in humour at what they're doing. Using me to manipulate Banner into agreeing to go into town, Logan starts being all dramatic about me needing food.

'We really shouldn't have you hungry, Gilly. It'd be breaking our blood oath,' Logan is dead serious and yet there is a gleam in his eye that makes me bite my lip to hold back my smile.

Banner just grunt-growls and demands for us to stay close before storming off in the direction of that warm looking pub.

Chapter Twenty Seven

The place is buzzing and quirky and kinda old school with all the wood accents and the fireplace and the squeaky tables and chairs scattered around the floor that look older than my grandma.

It's warm though and the food is definitely better than the small animals I've been eating on the road. Now, I'm no food snob but if I had to eat one more rabbit or fox I was going to turn around and run my arse back home. The hunt be damned.

There are more shifters than humans in the perfectly warm building and while the males sitting around the table eating and chatting seem relaxed, I know that we are in someone's territory.

Banner already went over to a group of massive cheetahs in the corner when we first entered about an hour ago and while they seem content with what Stuck Face has said, they keep looking over at us.

Well, at me mostly.

I can't help but think of the cheetah who hurt my pack and try really hard to not be one of those shifters who judges the masses for a handful of individuals actions. The cheetah pack in Sylo is small and they stick to themselves in their section of forest far from Farrowline.

It's also the first time in close quarters with so many stinky bodies and scents in days. Breathing through my mouth skilfully, I look up feeling eyes on the top of my head where I'm leaning over my bowl of piping hot stew eating like a starved person and sit blinking up at the dark eyes watching me.

Frowning and titling my head in question as I also haven't spoken much in days, and shaking the 'wolf' habits is hard, I find myself in a staring competition with the stone-faced male who I feel is judging me with his eyes.

Shaking his head as if he is disappointed by what he sees, I'm saved from telling Banner to do something to himself when the male next to me shuffles in his seat. That's when I feel the rising tension.

The hairs on my arms stand on end and I sit up and look over at Logan who is looking at his plate like he has stomach problems.

Dropping my spoon, afraid that something is wrong with the meal, I breath it in and find myself extra confused. There is nothing wrong with it.

'Don't,' Elliot grumbles softly from my other side and I sit like a fool, unable to understand anything that's happening. I have no idea who he is speaking to until Banner moves slightly in his chair.

Stuck Face looks extra grumpy and I have no idea what is going on.

'The storm is going to hit soon, Banner. We can't be out there,' the tone of Elliot's voice has my heart drop and that's when I realise what has the Coltonline males so tense.

Looking over my shoulder at the group in the corner that has now multiplied, I realise how fucking stupid I am. I actually let my guard down around these males and allowed them, allowed Banner, to take the lead. As a wolf in this group I am the least dominant so naturally she defaulted to the predators to ensure our wellbeing, but as a human...as I said, *fucking stupid*.

I hear one of the many cheetahs behind me say something about tits and wolf females being wild in bed and sit up in my seat. My hands clutch the table and I feel my canines descend.

A hand falls on mine, gripping it in warning and I'm left staring at the way Elliot is touching me while his eyes stay fixed on Banner. I don't know if I should be offended or turned on at the way he tries to control me.

'We will be stuck in the storm, Banner,' the sexy male states. 'I already booked us a room upstairs.'

That's news to me. Elliot went to use the restroom when we first got here and I'm left once again angry at myself for not being fully aware of what was going on.

Banner grunts. Logan throws the last of his bread in his mouth and indicates for me to finish up.

Without missing a beat this time, I rise with the males and don't put up much of a resistance when I'm hurried through the loud space and up the flight of stairs in the back corner after Elliot speaks to the pretty woman behind the counter. He throws her a gorgeous wink and then we are up the stairs, down a corridor, up another flight of stairs and another corridor before a door is opened and I'm pushed inside to a sight that has me freeze.

You've got to be kidding me.

'No,' I demand and I think it's the first word I've spoken in a very long time. The way Logan reacts to me speaking shows that I'm right.

'It's all they had. This town is one of a few along this route to the south. With the storm coming and all the guests downstairs, we're lucky to even get this,' Elliot says defensively and I glare at the subtle humour in his tone.

'I don't care,' I grumble while the three males make themselves at home in the very tiny space.

There is a very unimpressive mini fridge that I don't actually think is working. A kettle and toaster on the stained bench above the fridge that I wouldn't touch. A tiny round table with two wooden chairs and a bathroom that is big enough for one person to stand in.

I was dying for running water which makes the entire situation worse. But it's when my eyes fall on the main thing that makes me want to run and run and head back to Farrowline is the bloody bed.

Bed.

Singular.

The one and *only* bed that is taking up the majority of the space in this shithole taunts me.

The three males are too large for this space.

Logan throws me an apologetic grin before slipping into the bathroom after declaring he's the first to shower. Elliot is fiddling with something in the bag that he has been carrying. Banner is at the door behind my back doing something with the chairs and the table. He is moving it all to the door and I feel like an adolescent as I stamp my foot and tell him, 'I'm not staying here.'

The universe is taunting me because the wind picks up outside and the tiny, *what's the point*, window begins to rattle and shake with the storm that they all predicted hits, and hits hard. I actually groan out loud and slump down on the hard bed regretting my life choices.

'Cheer up, love,' Elliot whispers in my ear as he comes up behind me. And I do when over my shoulder he passes me a small bottle of liquor. 'We wont bite. At least not tonight.'

Chapter Twenty Eight

Laying on my back studying the stained roof, wondering how a roof can actually become stained, I wipe the tears on my cheek and try to control my loud emotions. My stomach hurts so much from laughter that I roll over, curl up and stare at the equally hysterical male beside me.

Studying Elliot's profile, I fixate on the perfect dimple on his left cheek. We've been playing twenty questions for the last hour and it's the most fun I've had in a long time. Being a little tipsy helps. There's something about Elliot, something so appealing and comforting that I can't quite put my finger on it.

Logan is snoring softly, he is sprawled out on the end of the bed. I've never met anyone who can fall asleep so easy and stay asleep with so much noise.

Despite everything, I don't feel uncomfortable sharing the bed. I think the alcohol has helped. And none of us are under the covers which takes the intimacy out of the entire thing.

On Banners growly demand that we stay in our clothes, with shoes on if we need to leave quickly, I'm now lying on the mattress fully dressed next to two males I don't really know. Banner is sitting in one of the creaky wooden chairs against the door to our room. I have no idea if he is asleep but his eyes are closed and his arms are crossed over his chest as he leans his extra-large frame in the poor chair. He is very attractive when he is asleep. He looks younger. Less...stone faced.

'Okay, okay.' Elliot sucks in a breath and takes another swig of the almost empty bottle that we've been working our way through. *It has really helped me to relax.* 'Where's the oddest place you've had sex?'

Leaning over him to take the bottle, I finish it off while draped over him. 'We said no questions about sex. It's tacky and tasteless,' I remind him and internally cringe when the voice in my head answers his question—which is in the shower. Jay liked sex at night and in his bed and once he spiced it up by coming into the shower while I was in there and it was the most exhilarating experience. I thought it was a turning point, but it was only once. A few days after we were back in the bed.

Elliot's very large warm hand lands on my lower back and I swat it away and slump back down beside him.

Logan snorts loudly in his sleep which sets off our drunk giggles again.

The wind is loud and fierce as it rattles the glass of the tiny window. The room is dark and quiet as the male beside me wraps his arm around my head and draws me close as a shiver races down my body. I warm up instantly drawing in his scent of leather, spice and a subtle sweetish, creamy almond kind of tone that doesn't seem quite right. It doesn't fit, but I push the annoying tracker nose of mine away and listen to the storm outside.

Elliot's breathing slows and soon I find myself on a bed with two sleeping males, unable to fight my heavy eyes.

I jump awake with a gasp, my heart pounding in my chest. It takes my sleep muddled brain a moment to understand where I am.

Frowning at the two sleeping figures beside me, my eyes instantly go to the glass window being violently shaken by the storm outside.

Assuming that is what woke me, I look around the tiny hotel room and wrap my arms around my body all of a sudden freezing despite the warmth that Logan and Elliot are generating with their bodies.

The door to the hotel room creaks open quietly and I brace myself and calm only a heartbeat later when my wolf and I recognise the male walking back in the room. Banner's large body blocks out the obnoxious light from the hallway before he shuts the door.

Those dark eyes land on me moments later when they travel along my body to fall back on my face with a frown. 'It's early. You should be sleeping.' He keeps his voice low as to not wake his packmates.

I point to the window as a way of explaining why I'm wide awake at this damn hour.

Banner is carrying a small paper bag full of goodies and my stomach growls instantly at the aromas that fill my tracker nose.

Banner throws the bag down on the stained table, dives in and grabs out a large pastry that he throws over at me.

'Thanks,' I mumble and with a small sniff of the chocolatey goodness, I get stuck in devouring the flaky wonder. 'Where did you get this?' I ask, truly in shock that he found something this good in a place like this.

Shrugging, Banner makes sure that nothing touches any of the surfaces in the hotel room as he rips apart the bag and lays out the rest of the small mountain of baked goods he has scored somehow. 'Bakers are up at ridiculous hours and I found one down the road. She opened early with a bit of charm on my part.'

'You, charm?' I snort and then gape at what has just spilled out of my mouth and shut the damn thing instantly.

Banner stiffens and then grumbles, 'just eat runt, before we have to leave.'

Nails sharpening, I almost ruin the perfect pastry in my hand but the male beside me stretches out and his hand brushes up against my back. The touch heats me instantly and I throw Elliot an eye roll because it wasn't an accident.

Lost in perfect blue eyes, Elliot grins. 'Morning, love.' Sitting up on his elbows, Elliot is all charm as he asks Banner what's for breakfast. His hand flies up and catches the pastry the arsehole throws him.

Logan rolls over with a growl of annoyance and I completely understand. The sun isn't even up yet. Cracking one eye open, Logan frowns. 'Did you stay in that chair all night, Banner? You were supposed to wake me for my turn to keep watch.'

Attention snapping from the pastry Elliot is now sharing with me, I take in the chair against the wall near the door and the male moving around getting his brother something to eat.

Banner sat up all night guarding the door?

I feel instantly bad for not taking any responsibility or realising that he was up all night and then I was rude when he was the one to get me food in this storm. But then I remember that he keeps calling me runt—so he can fuck off.

Declaring that it is my turn in the bathroom, I hop off the bed and leave the males to discuss the plans for our travel with the blizzard outside.

Braiding my wet hair and not wanting to touch anything in case I get some kind of bacteria and die, I'm busy thinking about my upcoming job in Coltonline when Elliot, who I can smell through the door, starts banging on the bathroom door.

Jumping out of my skin, I open it growling a 'what', and then freeze at the volatile and charged energy in the hotel room. One look at Elliot's grim demeanour has my wolf on high alert.

Logan is on his phone telling the crying young female on the other end that everything will be fine. I can hear her tears and her soft cries of how scared she is. Banner is throwing things into bags while grunting and grumbling to himself. I can smell his rage and his fear. Which does nothing to calm me down.

'Has she been taken like the others, Logan?' the female whispers as if the words are too horrible to say out loud.

'No, Gracie. I'm sure Maddy has just lost control of her wolf.' Logan looks across the room and shares a pained look with his brother who has now pulled out his own phone and dials a number. 'Did you call Dad, honey?'

'Yeah, he came around just before with mum and they told us that they will look for her, but then they left.'

Logan and Banner both tense. Banner picks up his device instantly.

'Father,' Banner growls when after two rings a male's voice comes down the line. 'Who is out looking for her?' Banner doesn't sound impressed with what the male on the phone is telling him as he rattles off names or how he explains how bad the storm is and how they don't have her scent anymore. After everything Logan told me about his parents, I find myself instantly disliking the Beta of Coltonline. I know that Maddy is their youngest sister and I curse at what I'm hearing about her being missing.

Elliot, while a little tense doesn't smell as worried as the other males in the room. I don't know him enough to judge so I brush it off because these things happen when you're dealing with adolescent wolves. However, with the issues Coltonline is having, I understand the need to panic.

We're about a day and a half from Coltonline and I look out the tiny window covered in snow and gulp down my anxiety before I move further into the room and look to Banner who has hung up the call and is now stacking the bags that we will be wearing. Clearly enraged after the useless conversation with his dad, he doesn't pay much attention to me.

'I can find her.'

Those black midnight eyes look up and catch me in their intensity. Logan opens his mouth to say something but I hold up my hand to stop him replying to what I've just said.

'Get me to your territory and I'll find her.'

I don't know where my confidence comes from but seeing Logan and the stone-faced male upset has stirred something in me.

Chapter Twenty Nine

My skin burns under the power of the ice that lashes my body as head down, eyes squinting, I stay behind the male leading the way through the blizzard.

My body is sore, my paws hurt and I think my fur is frozen. However, I don't stop.

The large, black-furred male wolf behind me is a solid wall as the next burst of ferocious wind is so powerful that I'm pushed backwards and right into his strength. Against Banner, my wolf bends into his body as the violent burst of wind keeps us from doing anything but curl up together and wait for it to calm.

We just have to keep moving.

So that's what we do.

Slowly and tirelessly.

I have no idea which way is forward or back, except if I stop moving, I know I will freeze to death.

It's heavy night and I only move because of the two males who have sandwiched me between their large and powerful bodies. Elliot is still in the lead, blocking as much of the damaging wind hitting my front. Not that any of us can fight a storm of this magnitude.

Time stopped holding meaning a long time ago and deep down I know that we just have to keep going. That we need to find the poor lost female in this blizzard.

When I finally spot the lights of a den up ahead and hear the blissful sounds of voices and wood cracking under fire, I almost whimper in joy.

My nose finally picks up more than just the smell of ice and the tones of the two predatory wolves keeping me as protected as they can, who I could now track and find wherever they go.

A little delirious, I wonder for the hundredth time walking in this blanket of pure ice and wind if Logan and Banner St Cloud realise what it means to have their scent locked by someone like me.

Mind drifting, I barely register the males taking me inside the den. I find myself on my belly on a warm, hard wooden floor. A perfect floor, surrounded by perfect walls that shut out the storm we have been traveling in for who knows how long. I want to kiss it and whisper sweet nothings to it. Having a very visceral reaction to the warmth and safety of a freakin' den, I close my eyes in exhaustion and soak in the heat from the blazing fire.

I barely hear the voices or make out the sounds that surround me. My nose is going crazy and yet it is numb and sore. When someone who smells like eucalyptus and ash bites my ankle in a command my wolf understands, I shift back to two legs and roll onto my stomach.

Logan is sitting just as close to the fire as I am, the black bags under his eyes and the paleness of his skin reflects exactly how I feel.

There are bodies everywhere. A blanket is thrown over my body by a figure who is frantically moving around the room. Nothing really makes much sense. I can hear Banner barking orders. I can smell too many new bodies. There must be about twenty wolf shifters in this room. Each one giving off way too much information.

After being in the wilderness with only three males and nature for such a long time, it's too much. I feel the bile just as my mouth beings to fill with saliva. Desperate and ignoring the pain that shoots through my body when I jump up, I spring for the door we just came through and hear a number of curses and shouts before Banner appears. He grabs me around the waist, half carries me to the end of a hallway and rips open a door. Now in a bathroom, I lean over the toilet and throw up. It's probably the most humiliating experience of my life having a male like him holding my hair back as I vomit.

There isn't much in my stomach so mostly it's just me dry heaving over and over again. It just adds to the pain in my muscles.

'Here,' Banner grunts and I blink at the hand that appears in my vision holding my tube of eucalyptus oil. 'Put this on.'

It is a command.

Wiping my mouth and falling to the tiled floor with Banner's help, I shake my head and pull my hair back into a high pony. Banner crouches down before me, taking up the space in the room.

Head resting on the wall beside the vanity, I close my eyes and try to control my nose.

'I won't be able to find your sister if I use it,' I tell the male watching me. Stone Face is frowning and I find myself captivated by the hint of emotion when I blink my eyes open. Mirroring his expression when I realise that I actually don't need the oil with his scent filling the bathroom, I take a deep breath and sigh.

'Sorry,' I mumble. 'That was a lot going from nothing to everything.' I have no idea if I'm making any sense but he nods so I assume he understands.

'I can imagine. We can wait if you need time. You're exhausted,' the confusing males says.

With our bodies close and his eucalyptus and ash scent in my nose, I find myself studying him properly. He is nothing like Elliot who looks fake in his handsomeness.

Banner is rough. His features are masculine. He has a strong jaw and thick eyebrows. His hair is dark and falls to his broad shoulders. The dominance dripping from him is hard to ignore, but for me, the thing that has me tilting my head in confusion is how he doesn't bombard my senses. There are not many shifters or humans that I come across that don't have so much going on with their emotions and energy.

For someone like me, who can read and pick up on all of those things with my abilities, it makes interacting so hard. But Banner—he is calming and solid. A male completely in control of his emotions and energy that I truly see him for who he is for the first time. Banner St. Cloud knows who he is and is confident in himself and it is refreshing.

'We're all exhausted. No, we need to find her. Just tell everyone to give me some space and show me her room.'

Banner doesn't flinch at my command, gripping my hands to lift me to my feet, I suck in a breath when my chest touches his. The male drops my hands instantly as if uncomfortable and steps back, which is hard given his size and the size of the room.

Grinning at his reaction, like he is afraid of such a touch, which I find super funny after days and days of nothing but grunting, I shake my head when he throws me that stone faced look as if telling me to grow up and leads me out of the bathroom.

It's eerily quiet as I move past the mass of Coltonline shifters who are standing in the kitchen on Banner's demand and follow him upstairs.

The silence and the fact that someone has opened a window despite the weather so that I'm not bombarded with all these new scents gives me a chance to take in my surroundings a little better.

The den is a typical cabin-house or so the human magazines at Farrow Group would classify it. There are logs as walls, the floor is solid wood and most of the tones in the den are brown shades. The straight flight of stairs has a tight turn at the bottom and as I walk up it, I look down on the large open lounge with the fireplace near the television on the back wall. The matching three seaters and the dark large armchair sit on top of a lush looking fur rug that covers the floor.

Everyone is piled into the spacious kitchen. The benches wrap around the wall and there is a small island. It's very open and welcoming and seems practical for a den with six wolf shifters.

Running my eyes over the group watching me, I try to see if I can find Banner's siblings. I look down the stairs at Logan who is watching from the bottom with a serious look about him and then catch eyes with Elliot who is beside the front door with two very intimidating, very 'predator' males who look like they've been in one too many fights.

Working through the scents in the air, I frown at the subtle honey tone that comes from them and realise it's the smell I scented on Elliot a few times. It's weird that I notice it and frankly it doesn't surprise me, my wolf and this nose picks up on some strange shit and if I analysed every single thing I pick up, I'd go freakin' crazy.

Chapter Thirty

Contemplating if it's possible for your lungs to freeze if you inhale too much ice and snow, I fight to keep my temperature stable.

Nose working on overdrive, I process everything that I pick up in milliseconds.

While a thick layer of frost covers this new, harsh and foreign landscape, my tracker instincts are unaffected.

It's the first time in my life that I feel free and unrestricted.

I feel like I'm whole. It's confronting when you thought yourself originally having balance and then to find out that you were wrong.

So wrong.

I know each and every one of the St. Cloud siblings now as I move through their lands. I've pinpointed every shifter who has walked on these lands and have linked them to the many at the den waiting to see just how good the Tracker of Farrowline is.

And I'm good. Really fucking good. Even with my body almost breaking I'm shivering so hard, I find her.

Maddy.

My wolf throws a look over her shoulder at the male guarding me from the trees. While he is keeping his distance, I'm fully aware of him and it might not be the time, but the human side of me is very intrigued at the way his presence hasn't disturbed my tracking.

Normally I need everyone in Farrowline to leave me alone to hunt or they mess up my head by distracting me. My mind can get very chaotic as it works through a massive amount of information every minute of every day. It takes a great deal of concentration to do what I do.

Breathing in the strand of scent Maddy has left behind, I pick up on something that might make the male behind me very upset and let my wolf take complete control. Fighting the instinct to throw my head back and howl to my pack who aren't here to help, I put my head down and hunt.

Flying through the trees, I move and turn and push my body to the limit. At one point I trip and almost stumble down an embarkment but am saved by the massive force of the black wolf trailing me. Banner catches me with his oversized, muscular body and propels me forward.

Getting my feet under me, I move harder and faster on the mighty noise Banner makes. He is telling me to keep going. To finish the hunt.

I don't know how it's possible but the temperature drops and I can feel my paws burn but nothing can stop me now that I have the scent of my target.

Maddy.

We jump over rocks and rivers and onto a land marked by someone other than Banner.

Sparing him a quick look to see how he reacts to being in another shifter's territory, I only keep going because he doesn't flinch.

The small dwelling comes into focus long after I smell it. I can barely keep going with the force of Banner's energy. It's as if he has let the dam on his emotions go. Long gone is the controlled male from the bathroom as he roars a sound that shakes my bones and sprints off to the hut-like shelter nestled in the trees. It's obvious that he was holding back, and I was running at full speed.

It's also obvious that Maddy is fucked because when I finally catch up, step up on the front landing of the dwelling and shift at the open door, I cringe at the verbal spray a very pretty, very young female is getting. The equally young male beside her looks like he is about to wet himself as Banner reprimands the pair colourfully.

Maddy hurries over and hugs her brother when he finishes and I feel the anxiety coming off her. Banner despite his rage, hugs her close, giving me a glimpse at another side of him.

Scanning the inside of this weird little structure, I'm quite impressed with the warmth held within the space without a fire going. There is a makeshift bed in the middle, a few bags of food and bits and pieces, and I know enough through the smells in the air that Banner has nothing much to worry about. These two were just hanging out.

When clear dark eyes lift and land on me, I try to give Maddy a look of solidarity behind her brother's back that has her smile and then hang her head when Banner growls. She steps back to her friend's side as if she knows what's coming.

Throwing me a look that tells me to stay out of this, I realise that the kind male from the bathroom is long gone and Stone Face is back. My eye roll is involuntary and poor Maggie gets in more trouble harder when she giggles softly.

'This is not funny, Madeline St. Cloud! You had everyone worried sick about you. You had Logan and I bring a member of Farrowline. Farrowline! Madeline! Out in this storm without stopping or thinking of her safety and ours to get here to find you. We thought something had happened. With everything going on you two thought that this was acceptable!'

I'm unsure why he has reinforced my pack name like that in his little speech and why Maddy is now hanging her head and the white-faced male beside her gaping at me. He reeks of fear and panic and I find it a little funny. It's clear that they're just two very silly, very adolescent shifters who just went to hang out and got caught in the storm.

Which is exactly what the young male starts stuttering when Banner demands that he explain himself, 'right. This. Minute.'

I bite the inside of my mouth when pictures of Dom and Liam and Oliver come to mind. This is exactly how they would react to finding two adolescents alone like this. Jay and I got into a number of situations when we were younger and had to listen to our elders tell us off for our behaviour, insisting that we were playing with fire because we hadn't heard the mating bond. We thought it would come.

I really, really thought Jay was the one. He was my best friend. Isn't that the foundation for a mating?

'We...we...just wanted to hang out and then the storm came and we couldn't leave.'

Bless him, the young male is so scared of Banner.

I cough when Banner's energy increases. It chokes my senses.

'And why Jake Carpenter did you think it was acceptable to bring my sister here to this particular spot? I'm not stupid nor am I that old to know what goes on here. The hut was not created by your generation as you all seem to forget.'

The pair share a look that just adds to my humour. I think I just found the 'make-out' spot in Coltonline.

It's a pretty good spot actually. The dwelling is tucked away in the trees and is covered with enough foliage to indicate that it has been around for a long time. Now more interested in the warm, cosy feeling of the place, my wolf seems very comfortable to stay here for a few days. The floors are wood planks, the walls are a mixture of natural and made materials. It's a big square with a pyramid roof. It's built around a massive, ancient tree trunk. There's a bunch of stuff that has been left over the years. And a mattress that needs to be replaced some time soon.

The wind banging the closed, makeshift door behind us rattles uncontrollably, drawing our attention. Banner finally stops lecturing and throws me an assessing look that I don't really understand until he curses and runs his hand through his hair. It causes a weird stirring to flutter in my chest at the sight.

'The storm is too dangerous to have us all out there. We'll have to stay here until it calms down. You both better thank Gilly for finding you. Neither of you have boarded up the roof. This place will not hold for much longer.' Banner gets to work fortifying the roof I am only just realising its caving a little near the tree trunk.

That's when I feel it. The adrenaline and thrill of the hunt completely leaves my system. I become very aware of how heavy my bones feel.

'Does that mean I can sleep now?' I ask the grumpy male who is now barking at Jake to start preparing the mass of blankets while he fixes the roof.

I take that as an indication to find a spot to sleep and moving past the two very unsure adolescents, I yawn loudly and crawl onto the bed and close my eyes instantly.

I feel a body next to me moments later and I nod when Maddy whispers, 'thanks for finding us.'

Throwing my arm over her and drawing her to my side because she is still scared even though her brother is here and she is safe, Maddy curls into my chest.

A wave of loneliness fills my soul. I miss my Pack.

Looking over her head, feeling eyes on me, 'can I sleep now?' I ask Banner because in this moment he is the leader. My wolf understand the hierarchy here.

'Sleep. You're safe,' his deep timber voice states and I take in the black depths watching me before exhaustion pulls me into oblivion.

Chapter Thirty One

'And this'll be your room while you're here with us.'

Giving the gorgeous young female what I hope is a warm smile, I stick my head through the door Grace is holding open and take in the room she's showing me.

We woke up with the sun shining today which was just typical to be honest. We spent days traveling in a blizzard, then hunting for a missing female who wasn't really missing in the damn storm, sleeping in a weird but very comfy dwelling, to waking up to a beautiful day.

Banner, Jake, Maddy and I headed back to Banner's den the moment we all woke. In complete silence.

It was awkward and a little funny. Jake ran away the moment we got close to Banner's territory and I think that may be the last time I see Jake while I'm here.

We entered the cabin just as Grace was beginning to make breakfast and she jumped straight into greeting me and showing me where everything is. I stood back while Maddy was reunited with her siblings. It gave me a moment to understand who I'll be staying with and to be honest, I fell in love with the St Cloud's instantly.

Grace has long, wavey, mousey blonde hair that falls to her curved hips. She has the same eyes as Logan. She is short like me and is surrounded by a warm energy only a den-maker can possess. She scowled at Maddy while hugging her close and I had an overwhelming need to claim the pair of females. My wolf decided instantly that she was keeping them. The other St Cloud males are equally as intriguing and full of life. Jesse and Mason are muscle heavy seventeen-year-old dominant males. They're very top heavy like their older brothers and have the same waists that taper in.

Very much like Logan, Jesse and Mason have shoulder length blonde hair with the same dark eyes. They were both very mischievous in the grins they throw me when Maddy and Grace finally broke apart and I was introduced. They all just stood there staring at me like I was some kind of superstar. Logan found it hilarious while Banner told everyone to get inside.

I couldn't help but chuckle at the look they all shared behind Banner's back and the love they all have for each other was infectious.

Walking into the bedroom, I head to the window on the other side of the wall and look out onto the new landscape.

Snow covers everything and while it's colder than anything I've ever experienced, Coltonline is beautiful. The trees aren't as dense in this forest. Snow gums fill the landscape amongst trees of varying heights. I heard a body of water in the distance on our walk back from the hut and ask Grace in which direction the river runs.

'South,' she tells me. 'We have a small section of the river that we have to keep clear and safe before it runs into the next territory.'

Contemplating my mission here, I mentally begin to draw an image of the territory in my head. I'll have to see everything soon and scout out the area.

I also need to learn more about Coltonline. I haven't really learnt the structure of this pack yet and plan to ask someone today so I don't get myself into trouble moving around when the hunt begins.

And I want it to begin.

I want to go home even if it means I have to watch Katrina's stomach swell with a pup that I always imagined would be mine or back to having no answers over who I really am.

My mind flicks back to how it felt yesterday on the hunt for Maddy. How free I felt. How content.

I shake it off instantly.

Turning my attention back into the room, I smile at the cosy-ness of it. The entire den has a very 'cabin in the wood's' kind of vibe.

The log walls, the rug on the floor is fur, the small tallboy is white and matches the posted bed in the middle which looks very pillowy. There is a single door on the other side of the wall and an inviting armchair in the corner. I smell my Pack instantly and quickly spy the row of bags against the right wall.

'Your things came about a day or two before you all showed up,' Grace informs me and I look over at the very perceptive female.

Closing my eyes, I take a deep breath to get a read of the room and then snap my eyes open.

Frowning deeply, I follow along when Grace tells me to. She shows me the other five rooms at the top of the stairs and the big bathroom up here that we will all have to share.

'Banner's room is downstairs at the front of the house. He has an ensuite and there is a small guest bathroom on the bottom floor too. So if this one is taken you can always go down there. We used to have a roster when we were younger to prevent arguments around the length of time we took in the bathroom but it went out the window when Mason and Jesse had an argument and shifted in the house. It was pretty funny especially when Banner got involved and made them both sit in two different corners of the den and think about what they did.'

Laughing along with the sweet female, we move down the stairs and into the kitchen where the rest of the family is preparing an early lunch.

Looking over to the back of the den where Grace points towards Banner's room, I frown again in confusion.

I smell...nothing.

There are no overpowering scents. No perfumes or candles or those cleaning products that when my mum uses them I have to stay wolf in the forest for a day.

No, everything is natural tones of citrus and fruits. And then I realise what had me so confused before.

Grace and the others don't smell either.

In fact, Banner and Logan, and even Elliot when we were travelling, they all smell just like themselves. Which is weird to think, but when you are me, smelling like nothing but your natural scent is very new. I don't know if it is coincidence. Do they somehow know how hard it is for me?

Shaking off my silly thoughts because no one would know how much it affects me when they use their perfumes and deodorants, or incense and powerful cleaning products, I sit down when Logan pulls out a chair for me.

The laughing and conversation flows around the table even if there is a few side eyes directed in my direction. Banner's face hasn't changed and he is actually reading a newspaper at the table like in those weird human movies Kurt, Gene and I would watch set in the olden days and I wonder just how old he is.

Smiling into my sandwich, I try not to make a big deal about everyone looking at me.

'Stop it,' Banner says into his newspaper.

Everyone looks up and over at each other. Eyes fly here and there. There is a moment of silence before they all burst into laughter.

Smiling wide, I put down my fork and look over at the gorgeous male beside me when he tells me that Farrowline has a bit of a reputation. 'Especially out here in the south. Your Alpha and his Circle in particular,' Logan finishes.

'I still can't believe that we are eating breakfast with a Circle wolf of Farrowline and you're a female and you're gorgeous and I want to be you when I grow up,' Jesse teases and I can't not laugh along with them.

It's a strange feeling to be amongst shifters who don't know me. Who don't know all the ways I've fucked up lately or look to me with sympathy for getting my heart trampled all over. 'I am nothing special,' I tell them all and then bite my grin when Gracie tells me that Banner doesn't like it when we lie.

I steal a glance at the male still ignoring us down the other side of the table.

'What's it like being a Circle wolf?'

'What's it like being the most revered Tracker in the country?'

'What's it like...' The questions go on and on while I contemplate the one that Jesse just asked. I still have no idea how they all knew about me being a tracker. So I ask, 'how did you know about me?'

The voices go silent and I watch Banner as he flips the top of his newspaper down to stare at me. 'What do you mean?'

'How did you know that Farrowline had a tracker?'

I would expect Banner to frown in confusion or raise an eyebrow or simply register any kind of emotion on his face and yet all I get is...stone. 'Everyone knows about the Tracker of Farrowline. Shifters talk. Farrowline interacts with many packs in the country. Of course we all know about the mysterious Tracker with the ability not seen in generations.'

Biting the inside of my cheek, I try to process. It is not unlikely for word of my ability to get out. Wolves from other packs come and go. We host events sometimes and Tobias is in regular contact with other packs. I find it weird though and a little unsettling to think that people talk about me.

We all eat in relative silence as I quietly chew on my food. This entire situation is weird and new and...fresh. Here in Coltonline I can be Gilly the Tracker of Farrowline. Something I couldn't do back home.

'Who is the biggest wolf?' Mason asks unexpectedly and the table erupts in noise. Mason gets told that he is asking a stupid question by the rest of the table because the Alpha of Farrowline is the most powerful wolf there is. So he must be the biggest. He is but Jax is a close second. He is our Gamma after all, the strongest physically in Pack. The one that ends the fights. The one we call to put his body on the line for Farrowline. I stay quiet, enjoying the attention.

'Who is the grumpiest?'

'Who is the best fighter?'

'What's Beta Dominic Knox like?'

'Who is the hottest?' Maddy asks and the table explodes in outrage while I laugh hysterically at the adolescent question.

Chapter Thirty Two

I watch Grace pull out items from my suitcase. She holds them against her body in front of the floor length mirror against the corner of my room and I wonder briefly what the faraway look on her face is. About to ask her, I'm distracted when Maddy claps and squeals as she pulls out the three magazines Mum must have packed at the bottom of my bag.

'We never get these in our small supermarket. We live in the middle of fucking nowhere out here. I have to read their limited articles online.' Maddy is jumping on the bed on her knees, hugging the pile of magazines like she just found treasure.

Chuckling at the way Logan appears at the door just as Maddy swears, he reprimands her on her language, reminding me of the males of Farrowline.

I'm sitting on the floor of the bedroom, folding my clothes, taking the time to get my mind focused on where I am.

'Settling in okay?'

'Yeah, I think so,' I reply, leaning over and snatching a pair of my panties that he teasingly picks up with the tip of his finger and winks at me. 'You'd fit right in at Farrowline,' I snap playfully and realise that it isn't much of an insult. Logan's face lights up as if I've just complimented him. He chuckles sexily.

'It's the twins birthday tomorrow and we might head into town, maybe grab a movie and some dinner, if you'd like to join?' Logan asks and I jump at the chance to be included.

'I'd love to, if it's okay?'

'Of course it's okay,' Gracie laughs. 'Jesse and Mason are a little in love with you already. Having a Farrowline wolf come to town with us would make them feel like they're the coolest shifters in the area.'

I can't help but light up at that. I want to shake my head and tell them all that I'm just an average shifter who happens to come from a well-known Pack. That I'm nobody special. I bite my tongue though. 'So is that what you guys do for fun around here? Go to town and watch movies?' I'm very interested and find it amusing when Maddy looks at me but seems to be holding back because her brother is here. Grace just agrees and tells me nothing fun really happens in the pack.

'There is a bar in town,' Logan tells me with a shrug.

'This place is stunning.'

Taking the hand Logan offers to help me step over a small stream of running water, I silently thank the shifter back in Farrowline who would've packed my luggage. It would have been Oliver, I'm sure of it. I found thick lined boots and a number of snow jackets and pants. All good enough for this weather. So when Logan asked if I wanted to go for a walk after breakfast and see their small section of territory, I jumped at the opportunity.

We have been walking and chatting for almost an hour as he shows me around the territory they control. It's very rocky and uneven, he explains while making sure that I understand that there are a number of drops along the east side of this section. I nod along, absorbing everything.

Drawing in every smell and using all my senses, I map out the entire area in my mind. My wolf is skilful in her abilities, not just the ones I was born with but the ones taught to me by Farrowline.

'We all have our own sections to defend. If you head that way a few kilometres, you will hit the boarder of neutral territory. That is our only exposed section and it's small in length. It's our responsibility to make sure that it is never breached. We defend our own areas and in doing so, the entire Pack as a whole.'

Trying to understand, I ask, 'but you can move around each section freely? What about your leaders?'

Logan having expected the question answers instantly, 'yes, we're all Pack. It's courtesy to let each other know if we're staying on their lands for an extended period of time though so if you are going to move around in your search just speak to Banner or myself and we will organise it. Banner will be with you for most of the hunt though. Only leaders can come and go and do what they please. Our Alpha is ultimately responsible for everything and everyone and owns all our lands. He and his family unit have a large section with multiple boarders that need defending. Dad and Mum, along with our Gamma are managing those lines with the absence of our Alpha and his daughter.'

'And what about you?' I ask Logan, throwing him a look to make sure I'm not going to offend him. He is a predator shifter and he doesn't have his own territory to manage, he doesn't have the same dominance as Banner but he is powerful.

'There aren't many sections left to give. We've had a number of prosperous years here in Coltonline and family units are established in these areas. Banner was gifted sections of my parents' lands. Our father, the Beta, owns the second largest section. His begins on our west side, over there,' I follow where he points. 'Our mother owns land on the other side of Dads. You'll meet them later this afternoon when the Pack comes together to discuss the next steps in the search. They haven't discussed with me about handing me any and it's not something you can just go up and ask for.'

We walk in comfortable silence while I process what he has just told me. Everything is so different here. However, while I don't necessarily think this is a place I could ever call home, I do fall in love with Coltonline.

'And what about you, Tracker of Farrowline, what is your story?' Logan asks unexpectedly while we hike and I get a baseline for the scents in the air.

'Nothing much to say. I'm pretty boring.'

'I don't believe that. It's definitely not what I saw in Farrowline.'

I can't decipher his tone. 'What does that mean?'

'Everyone loves you, Gilly. I swear the amount of shifters that came over and threatened to eat us if we allowed anything bad to happen to you was very high. And I'm male enough to say some of them were scary. The female den-makers in your pack in particular and the Beta's mate.' He visibly shivers.

I throw my head back and laugh at the way his whole body shakes with the memory.

'The Alpha's mother in particular was scary.' Whistling his appreciation of the female who means so much to me, I feel my chest swell with love for Mama.

'I didn't know they did that,' I confess. However, I'm not surprised hearing that Delfina had said something to them.

'You're not one of those shifters, are you? The ones that don't see their worth because they size themselves up amongst others and can't see their value? Because I'd be very disappointed if you were.'

Laughing, I sober up instantly because I'm *not* that kind of shifter. I know my worth. I've grown up with a pack and parents and an Alpha that have encouraged me and supported me to be myself.

I stop moving and grab the closest tree as I realise that I've been acting like one of *those* shifters that Logan has just questioned me about. It makes me angry that I've let Jay and what he did reduce me to this.

'Gilly?'

I jump at having Logan so close. His honey eyes study my face and I can only imagine what he sees. 'What happened with that male your mum was talking to us about?'

Gaping, I just blink up at him wondering if I've heard him properly. 'My mum spoke to you about Jay?' I'm mortified.

Grinning that very mischievous grin that brightens his face, Logan takes my breath away. His chiselled jawline is very similar to his brothers, their faces are the same but Logan's features are much softer. His energy is light and full of fun.

Biting my lip when I realise that also like his brother, Logan has complete control over his emotions, I grin because he is just perfect.

'What's funny?' he asks suspiciously, his eyes narrowing at me in a way that makes me giggle more.

'Nothing,' I declare and keep moving away from him, feeling a lot better.

'Don't think you got away with answering my question, Gilly. I know what you're doing,' he calls after me and I wave my hand over my head indicating that I heard him in response.

He growls playfully and runs to catch up to me, knocking me in the side with his hip.

Exploring the flora and fauna for hours, I look up with interest when Logan shows me Elliot's family unit's territory line. I can smell the sexy male and the two others that he was with at the den when we got back yesterday up ahead and ask Logan if we can go visit.

Logan doesn't hesitate and leads the way. It doesn't take us long before we spot the trio.

The tall, built males sit around an odd, shaped tree on a table that's looks to be built around it. The cold doesn't seem to affect these shifters. They wear thin long sleeve shirts and long dark trackpants. They're deep in conversation and it looks pretty serious. They don't notice that we are close.

Logan makes a deep noise and I realise he is making them aware of us. The three males come to attention. Each one looks ready to attack until they notice it's us. Elliot's face goes from serious and aggressive to open and inviting. His blue eyes sparkle.

Jumping up to come over, Elliot wraps a hand across my body, drawing me close and plants a kiss on my cheek. 'Gilly, love. You guys started tracking already?' Elliot pulls me into his side and I instantly mould to it.

He smells like male cologne and birchwood and that hint of something else that I can't name yet. I ignore the way it makes my noise feel scratchy.

Logan has already moved to the table and is shaking hands with the big, almost intimidating pair that I remember from the den yesterday.

'No, not yet. Logan was just showing me the St. Cloud territory,' I tell him and wave when Elliot introduces me to his littermates, Joshua and Laurence.

I get way too much from their scent and I try really hard to not scrunch my nose. I didn't catch my noise in time once with Kurt and I didn't hear the end of it for a month. I tried to explain it was the colouring shampoo he was using when he dyed his hair red that one time but fuck me, he didn't drop it.

So I keep my face as neutral as possible and not show how gross they smell. Like sex and cigarette and that damn other smell I'm getting frustrated about.

Elliot finishes with the introductions and looks down at me warmly. 'Well then, it's my turn to show you around my territory,' he declares and even though Logan tries to tell him that he can have me tomorrow, that we are needed back at den for a Pack event later this evening, Elliot brushes him off.

Chapter Thirty Three

'I'm surprised my cousins took you out to survey their lands, looks to me like they wanted to jump on the chance to show you that the St. Cloud family unit aren't involved in the disappearances you are here to work out.'

What? I have no idea if I heard him correctly as he is trudging through snow a few paces to my left. It doesn't sit well with me. 'I asked Logan to show me their territory,' I say, a little defensively.

Turning around with a mighty smile that has me believe that I clearly misinterpreted his words, Elliot starts telling me all about the section he has. Which I begin to realise is managed by his parents.

'We're in the process of dividing the land,' he tells me and I can smell the untruth and wonder how these strong, very dominant males must feel about not having much control over being given sections to be in charge of.

In Farrowline, we all own our territory. Each family unit has their dens and spaces around it that they can do with as they please but we don't divide the forest. We share and work together to maintain our Pack.

Yes, Tobias is our Alpha and it is he who is the leader, but that means nothing much in the way of land. Tobias would give up his den, his bed and all his possessions for any member of his Pack. So would Dom and Oliver and Liam and Easton and Delfina and even Ridley— who's a human.

Here in Coltonline they hold power through land. So what happens when there isn't any left for the next generation of predatory wolf shifters who need to have purpose?

It's a question that I push to the back of my mind to contemplate later. For now, I'm focused on the attractive male who looks very excited when we come close to a steep hill. Like a youngster, he beams at me and grips my hand, 'come, I want to show you something.'

His excitement is infectious and when his hand curls around mine, I know I'm not the only one that feels the connection between us. Butterflies form in my stomach for the first time in a very, very long time.

Pulling me around trees and streams and up the hill, we stop at the top and I gasp. The view is spectacular. There's an endless sea of white snow covering a gorgeous natural landscape. I see the dens scattered and built within the forest, most with smoke billowing from their chimneys.

I listen intently as Elliot comes up behind me and begins to point over my shoulder at various locations. There is a lake far off in the distance that Grace must have been referring to and I find the St Cloud and Elliot's den easily. The Alpha's place and the Beta are next to be pointed to. He explains all the other key points in Coltonline that I need to know about.

I'm so in awe that when I look up over my shoulder at the male who is smiling wide at the sight, I draw in his scent. The odd honey smell bites the back of my nose and I become very intrigued with the handsome male.

Blinking those clear blue eyes down at me, Elliot studies my face with hooded eyes.

Our faces are close. 'I'm glad you're here, Gilly.'

'Me too,' I reply softly and turn away when he leans in slowly as if to kiss me.

Reprimanding myself at having gotten caught up in the moment, I remind myself that I'm not doing this. Not without a mating bond.

Elliot squeezes my shoulders before moving off. I know he isn't upset, I can smell his arousal and his interest, not anger at me pulling away.

I watch as he moves around the area and contemplate if I might just have some fun here in Coltonline and try to put the events of the past behind me.

Hours later, Elliot throws me a pained look over his shoulder as his steps slow. We're close to Banner's den and I've already picked up that there are new shifters within the home. I don't know why Elliot looks so tense or why he throws me another odd look before he steps beside me.

'Just stay close,' Elliot tells me. He grips my elbow and leads me through the door with a mighty and friendly, 'hello.'

It's a show and Elliot is a great actor. Deep down he is uneasy and I think I know why when I spot the table full of elders.

Banner is at the head looking just as emotion-less as ever. Logan, Jesse and Mason are at the island sitting on the bar stools I never noticed this morning. They too seem uncomfortable with this situation.

Looking up the stairs, I spot Maddy and Gracie hiding at the top. It's all very odd.

Elliot is greeted by the many shifters around the table. He doesn't seem to care about the tension in the den or that there are a number of dominants looking at me.

Elliot leaves me and goes and slaps Banner on the shoulder before kissing a stunning female to Banner's left. I know who she is instantly. She has Banner's eyes.

A very dominant male at the other end of the table rises and I become the centre of attention. 'Tracker of Farrowline, we're so grateful that you've come to help us. Welcome to Coltonline.'

The male welcoming me is an older Logan. The Beta of Coltonline is not what I expected. With shorter light brown hair and the same gorgeous features, he has Banner's dark eyes and I find his smile very captivating. He exudes confidence and an energy that tells the world that he knows how attractive he is. When Logan explained him and hearing him speak about the situation with Maddy on the phone, I pictured him the villain.

'Please, sit.'

Thanking the Beta with a respectful incline of my head, I awkwardly sit in the chair beside his and force myself to not look around.

The Beta doesn't retake his chair, instead, he addresses the room as if this is an official meeting. 'Thank you all for your time tonight. We're here to welcome the Tracker of Farrowline and organise the best course of action in our search.'

'I think it is clear what has happened,' the fierce looking male beside Banner states. 'Our Alpha has left us. We are playing games here. There was no need to get another Pack involved in our business. Especially not Farrowline.'

A few looks are shared around the table and I have no idea if they all realise how much information I'm getting from them right now. I smell anger and resentment. I smell despair and grief. I smell...rage and fear.

Processing everything and sorting through the information bombarding my senses, I start to go all clammy.

It's horrible.

Until I look up and catch the black eyes of the male on the other side of the table watching me as if he knows what I'm thinking.

He does seem to do that a lot.

Raising an eyebrow, I fight the need to blow Banner a kiss to see a reaction and with a small grin that has those eyebrows lower slightly, I hold his gaze. Curious if he *can* read my mind, I start saying some really graphic and inappropriate things in my head just for fun. Which distracts me from the overpowering scents now up my nose and I'm able to stay in the conversation happening around me.

The Beta sighs, 'thank you, Rowan. We understand your thoughts on this matter and have already voted. Gilly is here and that is the course of action we will be taking.'

The conversation goes on and on about the best way for me to do my job. Sometimes its heated and other times it's civil. The Beta never sits down. He does listen intently to everyone that speaks. It is very respectful.

The female beside Banner, the one with black eyes, speaks up and everyone stops talking. It's clear she holds a great deal of power in pack. 'I think we should all take turns escorting Gilly around the territories. Each family unit can schedule a time for her to work through their lands—'

'I'll be the one to escort Gilly around,' Banner interrupts, drawing everyone's attention. There is a heartbeat of tension before his very unimpressed mother clears her throat.

'That is not your decision to make son,' she is completely without emotion when she speaks but I can hear the underlying threat.

Everyone can.

The Beta says nothing as his mate and son stare at each other and I can feel their history. Banner loves his mother, I can smell that, but he doesn't respect her. I'd never tell him what I get from his mum, it hurts my heart and I quickly look over to Logan and the twins. Difficult parents are not new to me. Easton and Delfina come from the worst pack in history and Ridley's dad is an absolute dickhead.

'I'm the one who gave my word to the Alpha of Farrowline to protect his female. I was the one to give my blood in an oath to forfeit my life if something were to happen to her, Greta. I will *not* be letting Gilly out of my sight.' Banner's words hang in the air and I don't miss the way he uses his mother's name. The elders all purse their lips, telling me that this is probably not the first time these two have gone head-to-head.

'You let her be with me this afternoon,' Elliot teases and then throws his head back and howls in laughter when Banner's completely black eyes narrow onto him before telling him that he didn't approve of our excursion and promises him it will not happen again.

I honestly don't know how I feel about being spoken about like I'm not sitting right here in the fucking room.

'Let's leave it there for now,' the Beta says. 'I'll speak to my son and let you know what the plan is. Thank you everyone.' It's a dismissal and everyone around the table knows it. 'Elliot, can I have some time with my pups. We will organise dinner next week,' he tells the male who hasn't moved from his seat when the rest of the table party headed out the back door.

Elliot nods, shares an odd look with Banner and then hops up. Throwing me a wink, Elliot leaves and I contemplate if I too should leave.

'Logan, Mason, Jesse, could you take Gilly upstairs please. We need to have a word with your brother,' Greta demands more than asks.

I don't miss the way the males don't move but look to Banner for direction. Greta's face hardens and we all practically run from the room when Banner nods at us to leave.

Chapter Thirty Four

We all stop at the top of the stairs and I comply when Logan grabs my hand and pulls me down so that we're sitting against the banister with Maddy, Grace and the twins. I get comfortable between Logan and Jesse and have to bite my lips to try not to laugh when Mason pulls out a bag of gummy lollies from thin air and the bag gets passed down the line of eavesdroppers. Legs dangling through the wooden posts, I take a handful and nearly lose control of my giggles at the hot-as-hell look Logan gives me when he takes the bag, grabs his own handful and passes it to Gracie who tsks and shakes her head.

'This isn't a game. Dad seems angry,' Grace reprimands quietly.

'Dad is always angry about something,' Maddy grumbles and leans over to take the bag of gummies. It's a very adolescent response.

'Banner is fine, Gracie. Mum and Dad can't do shit in his territory and Gilly is our guest. Banner isn't going to let anyone be in charge of her safety,' Jesse reassures his sister.

I go to respond but am cut off by the mighty growl that rips through the den, drawing all of our attention back on what is happening in the dining room.

'You did what!' the Beta rages. 'You gave a blood oath to the Alpha of Farrowline? *Farrowline*, Banner! For crying out loud. If things go bad, we do not have the pack power to defend you. Alpha Tobias Farrow and his Circle will tear you apart.'

I get a few side eyes and I wave their concern off. 'That's a little dramatic,' I tell them in a barely-there whisper even though I know it's not. Tobias and the others *would* tear this pack apart for me.

'Father, what I did, I did for Coltonline. I did for our Alpha and Sasha. And what I said is what is going to happen. You will all leave Gilly alone to do what she came here to do. I don't want interference. I don't want the Pack getting involved. We all voted. You all voted for me to be the one to go and ask Farrowline for help and so I went. I've done what you asked, now leave me to finish it.' Banner is one scary male and while I chomp on gummies and listen to the scents the others around me are giving off, I learn more about my surroundings.

The relationship between the pups and their parents is strained to say the least. There is love between the siblings. Deep, binding love.

There's a moment of silence before the Beta growls. 'Fine. But if this goes to shit, and let's be honest, it could very well. You're on your own. We will *not* support you if Farrowline come knocking.'

Gaping, I almost choke on the jelly baby in my mouth. I can't believe what I've just heard. His own father has just told him that if he gets in trouble with another pack, that his own wont help. It's despicable and I hate that the others don't flinch like they expect this kind of behaviour. That is so messed up.

'She is a Tracker, Banner. You know how flighty and irresponsible Trackers can be. Hide the alcohol.'

My jaw hits my lap at that and Logan makes of point of avoiding my eye. *What the fuck!*

'For shits sake Mother! I know exactly what Gilly is. We ran four days, practically the other side of the country to Farrowline for her.'

I have no words.

'I want to speak to Maddy about her behaviour yesterday with Jake,' Greta states, changing the conversation so quickly I get whip lash. I look over to the female who seems to pale at the hard tone of her mother's voice.

I hear chairs scrap back.

Grace grips Maddy's shoulder in solidarity.

'There's no need. I've spoken with her.' Banner's words drift through the den. He says it with such conviction that I find myself unable to do anything but smile.

'I think you forget that I'm her mother, Banner. You cannot stop me from speaking to her about her actions.' Greta is furious.

We're all listening intently.

'I can and I will. It's late and Gilly and I will start the hunt early tomorrow. I'll be starting at the Alpha's den.' Banner dismisses them so calmly that it takes a moment to understand that's what he was doing.

Logan and Jesse chuckle beside me. Their pride in their brother is infectious.

There are no more words.

The back door opens and shuts and like small youngsters getting caught eating sweets before dinner, we all look down at the male now standing in the loungeroom looking up at us.

Arms crossed and shaking his head, Banner does not look impressed and yet, he doesn't look surprised either. I can only imagine what we all look like. Our legs dangling between the balustrade clearly listening to their conversation.

No one speaks until we all lose the leash on our laughter and I happily join in.

Banner growls but it has no bite. His muscles bulge under his crossed arms. 'Go to bed, all of you. Maddy don't forget to finish your school project. Your teacher emailed me again this morning about your incomplete work.' Maddy nods and hurries to her room. 'Gracie, can you go to the store tomorrow with the other females. I've left some money on the table. I'd go but Gilly and I will be out most of the day.'

'No worries,' she smiles and follows Maddy to bed.

Grace is so sweet.

'I can go with her,' Mason offers.

'Thank you, Mason. Now go. Bed. All of you.'

Even Logan jumps up despite being a full-grown male.

Left alone after Logan winks in my direction and heads to his room, I blink down at the male now rubbing his large hand over his face. It's the most vulnerable I've seen him. I can feel the weight on his shoulders. I'm surrounded by shifters who carry immense responsibility every moment in Farrowline. I am a Circle wolf. I know.

'I wouldn't let them hurt you or your pack, Banner. Farrowline won't hurt you.'

Dark eyes shoot to me as if he forgot I was there. 'That had nothing to do with you, Gilly. My family unit has its issues like any other.'

Studying him, I get a good glimpse of why he always seems so serious. He is responsible for his sisters and brothers and his territory. And while I know, even though we have only really just meet, that he's very capable.

I'm also aware of how hard it can be being at the top. Being a leader. I'm learning the effort and emotional toll it takes.

'What did your mum mean about Trackers and hiding the alcohol?' I ask, not sure if I want to hear the answer.

Banner studies me intently. 'Don't listen to Greta St. Cloud. It is not about you. Trust me.'

I do and while I'm dying to know, I decided to let it go. I stand and turn toward my bedroom. 'Good night, Banner St. Cloud,' I whisper, knowing he can hear every word clearly.

'Good night, runt.'

Rolling my eyes, I huff and head to my room to ring my Pack and tell them all about my first day and what I've learnt.

Chapter Thirty Five

It's too fucking early and I bare my teeth at the male who nudges me in the side as if telling me to wake up. The sun isn't even fully up and it's so freakin' cold that even my fur isn't doing much to help warm me. I haven't even had my coffee fix yet and nothing good ever happens before a coffee. However, no matter how much I want to rip the oversized, growly black wolf to shreds, I stick to the plan for today. Which is to hunt.

There hasn't been any snow since the blizzard but the floor is still covered in white powder. Some parts are actually just dirty sludge and I come to the conclusion that I'm not a fan of snow at all.

Give me the sun and Farrowline any day.

Following Banner's wolf, we move fast through various territories until he slows and I find myself taken to a very large, and very impressive den. It is a great deal more modern than the one Banner lives in and I shift to two legs when I get to the top of the stairs. The wrap-around veranda is long and painted a brilliant baby blue. The white panelled den is eerily quiet and when Banner opens the door, I stand in the entrance and absorb the information that attacks me.

I pick up every wolf shifter from the male beside me to Elliot and his friends to every one of the elders at the dinner table yesterday, including Banner's parents.

Underneath it all, I get three new scents. Scents that are so embedded in the space that there is no denying that they are the owners, and from the energy I sense, it has to be the Alpha and his family unit.

Banner hasn't confirmed where he was taking me but I knew. I also know that the three shifters were last here about four weeks ago. In line with the information I've received already about the deaths and disappearance.

Having picked up on two female scents, I move slowly into the den. Banner is near the back door. He looks uncomfortable being here and I don't blame him.

'You can wait outside if it's easier, Banner,' I tell the unmoving male who has gone back to grunting at me as a form of communication.

'Just get what you need, runt.'

Grumbling what he can do with himself the next time he calls me runt, I do hurry up.

I move in and out of each room, admiring the décor and the beautiful features of the den.

'Where's the other female?'

Looking up from his phone, Banner frowns in my direction and I interpret that as a question along the lines of, 'what do you mean?'

'The third shifter who lives here?'

'Beth. The Alpha's mate. She has been staying with Greta since Sasha and the Alpha disappeared.'

'That's heartbreaking.' Fucking depressing actually. I can only imagine the state of the female who has lost her entire family. To lose your mate is said to be a pain like no other. You lose the other half of your soul. Males who lose their mates never stay in the world long after their females go to the next life. Females are said to stay if there are pups. They will stay and ensure their offspring are safe and secure before following their males. It's hard watching those females stay strong, knowing that there is a part of their soul that is gone forever. Images of Mama and Maree flash through my mind.

'Fuck,' I swear under my breath and look over at the male now nodding at me like once again he can read my mind. I've finally realised where he's taking me next. I'll have to speak to Beth. I will also have to grab the scents of the adolescents that have been killed and the one still missing. Which means a visit to their dens and potentially meeting some grieving parents. I know I have to, even if I don't want to.

'I have to meet the parents of the ones that were found dead and the one that is still missing.' I hate the words as they come from my mouth.

'Come runt, the hunt has begun.'

Groaning loudly, I gather up all my strength. 'Let's just get this over with.'

'Are you okay?'

'Not really.' I sniffle into the phone. I hear Noah squeal in the background and finally feel something other than the intense emotions of the past few hours. I went straight to my room and slammed the door once we got back from gathering as many scents and information as I could from around this pack. I instantly phoned Ridley. All I needed was to hear my Pack. The weak-heat-less sun is going down on this new world I have stepped into and it's been a long day.

'Oh babe, do you want me to get Tobias and the others to come and get you? You know they will. Oliver and Jax have already packed a bag of snow gear in one of the douchebag cars in case you ring. I'll tell them to get in the car and drive to wherever the fuck Coltonline is and get you.'

Wiping the water from my cheeks, I chuckle despite the ache in my heart. 'I'm okay, it was just really intense. You should've seen them Rid. The mother of the female adolescent that was killed hasn't left her den since they found her daughter's body. She barely spoke or looked up while Banner and I were in her daughter's room so that I could pick up her scent. It broke my fucking heart and I didn't think it was possible for it to be broken any more than it already is.'

Ridley sounds just as affected as me when she tells me that she is sorry. 'That would've been so hard. You're doing such an important job down there Gil.'

'I don't think I realised the magnitude of this hunt until I met all those parents today. The father of the one that is still missing hovered the entire time I was in his den. He showed me every piece of clothing his daughter ever touched to make sure I got her scent so that I could find her for him. When Banner told him that he has to be ready for whatever I find, he just said he understood but then jumped up and bought me her childhood teddy for me to sniff.'

Ridley makes a sound that has Tobias's voice come down the line. 'Gilly, do you need me to come and get you?'

'I have the keys to the car in my hand,' Oliver shouts in the distance.

'Maybe I'll phone Banner St. Cloud and remind him of his blood oath,' Tobias all but growls down the line.

It gives me more joy than it should to hear that Tobias is thinking about threatening someone.

'I'm fine. I promise. I have to do this. I have to find these missing wolves. It was just a hard day,' I reassure them and feel my anxiety drift away when my Alpha tells me that he is here for me 'no matter what'.

There's a soft knock on my door before a bright, cheerful face appears. Logan mouths if I'm okay. He walks right in and sits on the end of my bed when I indicate for him to enter.

'I gotta go. I miss you all. Can someone tell my parents and Gene and Kurt that I'll call them later tonight?'

Promises are made by multiple voices and I reluctantly hang up after Delfina gets involved in the conversation and promises that she'll be at my side in a heartbeat if I need her.

Logan is laying at the end of the bed and I pull my magazine out of his hand when he starts reading the section that tells you how to create the perfect up-do for the office.

Blinking those brilliant eyes at me, Logan studies my face and I can only imagine what he sees. 'Banner told me it was a difficult day.'

'He did?' I don't know if I believe that. After the last visit to the den of the female who died, he told me to get back to den and left me at the edge of his territory. He didn't say a thing. Just grunted and growled and told me to get washed up for the movie and dinner tonight. I didn't miss the small hint of grief he was trying really hard to cover. Banner St Cloud is good at controlling his emotions but I scented the pain he was trying to contain. If I found the visits hard, Banner must have had a worse time.

Jesse and Mason come in next. I haven't seen them yet and try to be cheerful when I wish them a happy birthday. Shooting Logan a look, he seems to understand that I don't want to be a dampener on their day.

'Should we start getting ready for the movie? We got to be in the trucks in half hour,' Logan says, jumping off the bed and high-fiving Jesse when he exclaims how excited he is for our evening out.

Chapter Thirty Six

Arm wrapped around Logan's elbow, I chat away with Grace and Maddy about all things fashion and watch as Grace fixes the zip on the designer boots I let her use. They were last seasons and I have about ten other styles in my bag—thank you Gene and Kurt for the outfits. They also added some racy lingerie and a nightgown that belongs on someone who is on vacation to a tropical island not here in the middle of nowhere were the sun doesn't seem to be able to heat the earth. Damn pair loved the sight of the three males who visited Farrowline, it's probably a note for me to let loose.

Not that I'd be wearing that stuff any time soon.

It's fucking freezing here.

The St. Cloud's, well the younger ones, thought it was super funny when I came downstairs dressed in five layers of clothes, including a practical coat I can imagine someone like Oliver forcing Gene and Kurt to pack in with all the stuff *they* would've decided I needed. It's only getting colder as the night goes on.

We're walking to the pub for a feed. It's the twins birthday. I felt bad that I didn't have a gift for them but they seemed happy when I promised to bring them to Farrowline once the hunt is finished and introduce them to the rest of the Circle. More than happy maybe. Ecstatic is probably the word to use.

We just finished off watching a hilarious movie in the small movie theatre. I think it was supposed to be a drama/romance. Boring really. However, sitting beside Logan and Jesse as they spoke over the main characters made the entire film enjoyable. They changed what the actors where saying to be more in line with a horror movie, it really added to the bland storyline. It was also fucking amazing when we looked over at Banner half-way through the film and saw him sleeping like some old male.

I feel like I've known these shifters my entire life. It's weird and comforting and even with Banner growling at everyone and waiting until I walked through the doors before him and reprimanding me just as much as his siblings when we got a bit too rowdy outside the cinema.

I've had an amazing night so far.

Stepping into the pub with Banner holding the door, I nod my thanks and smile at the sight before me. It's all wood panels and cowboy-style booths. The bar takes up the majority of the space and I follow the others as they head to the back area with all the families eating, a good distance from the alcohol. With Maddy with us, we need to stay in the appropriate section. Not that I mind. I've made a mental note to stay clear of alcohol while on this hunt and if I'm to be honest, I haven't felt the need to indulge as much being here with the St Clouds. Not that I think it means anything...I think.

Taking the seat Banner pulls out between Maddy and Grace, I'm too distracted by all the sights and smells that I'm barely aware of the show of chivalry. After I've absorbed the tall stage on the other side of the space, the large wooden floored dancefloor, identified multiple shifters and humans and pull out my tube of eucalyptus, I'm finally able to relax and dive into the conversation around the rectangular table.

We order. We eat. We laugh. Banner is teased mercilessly throughout the entire meal but it's very obvious that under it all his siblings adore the ground he walks on. Maybe even rely on him a little too much in my opinion. They asked him to open their drinks and I watch as they waited for him to fill their plates, the males included, before they eat. Each one not waiting for their big brother to serve himself before diving straight into their meals. They ate the moment he provided them with food. It's very obvious the dynamic isn't the typical sibling relationship. It's more parental on his behalf which is why he raises an eyebrow when I took my time handing him my plate and then waited for him to be ready before taking my first bites of roast lamb and vegetables.

Sitting across from me at the end of the table, Banner smelt uncomfortable and surprised. His subtle emotions made me frown and look at the table full of shifters a lot differently.

The responsibility Banner St Cloud has doesn't sit well for some reason and I contemplate what life must be like for a male like him.

Too bad he's a grumpy dick.

'Grace, there's a guy at the bar who keeps looking over here,' I whisper to the young female beside me and watch as her eyes widen. Her scent changes instantly and I cover my grin with my glass of soda. I'm so interested in what is happening that I try to work through everything her body is projecting loudly at me. Excitement. Nerves. Fear. A little arousal. Shyness.

Staring at her in my peripherals, I watch as she makes eye-contact with the human and see her face light up at the way he catches her staring back and waves. Her small little wave back is so sweet and I want to know everything.

I want to know his name. Where they first met. How long they've been flirting. If they are an item or if they are still new.

'That's Evan Bratman,' Maddy leans into my other side and whispers in my ear.

My excitement jumps. I clap quietly and do a little jiggle. I love this shit!

'Tell me everything,' I whisper back. Not taking my eyes off the man now trying to act normal even though he is fully aware that he is being watched.

'He's a human who works for the sheriff's department one town over.'

Oh a police officer. 'I do love a male in uniform,' I swoon and have Maddy giggling behind her hand instantly. It could also do with the small growl coming from each of the St. Cloud males around the table.

'Can we not?' Banner grumbles. I swear the male has been cradling the same beer for the past hour and looks bored. I want to smack him for some reason, maybe see if that rouses some kind of response.

Grace turns beetroot red and tells us to be quiet.

'Evan can't hear us.' I wave off her concern but picking up on her anxiety I decide to stop asking. However with each passing moment, I grow more and more desperate for information. If Kurt and Gene were here, we'd already be at the bar with the Evan guy, Grace in hand, chatting and planning their summer wedding.

I miss my friends.

The conversations around the table don't fully register. I'm so curious. I don't think I've ever been told to drop a snoop into someone's life. My social life thrives on meddling with packmates affairs.

Jesse and Logan are explaining something that I really don't understand fully but everyone else finds it super funny and I'm about to combust. I need to know more...I need to make Grace happy. I've claimed her. My wolf and I have claimed all the young St. Cloud unit despite only knowing them for like two days. It happens for wolves when we start to live in the same den. It's natural. We are pack animals. I could know someone an hour and claim them as mine to protect and care for. I might not be a full dominant but I have that aspect of my wolf's personality.

'Would you stop!' Banner grumbles from across the table and I flick my gaze from Evan to the grumpy moron.

'I can't help it,' I whine much to Logan and the twins delight. 'I'm sorry Gracie but please, I'm a major gossip and I really want to know what the deal is with Evan,' I blurt out. The table erupts in laughter and quiet, little Grace covers her mouth to giggle along with the others. She doesn't smell upset. I think she's actually a little surprised and excited to have someone take an interest.

I don't miss the glance she gives Banner and then catch the one she throws to the man chatting with his friends. He isn't staring anymore and I know it has something to do with the way Banner looked over his shoulder a few moments ago. I'm sure the poor human got the wolf eyes or something equally as frightening.

'Fine,' she sighs and I know she secretly wants to tell me everything. I clap again and am lost in her story about shyness and secret infatuation. I sit in rapture, 'oh-ing' and 'ah-ing' in different sections listening to her tell me how she tried to flirt once with him and it was awkward and then she just hurried away and hasn't spoken to him since.

Contemplating the complicated story of Gracie and Evan, I finish off my drink watching the human at the bar and come up with a plan that Kurt and Gene would fully support.

Her and I chat away about what I think she should do until Banner tells us it's time to go home and that I need a good night's rest as the hunt resumes early tomorrow.

Chapter Thirty Seven

I hunt.

For the next week, I absorb the environment around me both in human and wolf form and try to gather all the puzzle pieces of this hunt. I speak to Coltonline elders and adolescents. I sit in dens and listen to recounts but mostly I walk on four legs, nose to the ground, focusing on finding the missing Alpha and the two females.

Banner trails behind as I move slowly over the lands of Coltonline, using the scents of the missing and the deceased to try and find a trail. I did find a small hint of something on our second day, but when I shifted to two legs and told Banner he just stared at me for an uncomfortably long time before explaining that the exact location of where I was standing was where they found the two mauled adolescents months ago.

It creeped me out.

Today however, hasn't been very successful and the fact that I had a shit night's sleep last night isn't helping. Banner hasn't done anything but grunt and growl and the snow is making my paws hurt so when I circle back to the same spot again for the tenth time, I lose it.

Standing in the small clearing I have been coming back to over and over again, no matter what path I take, I shift back to two legs, clench my fists until my nails dig into my palms and scream up at the cloudy, grey sky in frustration. The next few words that come out of my mouth are not very lady-like.

'Fucking hell! Why do I keep coming back here! Fuck!'

Banner stops just at the tree line and leans against the thick trunk. He keeps doing this and its pissing me off more. That bloody look on his face. I just want to smack that arrogance right off.

This section of Coltonline is dense forest. Green, snow covered trees fill this area. I'm still within the Alpha of Coltonline's territory and that is why Banner thinks that I keep coming back to this area. There's a frozen creek to our left and a pile of snow underfoot. Nothing interesting or of use. I get some kind of scent that is confusing me. It doesn't mean anything to this entire situation. The area gives me the creeps though and I can't put my finger on why.

Originally, Banner and I searched this entire spot. He showed me a small area where packmates gather. There's a fire drum not too far from here in the trees with outdoor chairs. All spots Banner told me about and informed me are used regularly by the younger generation, Elliot included. Which could explain the weird scent I keep picking up. It's like the one I scented on Elliot and his friends and must come from here somehow. Not that it matters. None of this is helping the hunt.

'The Alpha came here often. Fishing in the creek is a pastime of many pack members. It's not weird that you would scent him here,' Banner says lazily. His thick arms wrapped around his chest.

'It's not that,' I respond through gritted teeth. Mumbling my annoyance at myself, I walk around in the clearing. If I wasn't so annoyed, I'd admire the area. 'I think my nose is broken! It's all this freakin' snow.' I kick the offending snow and hurt my foot when I smash into a decent sized rock even with my thick boots on and then end up jumping around swearing and cursing the universe.

I think I hear Banner chuckle and throw him an accusing glare that he doesn't seem too fazed about.

'Are you done?' he asks in that deadpan voice I've had to listen to for the last week.

'No,' I reply petulantly. Pouting, knowing full well that I'm acting like an adolescent, I stop hopping around and stomp over to the frozen creek. It's beautiful and I don't actually hate it here. I just...I'm confused. I miss Farrowline so much but there is something about being here in Coltonline that sings to me. Here I'm not treated like poor little Gilly who keeps fucking up and getting drunk and whose heart was stomped on. Whose ex is now mated and expecting a pup with the love of his life.

The actual reason why I couldn't sleep last night was because Banner's damn words back in Farrowline still haunt me. I'm a leader within the largest Pack in the country and yet, I have no idea what that means. And the dominants of pack don't see me as anything but the silly female who parties too hard. I give orders and they look to one of the males of the Circle. I'm not stupid. I see the subtle exchanges behind my back.

'I know what you must be thinking,' I whisper as I watch a small bird dance above the still, cold water. If I can't do this and find the lost Alpha and his daughter, who am I? If being a tracker is my purpose and the reason why I'm a leader in Farrowline, what is going to happen if I fail?

'And what is that, runt?'

Not even his offensive nickname offends at this moment. I'm doing enough offending of myself within my own head. 'That you didn't get the tracker you were searching for.'

'Is that right? Is that what I'm thinking?' I can't decipher his tone and frankly I don't give a damn. 'I think you'd be surprised what I'm thinking right now.'

That has me looking over my shoulder at him. He isn't against a tree anymore, he's staring right at me in a way that makes me feel all odd. My wolf sits up and tilts her head, assessing the male staring at us.

'Care to share?' I manage to say.

'No,' he replies smoothly.

I glare. He just stares, unaffected. My lips pull back involuntarily and a ghost of a smile whispers along his face. Damn handsome ass.

Attention going to the male I scent coming from the trees, Banner turns slightly toward where I'm looking. I shake off the stupid spark of emotion that forms when he saw my reaction and trusted my instincts to know someone or something was there. Elliot is a little too far for Banner's wolf to scent but I know he is there and will be here in about ten minutes.

'Elliot is coming, we can tell him how I'm a dud tracker who can't find your alpha.'

'Good, saves me a trip to his den,' Banner says so emotionless that I almost miss the fact that he made a joke. My jaw drops at the show of normalness and I grin when he scowls at me.

'What are you two doing out here?' Elliot asks as he comes from the forest. He has a wide smile on his face and I instantly want to go and hug him. Elliot has been to the St. Cloud den every day this week for dinner.

He is funny and friendly and invited me out this weekend with his fellow packmates.

'Following my broken nose,' I reply, watching the way Banner turns his back and heads into the trees.

'Your nose is broken?' Elliot frowns in confusion. His eyes go straight to my face.

I wave off the question, he doesn't get it. 'It's nothing. What are you doing here?' I ask, stepping away from the creek.

'Just scented you both here and was curious.' I smell a lie and try to work out why he's really here. Elliot throws me a majestic smile that lets me know he is here to see me. I blush. 'How is the hunt going?'

I groan and bask in his laughter.

'Do you want to come out tonight to the pub? Some packmates and I are going?'

'I'd like that,' I reply, feeling a little less heavy.

Banner appears back in the clearing and grumbles at me to stop wasting daylight.

Chapter Thirty Eight

'How did today go?' Logan asks over the noise of the pub. I shrug a nonchalant answer. 'That good huh?' he snickers.

'Let's just say that I'd love another beer,' I say too sweetly and wave the empty bottle in my hand.

'I gotcha,' he grins and grabs it off me. 'Anyone need a refill?' he asks the table of Coltonline packmates and heads to the bar with a decent order for more drinks.

'Don't worry too much about it, Gilly love. You're up against a massive task,' Elliot reassures me. Draping his arm around my shoulders, his touch instantly chases the stress from today away. I lean into him, absorbing his energy.

'Yeah Gilly, you're Farrowline. You could help us with our problems or not. You'll go back to being part of the most powerful pack in the country,' Laurence responds with a shrug. He's sitting across from me on the long table and I watch as his massive forearm flexes as he moves the beer to his lips.

'I don't really know what that means—' I begin and am cut off when Elliot says, 'it is an impossible task. The one that you are on.'

'It is?' I question and listen as the males around me joke and laugh about something I don't think is very funny.

'Yes, it is,' Joshua says as if I'm silly for thinking that it isn't. Out of the two males Elliot hangs with, I'm not a fan of Joshua. He is as big as Laurence but ruder. They both look remarkably alike and smell like cousins. They both have sandy coloured short hair, like almost cut to the skin and their faces are covered in a thick beard.

'This entire hunt is a fucking dumb decision. The Alpha left us,' Joshua bites out and I can taste his anger. Actually, he's giving off way too much information.

I don't reply and make eye contact with Logan from across the bar. He seems to read that I need him to come back and hurries over with our drink order. I take the beer he hands me and hope he can see the gratitude on my face.

'Anyways,' Elliot draws out the word, throwing the big male a warning look that I pretend I don't see.

'Now's probably not the time,' Logan warns and sits down beside me. I can feel the tension and for once am grateful when Banner appears at the end of the table.

'Now's not the time for what?' he asks, those eyes scanning the males around me and falling on Elliot. The male who hasn't dropped his easy-going smile, welcomes Banner loudly to the 'party'. His arm does drop from around my shoulders and I decide to keep all the questions bombarding my thoughts right now to myself.

The amount of information I'm getting is getting harder to manage and I wonder if Banner knows that Joshua and Laurence don't like him. Hate him actually. 'What have I missed?' At least I know that tone isn't just reserved for me.

'Nothing, cousin. Take a seat.' Elliot fusses about making room for Banner. Logan jumps off the seat next to me and heads to grab another one. He sits on the new one at the end of the table and I shuffle in my chair and move my beer when Banner sits between us.

This power dynamic is a little odd to me. All males around the table are pure dominant wolf shifters. None of them smell like an Alpha or a Beta but there's a power that surrounds Banner that none of the others have. It's strange to me to not be able to pinpoint what it is exactly. There's something with his wolf and human, a harmony that I don't think I've ever scented. He is so completely sure of himself, while I'm a fucking mess.

'So, why are you here?' Laurence asks the male beside me, his tone drips with contempt.

'Why? Is there a problem?' Banner challenges, the beer he raised to his mouth hovers while the two males stare. I look to Logan who shakes his head slightly and I'm guessing this is not the first time this tension has happened.

We all just silently drink for a few minutes while the pair work out 'who's is bigger'.

'We hunt tomorrow, Gilly. Early.' Banner says, just as I agree to another beer when Elliot stands and offers to grab the next round.

Again. Everyone goes silent. 'Let's have shots!' Elliot declares, breaking the weirdness around me. Everyone cheers and agrees and before I know what I'm doing, I'm dancing with Elliot to an old school song about shifter love.

'You aren't even trying!'

'I am!' I shout back to the unflinching male glaring at me from the damn tree line. 'I have no idea why I'm back here!' I growl, waving my hands around the fucking clearing where we got stuck at yesterday. I'm so hung-over, it's making me feel sick to my stomach. I haven't drunk that much in a very long time which is saying a lot but damn it was a great night. Elliot and his friends know how to party. We laughed, we sang karaoke, we danced and I have a fuzzy memory of making out with Elliot on the dancefloor and then leaning on Logan as he helped me into the den and to bed.

I can also remember Banner standing at my door with that fatherly disappointed look on his face and a promise to wake me up with the sun for the hunt. Which I now know wasn't my drunken mind that imagined him saying that, because he was at my bedroom door waking me up only an hour ago with the stupid sun.

'I need a taco and a kebab,' I groan, looking to the heavens for help. If I was with Gene and Kurt we'd already be at our favourite take-out joint eating our hangover food. But I'm not. I'm stuck in this freezing forest with the white snow and the frozen creek and the new scents and that sweet one that is starting to remind me of Elliot and his friends. 'Why does everything have to be so bright!' My head is killing me.

'Are you done? We need to keep moving.'

I bare my teeth at him and stomp into the trees to continue to feel like a failure. I can't scent the Alpha or his daughter.

I really don't think I can do this.

Chapter Thirty Nine

'How's the head?'

Logan chuckles at the disgruntled noise I make and sits down beside me on the wood steps that lead into the den.

Cradling a cup of hot cocoa that reminds me of home, I watch the snowflakes fall lazily to the ground. The sun is going down and it's been another failed day of hunting. Banner snapped at me to go back to the den shortly after my outburst in the clearing.

I spent the rest of the day with Grace and Maddy organising the large pantry here in the den that they stock for the winter. It was fun. I enjoy spending time with the two females. Maddy reminds me a bit of Jenny back at Pack and I can't help but remember how harsh I had to be with her the last time she went wolf and ran away. Maddy hasn't shifted yet which I'm secretly concerned about. I can tell that it will happen soon. She smells emotionally unbalanced which is why I'm out here drinking the cocoa Grace served everyone. Banner started nagging Maddy for not doing her homework. The argument from inside is getting louder and louder.

Logan sighs and I hand him my drink which he takes and holds in his hands. I can scent his frustration over what is happening and can't shake the feeling that Banner and Maddy might clash frequently.

'You all know she will shift soon, right?' I ask. They can't possibly think that she has any control over her emotions right now.

'We know,' he nods slowly. 'It's just different from when the twins shifted or when Grace did. Banner and I just wrestled and beat Jesse and Mason up to help them get over the antsy-ness you feel when it starts.'

I just laugh at that. Such a typical male response.

Logan gifts me a beautiful grin and continues, 'and Gracie, well she has always been a quiet soul, so she just kept to herself and when her wolf took over, she just walked the forest with Banner and I calmly.'

Nodding, I understand how hard it is for Maddy more than they would. I have seen it all in Farrowline. We're a massive Pack who are in each other's business. When an adolescent shifts for the first time, they are surrounded by Pack. Dominant wolves are led by other dominants and the less dominant ones are guided by the den-makers in our Pack. The Circle is there for them all, helping and comforting and guiding.

To shift is an experience that words cannot do justice. You're always aware of the beast in your blood, even as a small pup. It's not separate from you, it's in every thought and every action. However, a beast has to be fully grown before they can shift and take over the entire body. This happens in adolescence. I've heard it compared to human puberty. Emotions are louder. Thoughts are more chaotic and tempers are raised. It can be pretty confronting when your beast is a dominant which is what Maddy is. A bit like me, her human personality and her beast are a bit at odds. I'm not a particularly dominant person but my beast is strong in a way that no one else's is.

'You do know that Maddy's wolf is a dominant, yeah?' I question, wondering if the males can see what I smell.

'Yeah, we suspected for a while. It's just, Maddy is so...she is so...'

'She is your sister and you thought she'd be like Gracie?' I finish for him. It's a bit silly of him to say, but I get it. Dominant females are a particular breed of shifters. They're deadly and difficult and fierce and stunning to behold when given the room to explore their identity. Like Delfina and Nicolette and so many others in Farrowline. Each one is valuable and respected.

Logan just throws me a pained, *what do I do*, kinda look. 'You'll be fine,' I laugh.

'Jesse shifted once in the early days and he lost control. He ran away and we couldn't find him for days.' Shuffling closer to the male, I feel his muscles lose the tension that formed on the memory of what happened to Jesse when our sides touch. 'Banner went ballistic. He searched every hour until we found him almost on the other side of the region. Days away.'

'She'll be fine,' I reassure him again. Logan drapes his arm around my shoulders and I hear him breath in my scent. It isn't sexual, more like him grounding himself with a fellow shifter, an adopted packmate.

'How do you know?' Logan sounds so worried.

'Because I am here.' I grin up at him and expecting him to laugh at my joke. He just looks serious and nods like he sees the logic now.

'You're right.' He calms completely. 'We have the Tracker of Farrowline to help us.'

I look for the teasing and find none. His unwavering faith in me sits heavy against my shoulders, reminding me why I'm here.

'This is ridiculous! I'm not a pup!' Maddy shouts as she slams the door open, scaring the hell out of Logan and I and storms past us down the stairs.

'Are you sure, Madeline? Because the way that you are acting reminds me of your pup years!' Banner states in the fatherliest voice I've ever heard. It's comical.

Logan and I sit still, not wanting the huffing and puffing male behind us at the front door to notice us and maybe start telling us to clean our rooms or something. Maddy disappears into the darkness of the trees.

'Logan, please.' Banner sighs and the younger male hands me my cocoa with a grim smile and hops up.

'She has stopped just that way, where that bent weird tree is,' I tell the standing male who throws me a grateful nod before jumping from the stairs and jogging after his sister.

'I've got her,' he calls over his shoulder. He disappears in the right direction while I sit watching. I can feel the immense energy that is Banner at the door.

'You know she can't help it,' I say, mostly wanting to fill the space.

'I know,' he replies eventually. If I knew any better, I'd think he was worried or remorseful. 'It's harder with Maddy. They all went through this rebellious age where they didn't want their big brother to parent them and tell them what to do but eventually they all understood that rules are in place for a reason. I fear that Maddy is too big for Coltonline. That she needs room to move and grow and find herself.'

A little shocked to hear him speak so openly, I sit staring at the trees, absorbing his words. Banner St. Cloud is an arrogant ass but he is an awesome brother and male. To have taken on the responsibility to care for his siblings, at such a young age says a great deal about his character.

'You are a good brother Banner and a good leader.'

'It's cold out here, come inside before you get a chill,' he says, typical Banner style.

I throw him a look over my shoulder at the arrogance and glare at the way he holds the door open in invitation for me to walk through.

'You know when Tobias took the blood oath he didn't mean you had to trail behind me on every hunt or keep me from catching a sniffle,' I reply just to poke the beast who's clearly upset about the argument he has just had with his sister.

'Just get inside, runt of Farrowline.' His eyes narrow and I only jump up because it *is* fucking cold out here and the temperature is dropping.

Walking past him, I expect some kind of comment but he isn't looking at me. His eyes are locked on the forest where his siblings just went.

Half inside the warm house, I'm drawn to the laughter in the kitchen and the sound of the twins teasing Gracie for the way she keeps texting someone. We all know who the someone is, however, I hover, unable to walk further into the den. Banner smells like nothing but Banner. There are no emotions leaking through the cracks. No rage or sadness over the fight. There is nothing but steady silence as he continues to stare out into the night.

'They're still at the tree,' I say and hold my breath when he turns slowly to set those dark eyes on my face. I hate that I can't read him or understand the small nod he gives me. Or the fact that I wanted to reassure him that Maddy is all right.

Chapter Forty

'What's wrong?'

'Nothing.' I sigh into the phone. I can hear the noises of Farrow Group in the background of the call and sit on a broken tree not too far from the St. Cloud den. It's so peaceful here in Coltonline. The snow is bright. The birds are quiet and the tree dwelling animals are tiny. Nothing like Farrowline. Everything is vibrant and loud and full of a different kind of life.

'Gilly, what's wrong?' Oliver's deep, demanding voice leaves no room for me to stay quiet. I needed to talk to someone from Pack today. I needed to hear a safe and familiar voice.

'I don't think I can do this,' I blurt out. 'I've been walking in circles for a week. I keep coming back to the same spot that has no real meaning to this hunt.'

'Are you sure it has no meaning?' is his simple reply. I wish I was back at work in Farrow Group getting everyone lunch and taking my time eating so that I can socialise with Kurt and Gene.

'Yeah, I'm sure.' *Am I?* 'Actually, I have no idea,' I say, picking up a fistful of snow just to feel the cold against my skin. 'What I do know is that I'm getting nowhere in this hunt.'

'You've been there hunting just over a week, Gil. Jax takes longer to plan and then marinate meat for a single barbecue.'

I laugh, welcoming the feeling.

'Put me on video call, so that I can see you.'

Smiling wide, no longer feeling like a failure I comply and blink down at the handsome face that fills the scene. 'Missed my pretty face?' I tease and watch as those crystal depths narrow to scrutinise my face.

'You sleeping okay? Do you need me to send more of your smelling oils?'

'How do you know about my smelling oils?' I ask, I haven't spoken to anyone about what I do every day to manage my tracker nose.

He rolls those perfect eyes and I can't help but chuckle. 'I know everything about you Gilly.' I frown, unsure what the feeling is that sweeps over my chest. Maybe it's loneliness. I feel my face go beetroot red.

'Not everything! A female has secrets,' I fire back, loving that I can be playful with him.

'I know you females do.' That sobers me up. The reminder of his many conquests makes me all grumpy all of a sudden.

'Tell me what has been happening back in Pack. How are my mum and dad? Is Kurt ignoring my calls because he's still mad that I left?'

Oliver complies and I spend the next twenty minutes laughing over stories of home. In that moment, I watch a cloud roll across the sky and explore the feeling in my chest that while I miss Farrowline, I'm also very aware that here in Coltonline I can be something different...something more.

Around the table, the St Cloud family laugh and joke and hold out their plates while Banner fills them one by one with food. It's like a rotation system and happens every night.

Plates go from hands to hands until one gets placed down in front of you. Banner cuts up the meats and adds everything, ensuring that we're all fed before he begins to eat.

Stuffing my face, I listen intently to Mason who is telling me about what he hopes to do once school finishes in a few months. All the younger adolescents here in Coltonline study online, at their own pace. We have a handful of pack who do the same thing. It works for some and not for others.

'You know, I can get you an internship at Farrow Group if you really want to pursue marketing. We have a great team,' I offer, flicking my gaze to the male eating down the table briefly when his scent changes slightly. Banner isn't looking at me though and I think I may have imagined the spike in emotion.

'Really?' Mason is all but pouncing out of his chair with excitement. 'You can do that?'

Jesse slaps his shoulder. 'Of course she can do it. She is a Circle wolf of Farrowline.' I frown at the exchange. 'Don't you technically own the company? Don't all the Circle of Farrowline own all the business your Pack has?'

I go to respond and snap my mouth shut as I have no idea how to answer that question. It doesn't matter though because Logan jumps in asking Jesse how he'd know all of that. 'Everyone knows that. Just read a business article once in a while.'

'And when do you read business articles?' Gracie asks.

'At school.' Jesse shrugs.

No one seems to care that I haven't replied. They're all now arguing over information they have and have not heard about my pack.

'Eat your food,' Banner grumbles, stopping the nonsense talk happening around the table between the siblings.

There is a heartbeat of silence and I chuckle, smelling the energy bubbling under Mason's skin, get a side-look from Banner, and snicker when the adolescent blurts out, 'so does that make you super rich then?'

Banner growls in exasperation. Logan wipes the moisture from his eyes as he laughs so hard he can't breathe. Grace frowns and tells her brother that he is being inappropriate. Maddy continues to text on her phone, totally uncaring about us all. It's beautiful and uplifting and I find myself loving everything about this family unit.

Chapter Forty One

Taking the platter from Elliot, I pick at the assortment of meats and cheese to create my own little plate. Elliot and I are sitting cross legged on the floor of his porch, sipping wine and devouring a shit load of dairy. The day is dying and after hours of failed hunting, I jumped to come over and eat with him when he came over to save me from his cousin.

'I fucking love cheese!' he groans in pure ecstasy and I shuffle on the cushioned surface I'm sitting on. He is a beautiful male and I can't help but think about the way his mouth felt on mine as we danced at the bar. I'm sitting on the biggest, floor cushion I have ever seen, watching Elliot eat and I'm loving life right now. 'Life is so much better with cheese, isn't it?'

'Yep.' I laugh and throw another piece in my mouth.

Chewing and chatting, I slowly relax. The bottle of wine helps. A lull in the conversation has me stop and look out at the new snow falling from the sky. This place is stunning. Harsh but stunning. The chill is kept at bay by the heat lamps attached to the roof of the outdoor porch and I think we could use them in Farrowline when we have barbeques in the winter. That's the one thing I miss about home, the gatherings with everyone.

Here in Coltonline everyone is so separate. I only get glimpses of shifters as they move silently through whatever section I am hunting in.

'Don't hunt tomorrow, I want to show you something. A place in the territory that you'll love.'

'Yeah right. Banner told me that tomorrow there is a meeting with the leaders of Coltonline so we have to get up *extra* early to start searching.' I lean over to grab more cheese, completely concerned about food.

Elliot snorts as if he isn't surprised. 'So, where are you starting the search tomorrow? You two finished near the creek? Seems like nothing there helped.'

I groan loudly at the mention of the damn creek that I have circled back to for a week. 'Yes, thank fuck. We're heading closer to the Beta's territory.' Eyes rolling back at the sweet and smooth piece I place into my mouth, I smile when Elliot's hand brushes the hair from my face.

Staring up at him, I take in the mesmerising look on his face. 'Do you think maybe the Alpha just left us? Our pack has some problems that I'm sure Banner is keeping from you.'

Frowning, I have to take a minute to process what he is saying. 'What kind of problems?' *Am I here on some useless hunt where the Alpha just left?*

Shrugging, Elliot moves back and focuses on the food. 'Tensions have been high and continue to rise the bigger Coltonline gets. Everyone wants territory and there isn't any to give and most parents aren't willing to divide and give over their hard-earned lands to their pups.' I can't believe what I'm hearing. 'Like Logan, the poor male is a dominant and his brother gets something that he'll never receive. He fights for territory that he can't claim as his own. It's just sad.' He finishes by popping some fancy bread in his mouth like he hasn't just dropped a massive bomb on my entire hunt.

Eating my bottom lip, I try to work out if what he's saying is valid. There were leaders who openly said that the Alpha could have left in the first meeting in Banner's den. Laurence said it a few times at the pub and Elliot has educated me on the territory structure of Coltonline. Even Logan has mentioned it. *What if the issues in the pack got too hard for the Alpha and he really did just take off? Am I hunting a male who ran away from his responsibilities?*

'Would he be a male to leave his mate though? Why would your Alpha take his daughter and not the other half of his soul?' I question, observing the emotions leaking off the male. He is angry. Really, really angry. He is also a little afraid and I feel instantly bad for him. I can't comprehend the hurt my wolf and I'd feel if Tobias abandoned us. It'd be like ripping my own heart out. I don't think I'd survive it.

'I honestly don't know, Gilly.' I believe his words and go back to munching on crackers and cheese.

'Could he have left?' I snap at the male sitting at the dining table typing on his computer. I'm a little tipsy and feel a headache coming from the make-out session I just had with Elliot. His scent is odd and every time he is close to me it's like my nose and brain are trying desperately to find the connection of why he smells so oddly sweet like his friends.

The door to the back swings shut and I huff and place my hands on my hips, waiting for Banner to respond. All I get is those black eyes flicking to stare at me over the top of the laptop screen. Nothing. I get nothing from him.

'I want to know, Banner. Do you think your Alpha left on his own? Is this hunt a fruitless and colossal waste of time?' I'm pissed. I'm infuriated and I'm kind of hoping that there is a reason why I can't pick up on any hint of this male and his daughter.

'Anything is possible,' the arrogant ass says calmly.

'Are you joking with me?' I can smell the other Coltonline siblings in and around the den but ignore the fact that they are all listening. 'Why am I here then? If Coltonline has all these issues, why would you come and get me?'

I watch, with my arms crossed over my chest as Banner lowers the laptop lid slowly and leans back in the poor chair that has to hold so much dominant male muscle. He's an ancient tree trunk and while I 'sucked-face' with Elliot for an hour, I can admire the simple beauty of the male. 'You're here because I don't believe that he left. My uncle and I were close, Gilly. We did everything together. He only had Sasha and he knew that she wasn't born to be an Alpha. The poor female was...is,' he corrects with a look of pain on his features that has my heart drop. 'She *is* strong, but she is no alpha. Yes, Coltonline has issues and my cousin needs to learn to keep his mouth shut.' I watch as he rises from the chair and stalks slowly over to me. I strain my neck to look up at him but don't take a step in retreat as he gets too close.

Despite the position, I know he isn't being threatening and frankly I'm too stunned to move. This is the most he has ever spoken to me. That's when I realise something so stupidly obvious that I do take a step back and watch those black eyes follow my movements like the predator he is. I scent it on him like he drops the curtain he uses in his mind and body to conceal his emotions and his power.

'Fuck. It would be you. You'll be the next Alpha of Coltonline,' I whisper, knowing deep down that more is going on here.

'That is not information that I want spread around.' He is mad and I don't know if it is directed at me or not.

'Why?' I push, needing to know what else is going on here in Coltonline.

'Because my cousin is right, there are issues here in our pack that require me to keep quiet about this.'

'Who knows?'

'Only people I trust.'

I feel my face scrunch up. 'Does Elliot?'

His silence screams the answer at me.

I suck in a breath when the 'wall' he puts up blocks all the information that I was unconsciously reading. Studying the hard expression on his face, I realise that I may be way over my head here. My shock morphs into annoyance pretty quickly with his silence. 'How do you do that?' I demand.

'Do what?' Arrogant prick hasn't moved away from me.

'How to shut off your emotions so that you're hard to read or scent? No one can do that. It must be exhausting. You hide who you are every day, Banner. This is serious! It's freaking me the fuck out. If you need to hide who you are because of the issues in your Pack, then what does that mean?'

Banner searches my face and I don't know what he sees but he softens just a little. 'You're safe with me Gilly. No is going to hurt you or any of my family.'

I open and close my mouth, unsure how to respond. I have no idea what is going on. 'How do you do it? The others try but they aren't very good.' I wave my hand in the general direction of where the St. Cloud's are listening. 'It's annoying that I can't smell you,' I huff like an adolescent.

Banner is silent, his eyes roaming over my face before he makes a deep sound in the back of his throat that has my arms fall from my chest. 'That is a secret you'll have to earn, Gilly Sommers. Tracker of Farrowline.'

Chapter Forty Two

'You're very focused today runt.'

'I want to earn that secret.' I try to sound cool, like I don't actually want him to tell me what he was referring to last night but deep down I am dying to know. I want to know. I *need* to know. My damn wolf is a nosey beast. The fact that he can turn it on and off and I don't know how he does it is infuriating. A smaller hunt that I now find myself on. I couldn't sleep last night and ended up texting with Gene and Kurt until the early hours of the morning.

'I would've told you about the secret earlier if I thought you'd work harder.'

Ignoring him completely, I look around at my surroundings. I haven't been to this side of Coltonline. The trees are scattered around this area and I can't smell a living being for miles. We are up in the furthest left corner. A territory owned by the Beta. There is something on the wind here. Not the Alpha or his daughter, but something. The ground has been rising slowly and I know by the way the earth smells that we are heading towards a rocky edge. The terrain isn't flat snow like the other sections I've been investigating. There are boulders and small drops everywhere. It's harsh, yet pretty.

'If you insist on following me everywhere I go, at least try and stay out of my way,' I snap back and bend down to look at a funny looking branch on the floor. There are trees here in Coltonline that I've never seen before and I find them fascinatingly beautiful.

'Have I been in your way?' Banner insists.

Again, I ignore him because he is right to question what I said. He has never been in the way. Actually, there are times when I forget that Banner is following me which is strange because I normally hate when I'm trying to track for Farrowline and Tobias sends others to 'watch over me' when I'm on a hunt. They all get in the way and muddle up my nose. Banner though, I sometimes forget that he's there in the shadows watching me.

Rising, I continue to follow my instincts. Which take me all the way up to a ridge. Standing on the edge of a sheer drop, I look hesitantly down at the rocky, snow covered fall and try to work out if this is a place of significance or not. Today we're on the Beta of Coltonline's lands, Banner's father is close but has kept his distance for reasons I don't understand. His mother on the other hand came over just as we crossed into the territory to ask us for an update on the hunt. She was cold and unmoving and I hated the way Banner didn't react to her clipped tone or subtle, snarky comments like he expects these things from her.

'Your dad is close.'

'I know,' is all Banner says. 'He will keep his distance.' He's not far from where I stand, looking over the cliff face. He seems bored and pulls out the phone that begins to chime in his back pocket with a look of annoyance on his face. I watch him in my peripheral vision. He answers the phone with a huffing, 'what?' and proceeds to bark orders to one of the twins about what they should do after Maddy yelled at everyone and left the den.

Banner hangs up with a grunt of annoyance that has me look up at the show of emotion. I even smell exasperation. 'You know she can't help it,' I offer, and bend down to brush my hand lightly over the packed snow to see if I can mess up the lack of any real scent markers. I followed a very subtle scent in the beginning, it was the Alpha's daughter but it didn't go anywhere.

'I am fully aware.'

'Are you?' I quip back. 'She is a dominant adolescent who is on the verge of a shift. When she does, her wolf will take over and the way you handle it will have a lasting impact on the kind of relationship you and Maddy have in the future. If her wolf doesn't like what your wolf does, it could affect your relationship.'

'I raised Maddy from a pup. I handled the twins and Gracie's first shifts on my own, I think I know what I'm doing.' He is fucking infuriating.

Rising, I clap off the sand from my gloves and shrug in annoyance. Moving slowly further along the edge, I have no power over the words that spill from my lips. 'Fine, don't listen to me. I'm telling you that I've witnessed many a shift before in Farrowline. I know I haven't raised pups or have had the responsibilities that you have but I know what I'm talking about! You don't have to listen if you don't want to.' I end with a grumble and then step into what I can only assume is a small animal hole. I tumble sidewards, my wolf responding quickly and yet not fast enough that there is a moment where my face drains of all colour and I fear that I'm about to fall to my death.

Strong arms catch me around the middle, pulling me backwards into a hard body. We hit the packed snow hard and I huff out a breath as it's knocked out of me.

Lying on top of Banner as he hold me firmly to his chest, I feel his heart beating rapidly underneath me. I feel his wolf against my body, rippling and changing under my touch. We both lie like that, trying to get over the shock.

'What was that! Will you watch where you're going!'

Rolling my eyes, I push off his chest and know I'm only able to because he lets me. Sitting my butt into the snow, I try to catch my breath. I'm shaking with adrenaline.

Banner jumps off, his chest all puffed out as his damn lecture starts about how he is not going to tell Alpha Tobias Farrow that he lost me over a 'damn' cliff edge and how he will not allow me to be harmed here in Coltonline.

'Yeah, yeah,' I mumble and brush the snow from my black pants. I'm still rattled over what could've happened. He is still bloody going and I push myself off the floor. Looking down at the cliff, I shake my head, that could've been bad and I look over at the male pacing a few steps away. 'Thanks for saving me, Banner.'

His, 'hmmmm,' annoys me, but I still smile.

'There is nothing here. We should move on.' I need to get away from this cliff edge.

'Lead the way, Tracker.'

Chapter Forty Three

Shedding one skin for another, I crack my neck and wait for the male beside me to do the same. I'm absolutely famished and hate that I have to go to this Coltonline meeting tonight. I miss my Pack so much and every interaction I've had with various wolf shifters on this hunt has been strained and awkward which is how I feel walking into the Beta's den.

Too many eyes flick my way and I fight the need to move closer to Banner. I don't like the way Greta sits amongst a group of elderly males and females, all dominants, all unimpressed that I am here. The Beta stands at the end of the room, the entire living area has been prepared for this meeting. Chairs and lounges have been moved to the sides of the room and are scattered around the place. Most of the seats are occupied and I notice the many faces from the meeting when I first came to pack. The male who demanded that the hunt I am on is a waste of time throws me a glare. He smells like that sweet scent Elliot and his friends have and I put it down to the fact he is clearly close to Elliot as the male is sitting beside him. He throws me a wave. Nodding in return, I'm not in the mood to go over and talk to him.

Taking the seat Banner holds out in the back corner of the room, I plonk down and nod when he tells me to stay. I watch him move over to his father and try not to make eye contact with anyone, especially the two dominants to my right who smell of aggression and trepidation. There is a vibe in this room. An energy that has the hairs on my arms stand on end.

Looking around the room, I notice the pictures on the Beta's walls. He isn't really much of a decorator. I see the family photos. Banner and Logan with the twins. Maddy and Gracie beside Greta. The Beta and a male with salt and pepper hair in front of the den with their arms around each other. It's all very...normal and yet there isn't one photo of the family together. Not like in my parent's den. There are photos everywhere of all members of Farrowline. Oliver and me at the lake, eating ice blocks. Tobias, Ridley and Noah. My parents and I on vacation. Jax and Easton flipping burgers at a barbecue.

Coltonline is weird.

The Beta eventually starts the meeting and Banner sits down heavily beside me, blocking me from the majority of the room.

'We meet because there was a loner found not too far from our Alpha's territory lines. My mate and I were able to contain the situation.'

Shocked, I look up at Banner and take in the hard expression on his face. He clearly had no idea about this.

'The concern is that the loners in these areas have found out that we don't have an Alpha. And a pack without an Alpha is an unstable one.'

The room erupts in demands of action and change. I sneak a glance at the stoic male beside me again, trying to read his features. He must have a good reason to hide his alpha energy. 'We need to either find the Alpha or declare him gone and move on.'

'We voted for the hunt, we let the Farrowline tracker do the work.'

'We should never have gotten another pack in our business.'

'Declare a new Alpha! I choose Elliot Colton.' That was the male who clearly doesn't like me and I watch behind Banner's body as Elliot grins and then raises his hands in flattery.

'I am honoured my name has been called but we should continue to look for the Alpha.' The grin on his face has me feel odd. Turned off, maybe. He's clearly loving the idea. Laurence and Joshua are both nodding like he should be the next Alpha. It's a little absurd that they all think they can just name an Alpha. It doesn't work like that. An Alpha, like a Beta or a Tracker, is born. There is no one in this room that smells like an Alpha. Only Banner, if he allowed that curtain over his power to come down. It's so strange that he would keep his true self hidden. I have no idea how his wolf can stand being leashed like that. I don't know if it's impressive or sad.

The Beta to his credit allows everyone their space to vent and share their thoughts. Banner doesn't move. No one is calling his name, obviously. It goes on like this for a few minutes before the Beta gets control.

For an hour, I sit, secretly judging this weird pack. There is such a divide here. Some shifters want to move on while others want to keep looking.

When the arguing dies down, Banner indicates with his head for me to follow. 'Come on, you are hungry.'

Excited now at the thought of food, I trail beside him until we get back to his den and he starts to make us both a sandwich with the works. Banner feeds me first, fussing around getting me a soda and extra dipping sauce for the sandwich before he eats his in silence across from me.

'Wow! You could have fallen to your death! Babe, be careful!' Ridley sounds more amused than anything else, she had me explain the way Banner saved me three times. 'He is a very attractive male so I'm sure it wasn't too bad.'

Pulling the pin from my mouth, I fix the bump that has formed at the top of my head from my ponytail. 'It was nothing.'

'Doesn't sound like nothing.' Ridley is in her bedroom folding clothes and I can see Noah in the background of the video chat playing with his favourite stuffed wolf. Oliver gave it to him and the young boy is obsessed with it.

'Please, he's a grumpy old male who grunts and growls.' I finish off my hair and sigh. 'He *is* nice to look at though.'

Ridley's laughter filters through the device resting up against the long mirror on the wall that I'm sitting in front of trying to get ready for a dinner with the St Clouds at the bar. 'He sounds like every Circle wolf here in Farrowline.'

'Who is nice to look at?' I can't help but smile wide at the face that appears in the screen. I miss my Alpha so much and even through the phone I can feel his love and affection.

'How are you, Gilly?'

I have to get control over my emotions before I respond with an, 'I'm okay, Alpha. It's just...this pack is weird. There's more going on here that I don't understand.'

He frowns and a new face appears behind his massive shoulder. 'What does that mean? Are you safe?' It's a skill Oliver has that even through the phone I am powerless to not answer him. I tell them everything...well, except the information about Banner, I keep that to myself.

Chapter Forty Four

Arms around Elliot, I dance and sway against his body. There is a local band playing live music at the bar and it is brilliant tonight. Logan is close, dancing with a female I haven't met before. He doesn't seem too interested because his gaze is locked on the pair closer to the stage. Gracie is pressed shyly against her human man, Evan, and I just want to squeal with joy. It took about ten minutes of convincing and then promising to go out on the dancefloor with Elliot before she accepted his invitation to dance. Elliot and I have been teasing Logan for the past twenty minutes as we act like fools. I love how relaxed it is with Elliot. He kisses my neck and asks if I want to hang out at his den later tonight and I laugh loudly and tell him I need a drink.

Shaking my head, feeling light and happy, I slump down on the seat beside Banner, who doesn't look too impressed by what's happening on the dancefloor. I don't need to look to see what has him frowning and go to grab the pitcher of water on the table. Banner beats me to it and pours me a glass without looking at anything but his dancing sister. I take it with a grin and openly watch him.

'She's fine, Banner,' he grunts in response and I shake my head because I feel I understand what he's just said to me. Which is 'mind my own business'. 'Gracie deserves to be happy. You aren't one of those human-haters are you? Because if you are, I'd be really disappointed.'

'Do you ever stop talking?'

I stop to think and then stick my tongue out at the male now side-eying me. Leaning back in the chair, sipping at the cold water, I observe the twins playing pool on the tables in the back corner. Maddy is underage so she has to stay within the family friendly section of the pub. The table Banner snagged is in that section but is close to the alcohol serving areas.

'I want us to start looking on the south side of territory. Doug might give us a problem but it isn't his lands so we should be okay. Just prepare yourself.'

I have no idea what he is talking about. 'Who's Doug?'

Banner takes a drink of his beer before answering. 'He's the male who threw Elliot's name into the room for our next Alpha.'

'Right, that male.' He's a creep. 'Could a pack actually just nominate an Alpha like that? Even if they don't smell like an Alpha?'

Banner shakes his head in exasperation. 'I think some shifters around here reckon they can.'

I take another drink just to process. 'It doesn't work like that though.'

'I know that. You know that. I don't think they care.' Banner sounds like he could be mad. Maybe. It's hard to tell.

'Why are they all so angry? The dominants in your pack.'

I don't think Banner is going to respond until he says, 'territory.'

Enough said.

I watch Gracie and Evan dance and drink my beer slowly. 'They are good together. They smell like they are in love,' I tactfully say to test his reaction.

'I think Gracie needs to focus on her studies.' His response has me smile into my beer. Typical dominant male nonsense. Grace is doing a university course online.

'You know she is not an adolescent, Banner. She is full grown and she is in love with that human male.'

'Love means nothing. You should know that.' His words are a slap in my face.

I'm fuming. 'You're a prick,' I bite out, stealing some of the chips from his plate and pop them in my mouth before I say anything more. Furious, I snap, 'what did my mum tell you?'

Banner doesn't respond right away, he's monitoring every move Evan makes with his sister. The poor human is very aware of the male watching him too. 'That you were stupid enough to get a mating bond confused with adolescent infatuation.'

I should be baring my teeth and showing him my canines. I should jump the table and slash his face. Instead, I sit and absorb his words feeling like I'm being reprimanded by my brother or something. The shit thing is that he is right. I did get the two mixed up and every person in Farrowline knows it.

'I was dumb,' I confess.

'Yep, it sounds like you were.'

This time I do show him my teeth. 'That's a bit harsh. I was in love with him.'

His typical, 'hhmmmm', response is infuriating. 'It's none of my business, but I think it's a silly thing to try and find your mate when you don't know yourself first. I just hope you don't get confused here on what is lust and friendship and what is true, binding love between two souls.'

I don't miss the way his eyes flick to Elliot and I scoff. 'You're right,' I state, rising and dropping my beer on the table. 'It is none of your business.'

Chapter Forty Five

Sitting in the tray of the pick-up truck with the twins and Logan, one of their phones is playing music and we shiver and laugh and keep the party going. Banner is driving and the females are in the truck with Elliot. There is another pick-up ahead of ours and the snowy wonderland flies by as we head home on a well-used dirt track through the forest to Coltonline.

The sky is lit up tonight and for once there isn't a dark, snow-filled cloud blocking the full moon. It shines down on us. Illuminating the world. Stars twinkle and I find myself feeling calm. I feel like myself again. Like everything that mattered and weighed me down has been pushed from my mind. Which causes guilt to creep into my mind.

I love Farrowline. It has my heart completely but it also holds so much history for me.

Lost in my own thoughts and staring out into the darkened woods, I contemplate my life choices and then sit up to attention when my wolf comes to the surface. I smell danger.

The entire world slows down.

A mighty howl rips from my throat as I give myself over to the wolf who reacts like the hunter she is. From the trees, an animal leaps toward the truck, his trajectory is clearly to the tray and I rise on my knees, hand now morphed into claws and swipe out just as the cheetah dives towards Mason who is sitting at the end of the tray.

My claws take him down, ripping the skin from his monstrous face. I feel the impact through my body. The cheetah cries out in pain and surprise and disappears under the truck.

The vehicle turns sharply and I hit the side of the tray and am only saved from going over because Logan reacts and grabs me.

Heart pounding, I fly from the car and shift beside the males who mimic my actions. I face off with the line of shifters now observing us from the other side of the road. Loners. The other vehicle has stopped and the two dominants from that truck are now behind Banner and I, watching our backs and the females left in our car.

I count three shifters but can smell two more in the trees. They are the biggest threat.

Stepping slightly into Banner's side, I flick my gaze to the trees to our left and try to communicate where he and I need to have our attention. To the male's credit, he seems to listen. Banner's beast grunts and Logan and Elliot appear beside us. Their teeth bared, growling a warning to the loners.

A heartbeat.

Two.

And then all hell breaks loose.

Fighting is not my biggest strength but I am a tracker. A hunter. So when Banner takes on the bigger of the two bear loners, I engage with the female one.Completely surrendering to the wolf, I use her nose to keep the advantage. I smell every one of her moves before she makes it. Each time her weight shifts, the ground under her paw lets off a scent. Every breath she takes tells me when she is preparing to attack and every time she does, I evade her massive, razor sharp claws and teeth.

It's a dance. Yes, a different one than the one I was enjoying with Elliot, but a dance none-the-less.

The bear gets grumpier and grumpier, unable to understand why I'm always one step ahead of her that she doesn't see the male wolf come up from behind.

I might be a dominant but I still turn my head when Banner finishes the fight.

I look back when he is on two legs beside me. His hand in my fur, completely shocking me into not moving or reacting. Large hands work their way clinically over my back and to my side.

Banner steps in front of me, uncaring that my teeth are close to his neck and grips my face in his monstrous hands. They are warm and calloused and I wish he'd drop that curtain over his scent so that I can draw him in.

He checks my body thoroughly, ensuring that I'm not hurt and I shift when he finally steps back.

Standing before him, blinking up at that stone face, I feel something change between us. Like he sees me in a new light.

'Don't worry, Banner. I'm fine. You don't have to worry about Farrowline or Alpha Tobias coming for your head,' I tease...kinda. Actually, I really want him to care if I'm hurt or not. In that moment I realise that I want to be part of the shifters that Banner takes care of. I want to live next to his energy and be important to him.

'You fight well, but you need to improve. You are a hunter, Gilly Sommers.' He is all serious and unfazed by what has just happened. Typical

Banner style. I sigh, unsure why I thought we'd have a beautiful moment where he told me he was happy I'm safe or that he cares. 'Tomorrow, after the hunt, we start training.'

He walks off on that bombshell and barks at me to follow.

CHAPTER FORTY SIX

I rub the sleep from my eyes and take in my surroundings, the sun is barely up. I stand at the edge of his territory muttering how much I hate him right now. We were up all night trying to calm Gracie and Maddy down. Mason was in a mood too, he knew that he was close to being very hurt and it shook him, I think. I woke to him standing outside my closed door. He didn't say a thing, only threw his arms around my body and held me tight. He didn't see Banner watching us from the top of the stairs. Everyone is very aware of the danger we faced and I'm just so glad that I was there to protect these beautiful shifters.

The oversized male, with his emotionless scent, hasn't said a word as he led me through his territory and to the very point where Coltonline ends. There is something about him this morning that is weirding me out a little though. He waited for me to shove a breakfast muffin in my mouth without complaining of how slow I am, which he does every morning, and when I asked him to slow down just before when my energy just couldn't keep up with him, he listened. I asked him to do the same thing for me two days ago on the hunt and he ignored me.

Hugging myself, feeling the cold, I try to work out what we are doing. 'What is going on?' I yawn. 'You said I could sleep today and we'd hunt tonight.'

'We will hunt tonight.' I want to hit him so bad and he knows it because those black eyes come down to land on my glaring expression. 'Do you want to know the secret of how I know how to block your tracker senses?'

I perk up at that. Standing tall, I nod profusely. Almost begging with my head. I actually think he rolls his eyes at me and I gape as Banner steps from his territory and heads into the trees. *Did he just show emotion?* I practically run after him to keep up. I'm all giddy and eager. Like a small pup.

We walk for an hour. My endless questions are ignored and I'm about to turn around and walk back when I smell the subtle strand of life up ahead. Stopping, I lift my nose and look over at the shifter observing me. 'There is a male wolf out here.' I point in the direction where we are heading.

Banner nods once as if approving what I've just said. 'My uncle will be annoyed that you scented him.'

'Your uncle?' I question and run after him again when he strides away from me. 'Who is your uncle and why does he live outside of territory?' I ask his back. I don't need him to answer though because when we get to a clearing, I slow down and frown at the sight of a single, small cabin nestled comfortably in the trees. The roof is covered with snow. The cabin is on stilts and there are wood steps leading to the front door. For some reason, the structure doesn't seem out of place within the winter wonderland of the landscape. This place holds a number of scents. A few that have my lips pulled back in rage but when I start to tell Banner that we shouldn't be here, a male appears at the door to the cabin and he doesn't look particularly impressed to see us. He smells like...nothing, and I take a small step closer to Banner on instinct at the hostility radiating from him. I've seen his face before. In a photo in the Beta's den.

'I told you not to bring her here,' the new male calls. He doesn't seem happy.

'You said I shouldn't, not that I can't,' Banner shouts back, he seems to pick up on my hesitancy because he turns slightly so that he can place a hand on my lower back. The touch surprises me. 'Come, I want you to meet George St Cloud, my father's brother. He's a tracker, like you.'

Stunned, my gaze flies to the scowling male at the door.

I've never met another tracker before.

Sitting beside Banner on the two seater lounge in the open living room, I sip at the sweet tea his uncle gave me and look around. Everything is neat and tidy with no powerful scents in the air. It's actually refreshing and I find myself no longer anxious about being here in some new male's den. Banner's uncle, George St Cloud is a tall male. He's has lean muscle and salt and pepper hair. He looks exactly like the Beta of Coltonline. George is older though. Maybe in his late fifties, the male groans when he sits and stands and hasn't stopped moving around the cosy space getting us tea and biscuits. For someone who didn't look keen that we were here, he has been very accommodating.

He sits across from us, silently stirring his drink while I cradle the floral China in my hand. It's like he bought out the nice serving wear and it makes me warm to him. His gaze keeps flicking to me and then back to his nephew. Banner hasn't said much and I see where he gets his 'silent type' routine from.

It's odd that he doesn't live within Coltonline though.

Clearing my throat, I place down the teacup on the matching saucer sitting on the small rectangular coffee table between us. 'So, Banner tells me that you are a tracker?' I have to say something to break the silence. It's killing me.

'Yes,' is all he says.

Trying really hard to be a good guest, I grow more and more impatient.

'Just ask him, already!' Banner grumbles, clearly over my energy.

I throw him a glare and then blurt out, 'how do you cut off your emotions like that? It's infuriating for a tracker but the power is amazing,' I blurt out, *needing* answers. 'What else do you know about our abilities?'

Shrugging, George brushes off the question with a simple, 'you can learn how to do anything if you practice. You are young and have much to learn, Farrowline Tracker.'

'Teach me!' I blurt out. 'I've never interacted with another tracker before.'

George sips his tea and watches me intently. 'From what it sounds like, you don't seem to need my help.'

'You can teach me anyway. It doesn't seem like you have much else going on.' I look around the cabin and see the pile of empty alcohol bottles in the corner and feel the colour drain from my face. Then it hits me. Straightening, I ignore Banner's growing tension. 'You're a loner.' How did I not put this together when we got here. *Is this what my life is going to be like? Drinking alone in my little den, pack-less and isolated?*

'I prefer recluse,' is his smooth response.

'Is that any better?'

'No.' I watch as he brings the teacup to his lips. His black eyes are fixed on me, waiting for my reaction.

'I shouldn't be here.'

'Why not?' Banner questions angrily.

Seriously! 'Because he's a loner. *You* shouldn't be here, Banner! After everything that happened last night—'

'I had nothing to do with that,' George grumbles.

'But you clearly know about it,' I half shriek in his direction. 'The scents of those loners are out the front, so don't lie.' I smelt the bears and the cheetah outside the moment we got here. I should have reacted then.

'Hmmm,' the older male says, placing his tea down. 'You are good. I cleansed the area after they left. However, you don't know what you're talking about.'

'I don't?'

'No,' Banner replies for his uncle. 'Gilly, George is a loner by choice. It got too much for his tracker abilities to be around pack and decided to live off the grid, away from the protection of pack, but close enough to help if needed. My uncle is the most loyal Coltonline male you will find.'

Shaking my head, I try to process all this information. I've been raised to hate loners. To believe that they're our greatest threat. The damage done to Farrowline has been so huge since we became their target.

Rising, George draws his focus from me to his nephew. 'I will begin her training tomorrow. Bring her here early.'

'What?' My jaw hits my lap. He can't seriously think that I'm okay with this.

'Gilly, my nephew said that you saved Mason's life and fought to protect our family unit. I can train you to hide your scent and read a fight in ways that you could only imagine.'

Opening and closing my mouth, I have no idea what to say. I want to learn. I really, really, want to learn. 'Just like that? You will teach me, just because I saved Mason once?'

'It's part of the payment. The other is that you find my cousin, the Alpha of Coltonline.'

CHAPTER FORTY SEVEN

For a week and a half, life in Coltonline goes around and around in circles.

I hunt. I find nothing. I listen in on Coltonline meetings that go nowhere. I go to George's den in the afternoons and sit and listen to him try to get me to calm my mind and I hang out with the St. Cloud's and Elliot and his packmates.

Gracie and Maddy are amazing females who sit on my bed every evening when I get back from George's cabin and watch movies on my laptop. I play video games with Jesse and Mason and go out on patrols with Logan. Banner is a constant presence always at my back, keeping me safe and staying out of the way while I hunt and life feels good.

It's been an hour of sitting on the freezing path leading to George's cabin, trying to follow the older male's instructions to meditate. Sitting still for this long is not something that I can do comfortably, I'm all antsy and fidgety, and I want to burst out with laughter because George keeps making heavy, controlled breathing noises.

'Stop it.'

'I can't,' I wail, eyes flying open.

The tsk he makes has me miss Mama and my mum so much. Now those females know how to tsk.

'Why can you not be left with your own thoughts?' George asks unexpectedly. He has a damn teacup beside his crossed leg and it must be freezing cold now.

Shrugging, I hate the way the question makes me feel. It's confronting.

'Shrugging is not an answer. You need to learn to be alone, Gilly Sommers. You need to become more in tune with your own body. Your wolf and your human side must have harmony.'

'Is that why you live in isolation as a loner?' I ask, stretching my legs out.

'It's part of it.' I roll my eyes at the non-answer.

'Why haven't they asked you to track the Alpha? You're related. You could find his scent.'

Huffing a laugh, George picks up his teacup and downs the rest of the liquid. I know what's in there, that the brown liquid isn't tea. 'I'm a drunk. I'm anti-social and I left pack.'

I fiddle with the rim of my own teacup. I was given tea. 'Drinking helps, doesn't it?'

'No,' George states, his black eyes colliding with mine. 'No, it doesn't. It's a cheap wall to hide behind. I'm not strong like you, Gilly. I am half the tracker you are. I can smell your wolf and she has me intimidated. However, you are untrained and young. And you wreak of sadness. Tell me what happened.'

'You don't want to know,' I mumble. I don't even know this male. I'm not going to spill my issues to him.

'We have to start on the inside before we can project our skills on the outside.'

'Have you been crying?' Oliver's tone is harsh and full of emotions. A bit like me since I got back from spending the afternoon with George. 'No,' I lie and smile when he growls. My lip wobbles and I catch it between my teeth. I feel raw and needed Oliver. 'I wish I could jump through the phone and hug you.' I need to smell his sandalwood and citrus scent. No matter how much I enjoy the change being here in Coltonline, I miss my pack with an ache that hurts my soul.

'Gil, you have no idea how hard it's been without you around. I know the entire Pack misses you terribly. I miss you terrible.'

'You do?' I sniffle.

I watch on the screen as Oliver's brow furrows. 'Do you need me to come and get you? Just say the word and I'll be there.'

'No,' I say, meaning it. 'I have to finish this hunt.' I haven't told anyone about George the loner yet and deep down, I don't want to share that with them yet. I want to come back to Farrowline as a new female. One that can manage herself and help lead the Pack.

Chapter Forty Eight

I'm getting good at meditating. Despite how hard it was opening up to George, who is a remarkably great listener. It did feel good to get everything off my chest that has been weighing me down.

Watching individual snowflakes fall around me, I follow instructions and scent each one. Closing my eyes, I snatch them out of the air, one by one. I know I have an audience. I've had an audience every day for the past week.

'You're learning quickly.'

'I'm determined.'

'That you are,' George says, huffing as he sits down beside me on the mat on his pathway. He has tea for me and places it beside my thigh.

'Why does Banner have to hide his power and scent? Why would you teach him how to do that?' I ask, not sure where the question comes from. This damn loner makes me feel comfortable.

'He is too big for this pack. My nephew is one of the good ones and this pack...well, I'm sure you'll see.' I know he is not telling me something important.

'What does that mean?'

He just throws me a look that tells me that he isn't going to answer. 'Focus on your breathing. We are going to try and create that barrier over your scent.'

I perk up, no longer caring about the mystery that is Banner St Cloud. I know I will get to the bottom of it one day.

Groaning in frustration, I swat at whatever is touching me on the shoulder and snuggle under the covers and try to go back to sleep. The fucking shaking doesn't stop and I finally blink one eye open and hear a voice. 'Gilly. Gilly!'

'What?' I grumble, rolling over to the male I know is standing over me. Glaring up at him, I notice two things in the space of seconds. It's dark outside still, and I can smell fear and worry. Fully awake now, I sit up quickly, taking in the clothes he is wearing and the way his brow knots together. 'What happened?' I'm already jumping out of bed before he has time to step back. I reach for the jeans on the table listening to Logan as he starts to tell me. 'Fuck!' I exclaim, bouncing around, trying to pull on my socks and then shoes. 'How long ago did she turn wolf?'

'Like fifteen minutes, Banner is out there, but she took off.' The poor male indicates to the darkness and the snow falling outside the window. 'We can't find her, Gil.' His fear and anxiety is choking. I grab for the vial of the smelling oil, very aware that I haven't touched it since being here.

Pushing the reasons why I don't need it to the back of my mind, I walk towards the distressed male and wrap my arms around his middle. 'I will find her Logan. I promise.' And I do. I will find her and there's no doubt in my mind.

Rushing down the stairs, I ignore the frightened looks on the faces of the twins and Gracie.

'Banner told us to stay,' Jesse states. He is mad.

Hand coming up to grip the back of his neck, I squeeze it reassuringly. 'It's best if we only have to find one wolf tonight. I'll get her back.'

'We know you will,' Gracie responds quietly and I run a finger down her cheek so that she knows that I am here for her. She leans into my touch.

Pushing open the front door, my attention snaps to the massive wolf that comes from the trees. Banner grunts and growls, telling me that I need to hurry. Clearly he can't find her.

'You follow my lead,' I say before I do anything. The noise the wolf makes in response has me wrap my arms around my chest in annoyance. 'I'm being serious Banner! If you go out there all angry and dominant male, asserting your authority, you will do damage to the relationship you and your sister will have moving forward. She's a dominant female. This is a new ballgame for you. I have dealt with this myself and have supported more adolescents than you can imagine.'

There's a heartbeat of silence, where Banner tries to stare me down but I hold it. He can throw around his dominant weight all he likes, I'm not backing down. I have the higher ground, I know the power balance between us. I stare down at him, waiting for him to comply.

'Fine,' he grunts out eventually and while I'm shocked beyond belief, I hide it with a simple nod. Fuck but there is a part of me that wants to rub it in his face that he is conceding to me. I don't though. I'm the bigger shifter. I'll call Ridley later and gloat, but he won't know that. 'But if there is danger, I'll take back the lead. Do you understand?'

'Fine,' I mimic and then we shift.

Sprinting through the trees, my wolf throws her head back and howls in joy at being let free under the falling snow. Despite the temperature and the way the pads of my sensitive paws are frozen, I feel invigorated. With the main hunt being an absolute flop at the moment, having the scent of my prey clear in every morsel in the air and on the ground, I feel good.

My wolf feels good.

This is what I'm born to do.

Turning my head slightly as I run through the trees, I see the large, black beast keeping a small distance to my left. Banner is following and if I'm being honest, I have no idea how long he has been there. The human and wolf in my soul comes to an agreement that I will be asking him again how he so easily hides his scent.

We pass Coltonline territory with a quick jump, always making a point of staying on Banner's lands. I lead us into the unclaimed lands around the pack lands and into thicker trees. Constantly aware of what is going on around us, I growl loudly at what I catch on the wind and bark towards the male, warning him that we are close.

Breaking through the next row of trees, we're far from territory and we come up on a female rushing through the trees, her dark fur is remarkably like her brother, and it's beautiful. She's running hard on four legs, almost gliding through the forest without a sound. Her scent is intoxicating. It screams to the world her wolfs ecstasy of being free. The small female looks over at us as we comes up beside her, one on each side. She quickly looks away at the dominance she must see on our faces. I can smell the power on her. She is still young and right now is completely beast.

Banner makes a move that has me throwing him a pointed look over her head as we run. I wait until the hardness and anger in his eye softens and he dips his head while we follow easily alongside her.

We run for miles. No rest. No communication and no aggression. I don't know where we end up but when the adolescent wolf stops running, I stand beside her and watch as her ribcage heaves with each breath. Banner steps over to her when she finally seems to realise that we are still with her and her wolf makes a soft sound of sorry. The pair share a loving moment when their beasts rub against each other, showing affection and acceptance.

When they are ready, Maddy comes over to press her small side against mine and I nip her nose in play, tagging her, and run. Her yelp of excitement fills the unknown forest and with Banner standing watch, we both play in the snow and wrestle so that Maddy can get to know her beast and the magic of being what we are.

Chapter Forty Nine

Having spent the afternoon with Elliot and his friends, who I may have judged a little too harshly to begin with, I find myself in the kitchen beside Gracie who is anxiously making dinner. Not sure what is wrong with her, I try to help out as much as I can.

'You okay?'

Nodding with a quick, 'yep,' I know that it's a lie and I don't need my nose to tell me. It does. Lying smells like eggs. It's gross.

'Spill!' I demand playfully, removing the knife in her hand and taking over the chopping vegetables. Gracie heads to the sink and starts washing plates that don't need to be washed.

'Is this about last night? You know Maddy is okay, yeah? Logan and Mason are on a run with her. She will stay wolf for a few more days until she can take control and she will shift back and be the young, sweet, female we all know and adore.' Grace chuckles. Maddy is anything but sweet. I get the desired response though and my wolf feels better for it.

'It isn't about Maddy. I knew you'd find her.' I don't know how to respond so I just chop the row of vegetables.

'He is my mate.'

I gasp and swing around, dangerously holding the knife out between us. 'What?'

'I heard it on the dancefloor the other night and I have been panicking ever since.' I watch as a tear runs down her face. Dropping the knife on the bench, I hurry to take her into my arms, wet hands and all.

'That's amazing news, Gracie. Congratulations.' I pull back so I can understand her rolling emotions better. 'Why are you sad, babe?'

She shrugs and fights her wobbling lip. 'He is a human, Gilly. He has no interest in living in Pack and he doesn't seem to feel the same way I do about him. Would he even know what a mating bond is?'

'Gracie, trust me, he feels the same way about you, even though he is a human. He will understand.'

'How do you know?' She sniffles.

'Because I smelt it on him. Love. Devotion. Passion. Honey, he is so smitten with you babe.'

'Really?' she cries softly and I pull her back against my chest.

Rubbing her back I tell her that a human mate is no different to a shifter one. 'Look at Farrowline. Our Luna is a human and we are all better for it. She helps us all to stay connected with our humanity.'

'What do I say to him? What do I say to Banner? I doubt he will like a human man coming to live with us.' Poor Gracie, she is so confused.

'Babe, your brother is a complete ass but he loves you with all of his heart,' I say, fighting back my own tears. 'Just tell him. You may be surprised.'

'Yeah?' she whispers into my shoulder. It's all wet from her pain, however I don't care. Gracie is mine just like Maddy and Mason and Jesse and Logan. Even Banner. They are all mine now.

It's late when I push the front door open and spy the male sitting on the top step staring into the darkness of his territory. His broad frame doesn't leave much room for me but I still head out and sit down beside him. Passing him one of the beers in my hand, I wait for Banner to take it before I start drinking mine.

We sit in silence, enjoying the beauty of the land before he sighs dramatically and tells me that Gracie spoke to him.

'And?'

'And what? I have no idea how this is going to work. Coltonline is on a knife's edge at the moment. Bringing in a human to Pack is not an easy decision.'

I contemplate what he's saying and feel I might be misinterpreting his tone. 'I think that if the *Alpha of Farrowline* can choose a human mate and we can accept her as our *Luna*, than Coltonline can let Gracie and her human live here.'

Banner growls and I realise I did misinterpret his meaning. 'I mean that I'm worried if we don't find the Alpha, things will change around here, Gilly. It'll change in a way I fear will leave my family vulnerable.'

Frowning deeply, I hesitate before responding. He called me Gilly and not runt. It's freaking me out. 'You think that you're in danger because of your alpha energy? You think something really bad happened to your Alpha, don't you?'

Banner places his beer down and looks briefly towards me and I almost collapse at the emotion written on his features. It makes me instantly panic. 'I think we need to find the Alpha of Coltonline and I think we're running out of time.'

Chapter Fifty

'Move your legs. Use your nose!'

'I'm trying!' I shout back to the ass watching from his cosey position on the porch, sipping alcohol from his teacup. Sweat is leaking off me and I glare at the male grinning widely at me. The attractive shifter is loving this activity and I would be too if I wasn't so damn sick of being yelled at and thrown on my arse.

'Again!' George demands and Banner and I go back to our sparring session and I once again, end up on my arse in the snow which has been slowly melting for days now. I'm actually not feeling as frozen lately and I love it. 'Gilly, every scent can be used in this fight.'

'How can I win when he is a brooding, Alpha energy, jackass, who is five times my size.'

Banner's eyebrow rises in question, 'jackass?' he mocks.

'Yes.' I take the hand he offers and clap the white powder from my butt.

'Again!' George says and I throw myself back into the fight, thinking through each move he makes and adjusting my behaviour with each call George shouts about using my nose and my other senses. 'It's not about physical force. That is cheap fighting!' he yells just as I jump back to miss the way Banner swipes his big hand at my head. That would've fucking hurt. 'Any shifter will underestimate you, Gilly, but they would be wrong.'

Falling into the space in my mind where my wolf and human live together, I become hyper focused on the way Banner moves. I can smell his moves but can't seem to win over his sheer size and force.

'Focus more, Gilly! Feel the scent! Allow your wolf to accept it.'

Nothing George is saying makes sense but I stick with it. I dodge and barely keep out of Banner's reach and the male is holding back, I know he is. It's frustrating and annoying that George is right. A dominant sees me and thinks I'm powerless, that I am no match. The Farrowline dominants do it to me all the time. They question what I say. They don't follow my orders and it pisses me off.

My rage simmers and boils over.

I'm moving without much thought and swing out my leg and connect with Banner's midsection. The male huffs and steps back in surprise.

'Yes! Use it Gilly! See the scent! See the colours of the world!'

That makes no fucking sense and I swing and dodge and swing some more. The battle between us is growing more and more heated. I hate the corner I'm put in. I hate the image of Gilly Sommers that I left behind in Farrowline. I don't want to go back and be her again. I am a Circle wolf! I am...

The world slows like it did with the loner attack and before my eyes, colours seems to change. They brighten and dim and enhance. I see, taste, feel the scents in the air. Stopping, I'm fully aware of Banner pulling back a hit he was about to throw and only because I can see him in perfect colour. I see his emotions and his Alpha power. He's a rainbow and I stand with tears dripping down my face, overwhelmed by the scents in the air. I fall to my knees. Banner is beside me and I can hear George telling him to let me go.

'She has to feel this Banner. She is seeing in true colour for the first time.'

Everything is so beautiful and terrifying and I know deep in my heart that I will never be the same after this.

Not ever.

For the next two weeks, I learn to become a tracker. I find out skills of myself that I never knew I had and I embrace the part of my wolf that I've misunderstood my entire life. Banner and George help me as I play the older male's stupid tracking games and I find myself more attuned with the world. I can pinpoint the time of day to the minute. I can sniff out anomalies in the air and see the world in colour. Strands of light illuminate the world, providing me with information that means I could close my eyes and track anything. Which is George's favourite game to play. I'm blindfolded and left in unknown areas around the cabin and I have to evade Banner and George as they stalk me. We even played with Logan last night and it was the best fun I've had in such a long time.

Every morning when I dress in front of the mirror, I see a change in my features. I'm fitter, leaner and have built muscle on my arms, legs and stomach. My skin glows with a healthy light that I put down to not consuming alcohol in weeks and feel more connected with my wolf than I ever have.

It's different and I can't help but think how everyone back in Pack will react to this new version of Gilly. The Tracker.

Chapter Fifty One

'You're quiet tonight.'

Nodding, I throw Elliot an apologetic look and go back to trying to focus on the movie we are watching in his loungeroom. It's some action film that doesn't make any sense and the main character has his shirt off for some reason. Elliot has no idea the work I'm doing with George. Only the St Cloud siblings know. He is a loner after all. 'Sorry.'

'You don't have to be sorry. Are you okay? Did something happen on the hunt today?'

'No,' I respond. He always brings up the hunt no matter how many times I ask him not to. I don't need to keep getting reminded about my failure.

'Talk to me,' Elliot commands softly. He leans over and runs his hand down my face to catch my chin. Making sure that I'm looking up at him, Elliot smiles warmly. 'Tell me what is going on. You're worrying me.'

'I'm just tired and maybe a little homesick.' I'm not lying. I missed a call from Delfina and Ridley today and I haven't been able to get them both on the phone. I tried Oliver and even he didn't answer. Now my phone is dead and I won't get to speak to anyone tonight.

Elliot's face softens. 'Gilly…' he starts and leaning forward places his lips on mine. I return it. Loving the connection until it becomes a little too much. Before I know what has happened, Elliot leans me back until I'm laying down under him. His hard body pressed against mine, his hands roaming under my shirt, setting me alight. I nip at his bottom lip and moan when he returns the action. His mouth lingers at my neck, his hip grinding into mine before I regain my senses.

'Elliot,' I mumble, trying to push him off but not really using much force. His body feels so good against mine. I've been craving this kind of attention for such a long time but now that I have it, I want to put a stop to it. I can't help but hear Banner's damn words in my head though about getting confused again.

'Elliot,' I say a little louder when that warm, masculine hand creeps down to the waistband of my trackpants. 'We need to stop.'

'Why?' he asks my neck, trailing kisses up to the underside of my ear. It causes a shiver to race down my spine.

'Because we are not mates,' I blurt out like an embarrassing fool. The male pulls back and stares down at me and I wish the lounge would open up and swallow me whole.

'Do we have to be mates to have sex?' I see the confusion on his face.

I force myself to stick to my convictions, I nod painfully. I will not make the same mistakes I did with Jay. Elliot is kind, he is attentive and he is hot with a capital H. However, I have fallen for all that in the past and confused friendship and affection with immature beliefs of mating and true love.

'It's my new rule in life. I'm not going to do this with anyone but my mate. I can't,' I state with as much confidence as I can muster. Damn life rules. Damn Jay!

Elliot pulls away, I see the colours of his emotions as they play on my tongue. Hurt. Confusion. Disappointment. 'We could be mates.' My heart flutters and I almost tell him to forget what I've just said and take me here on the lounge. 'I like you Gilly. I like you a lot.'

'I like you too.' I really, really do, and if it wasn't for Jay, I'd be welcoming his touch right now. 'I'm sorry,' I begin and bite my lip when he tells me not to be silly. I sit up and fix my clothes just as he rewinds the movie so that we can watch the parts we just missed.

'We can take this slow, if that's what you need.'

'I do.' *Could he be any hotter?*

Turning serious all of a sudden, Elliot throws me a look I can't decipher. 'Gilly, do you think that you will call off the hunt soon?'

Sitting up, I have to process before I can find the words. 'What? I don't understand?'

'It's just...you know I think it's really important that we find the Alpha and Sasha but I agree with the packmates who think it's time to move on, you know?'

I don't react. I just listen.

'Coltonline is so broken and we need a strong leader and I just think that maybe Banner and the Beta need to look to the future. Do you agree?' He raises an eyebrow in my direction, waiting for me to agree with him.

'Who'd be the Alpha though? There's no one that I have scented that kind of power on,' I lie. Banner could be the next Alpha of Coltonline.

Elliot doesn't seem to like that response and rises off the lounge quickly. He moves over to the small kitchenette. 'I believe an Alpha is more than just a strong beast.' Damn, I hit a sore spot. I watch over the back of the lounge as he picks things up and moves them around the countertop. 'I'm not saying I could do it, but if that's what the other dominants want, then I will. You know?' His eyes are all wide and furious as they look over to me and I nod without uttering a word.

'And I could fix things around here,' he states, throwing some clean mugs into the sink.

'What needs to be fixed?' I ask softly.

'Territory distribution for one thing. This older generation needs to share with the younger ones. We are all valuable as dominants. Don't you think?' He doesn't wait for me to answer. I have heard other Coltonline shifters speak like this on a number of occasion but hearing it from Elliot feels different. He grips the counter and I watch as his shoulders heave and then slump. Looking over at me, he gifts me one of his flirtatious grins. 'Sorry, love. I got all heated and passionate. I just...' I track him as he walks back over to the lounge. He sits down heavily and throws his arms over my shoulders. 'I just wish I knew what happened to my Alpha. I'm worried.'

I taste eggs. Schooling my face to be neutral, I nod and swallow down the unsettling feeling that forms in my chest.

Chapter Fifty Two

With the snow melting away and new sprigs of green covering the forest floor, I let Elliot take my hand as we stroll through the territory. More animals run through the trees and new sounds and scents are available to explore. I have been given the morning off by Banner who had to help the Beta with some pack business and I am not complaining. He did tell me he'd catch up with me soon though, so I'll enjoy this while I can.

Elliot leads the way and I have scoured every inch of this place so I know exactly where he's taking me. To the freakin' creek! The fucking clearing that always gives me headaches. I know that it is a section on the Alpha's land where the younger packmates hang out sometimes.

I haven't been back here since my last tantrum over my nose taking me there for no reason.

Stepping into the clearing, I stop and take in the beauty of it. The ground is no longer thick snow but gorgeous white, snow drop flowers, they are scattered all over the thinning white powder. I love the fact that the creek is running loudly. There are still frozen sections and melted sections and I find myself falling more and more in love with this place.

Elliot throws a smile over his shoulder and I know Laurence and Joshua are at the meet up area. A few others are there too. He drops my hand, starts explaining how we're going to cook up the first barbecue of the new season and heads in the direction of the other males, who I can't see yet as they are behind the trees and I take in a deep breath.

I choke.

Throat closing up, I grip my throat, unable to draw enough air into my lungs.

Everything bombards my senses at once and I stand in my own personal hell and then I feel it. The moment my world comes crushing down around me. It falls, catches alight. Before my eyes, the world explodes in colour, painting a picture of a scene so horrifying that I almost fall to my knees. The pain and suffering that occurred here has left a scent signature. Staining this beautiful landscape. Tears stream down my face as I witness, second hand, the betrayal. The murder of an Alpha who I have learnt was a good male and his daughter.

Pain races up my spine.

Elliot continues to go on and on, his smile electric and bright as he throws it over his shoulder at me again but I can't hear a single word.

The realisation of my stupidity hits me hard. My feet refuse to move as I stand gripping my stomach. I rush to the nearest bush and throw up everything.Sweat beads and pours down my forehead as I heave. How could I be so dumb. They smell like snow-drop flowers. The odd sweetness of their scent and under it...oh my fucking heavens, I smell in colour and its making me vomit again.

Involuntarily jumping when a familiar hands falls between my shoulders, the fear that grips my heart it debilitating. I jump off my knees and rush to put some space between us. My back is to the creek and I blink up over at the male watching me intently, there is a line of males behind him now. Elliot's friends. So many males from this pack. All of them with the scent that marks them as traitors.

Elliot's head bends to the side and his features twist into a wicked grin that has my heart pound in my chest. It's fucking freaky. 'Oh no, Gilly love. You worked it out, didn't you?' his voice, his demeanour, all of it is different to me now. Like a villain in a movie, he seems demented.

'You...why?' I ask, hating the catch in my voice. There's way too much information to process at once. I have whiplash. I'm staring at a male that I was making-out with last night, wishing that I would hear a mating bond with. A male who has committed one of the most disgraceful acts a wolf shifter can do within pack. Killing an alpha goes against everything we stand for.

With my focus locked on Elliot's I forget to use my senses and only catch the movement of the males behind him because of the colours that play and dance toward my nose.

I flick my gaze, left and right, to see two males on either side of the clearing. Baring my teeth in warning, I realise quickly that I am surrounded. With Elliot blocking my front, four males on my sides and the flowing creek to my back, I can't help but find the poetry of this moment. This is where the Alpha of Coltonline and his daughter took their stand amongst these males. The magnitude of this mutiny is devastating. Each one of them never kept it a secret in any Coltonline meeting that they want to move on, and now I know why.

And then there is Elliot. Sweet, funny, adorable Elliot.

It's genius really. No one would ever suspect that he's involved in this. Him and his gang of monsters are dangerous because they aren't noticeable. I see their entire plan now. All the comments. The anger towards the way this pack is run. The sweet scent that follows so many of these wolf shifters, their faces flash in my mind. At the meeting, Elliot's name was mentioned as the next Alpha of Coltonline.

I'm angry. Furious actually. 'You killed them so that you could be the next Alpha of Coltonline!' I throw the accusation at him, keeping my wolf close to the surface so that she can monitor the males surrounding me.

Nodding, Elliot's smug expression is enough to make me growl.

'You're a fucking idiot! Delusional! It doesn't work like that!' I shout. 'How do you expect to be an Alpha with a wolf that has mid-level dominant energy,' I spit the insult, hoping it hits hard and watch as that wicked smile morphs slowly to rage.

I take an involuntary step back as a communal growl of aggression filters through the males surrounding me.

Chapter Fifty Three

I never thought that this would be my ending. That I'd die in a territory that wasn't Farrowline.

In this moment, standing before a group of dominant males who shift into their oversized beasts, one by one, I find myself wishing I was home. Wishing that I could ring Ridley again and speak to my mum. To hear Kurt and Gene argue over what we're going to eat for lunch and wishing...my heart flutters in my chest at the face that flashes in my mind's eye. A face that has me curse my own stupidity. It's a moment of clarity that floors me and gives me new purpose despite how confronting the spark of realisation is. It's impossible and yet, it all makes sense.

'You ready to meet your maker, Gilly Sommer, Tracker of Farrowline?' Elliot asks and I throw my head back and laugh.

'How fucking dramatic!' I cackle. 'Just fight me already, you pin-dicked arsehole.'

He roars in my direction and runs at me but I've already moved, having seen his intention in the way George and Banner taught me. I dance, never letting Elliot near me so that when he stops and we are back in the same positions we started, my back to the creek and his to the males watching us from the trees, I smirk.

Elliot grins back. It's a little distorted and feral. 'You're good, I'll give you that.'

'Honey, I'm more than good,' I reply and we go again. The male getting more and more frustrated as the minutes tick by and he's unable to touch me. The world is full of colour and I never let the creek leave my back. I stay human because Elliot does and because I know what's coming from the trees. So I keep it up. I evade every move he makes, keeping my distance and keeping his focus on me and not the male who appears to my left and barks a sound that has Elliot spring away from me until we are both in our original positions again.

Breathing heavily and thankful for every training session I had with Banner and George, I take a moment to gather myself for the real fight that's about to happen. The massive black wolf shifts to two legs and I have never been so happy seeing that grumpy bastard as much as I am right now.

Banner's gaze passes over the scene, the wolves that were standing to my left are now stomach flat to the ground in submission. New tears spring to my face because the barrier that Banner keeps over his power and emotions is gone and fuck...his Alpha energy is next level amazing— like Alpha Tobias Farrow amazing.

Banner slowly steps into the clearing, not rushing and holding the complete attention of everyone in this area. Logan comes up to my right as does the Beta of Coltonline, Greta and a handful of other dominants. Each one shifts and stands like soldiers around the space, their focus locked on the male who has now declared himself as the next Alpha of Coltonline. The confusion and shock is communal.

I don't know if it's obvious what's going on between myself and Elliot. I think Elliot works that out too because he jumps on that advantage to start spurting lies.

'Banner, I'm so glad you're here. This female went crazy and attacked me. I have witnesses.' Elliot's arm goes out to indicate his friends who are all no longer in wolf form, who are all staring wide-eyed at the mighty male still walking closer. Two fall to their knees, the other's don't move and with a smug satisfaction I think I'll remember forever, I grin in victory at the traitor who slowly works out that he has no allies. Elliot goes silent, glaring at his packmates.

'Tell me,' Banner states, in what can only be described as an 'alpha arsehole voice', it makes me so unbelievably happy.

Elliot, the fuckwit that he is, starts ranting and raving again about how I am the instigator and how they should never have allowed a member of an outside pack to be on their territory.

He shuts his mouth quickly when Banner growls, 'enough.' Those dark eyes are all wolf as they look to his cousin. 'I was asking the Tacker of Farrowline.'

Elliot cowers back a step and I want to whoop and dance around in joy. 'It happened here,' I declare, pointing at the space between Elliot and me. The adrenaline from the dance-fight is wearing off and I feel the pain of the memory scents all over again. 'They attacked them. From what I can gather, Sasha went first and the Alpha couldn't defend himself against multiple wolves. It wasn't quick and the blood that marks these flowers will stain this soil for generations.' I feel the tears stream down my cheek and cover a sob when Banner stands next to me.

Hand rising slowly, he catches my tears. One after the other. We stare, eyes locked, his pain and grief on display like his alpha energy. It mimics my own because while I didn't know his uncle or cousin, I can feel the heartache of this betrayal. I can see from the scent that the Alpha of Coltonline fought hard to protect his pup and it breaks me to think that his body, that her beautiful body, were thrown into the creek to be lost forever. The water here runs fast and furious. Their bodies could be anywhere.

'I'm so sorry, Alpha Banner,' I whisper and lean into the hand that cups my cheek. I use his title loudly and proudly. 'He fought to the end. A male whose name should never be forgotten here in your pack.' I've lost an Alpha. Farrowline lost Alpha Caleb Farrow a number of years ago and the pain is still there. It will hurt forever.

I can hear a few murmurs from the new group and watch as the most senior members of the pack storm over to take their position over the one who committed this crime.

Banner's gaze is soft and holds too much emotion. 'Tell me the names of the shifters who did this.' It isn't a demand, more of a plea for answers.

'How would she know! She has no proof!' Elliot shouts, he starts on a rant about loyalty and trustworthiness.

I take a breath, knowing the weight of my words right now. Knowing what it will mean for the shifters whose name I will condemn to the same fate as the male and female they so brutally murdered. I only get a hold of myself because of the way Banner nods reassuringly at me.

'Elliot Colton,' I say, my voice ringing out throughout the forest. I speak the truth and they all know it. I spend the next few seconds damning seven shifters. Including Laurence, Joshua and Hugo, who never hid their hatred of me being here. I guess I know why now, they were so afraid that I'd find out their secret.

There is a hush over the area when I finish. The energy coming from the Beta and the others is violent and I know the leash over their wolves is thin.

'Go back to the den, Gilly,' Banner says kindly, he leans in and kisses my forehead and I want to throw my arms around his waist and make sure that he is okay. He didn't want this, he didn't want to be Alpha, and I have had a hand in deciding his fate too today. I hate it.

'I can—'

'No.' Banner shakes his head. 'This is a Coltonline matter.'

It's not offensive but it does hurt a little and I nod and do what he instructs. He *is* after all, an Alpha.

Chapter Fifty Four

Jumping from the top of the stairs, I practically run to Banner the moment I can see him. The male looks tired, like he has aged ten years in one afternoon.

I stop just short of his body, taking him in with a deep concern. 'Are you okay?' I ask stupidly, knowing that he is anything but.

He gifts me a soft, rare smile. 'It's done.'

I'm not expecting the emotions when they come and I'm powerless to the tears. I've only been here for a short time and feel stupid having these feelings. Banner should be crying. Logan should be the one breaking down but all he does is walks past where we stand, rests his hand on my shoulder in a friendly gesture before he heads into the den. Not me. I don't have the right to feel this much.

Banner doesn't hesitate but wraps me in his arms and holds me against his warmth and power. I weep for the loss of an Alpha, for the scent memories that will forever haunt my dreams. For the loss of a male I cared about. For an Alpha that I loved and lost in such a traumatic way. I cry for Banner and how much his life is going to change and I cry because it means that my hunt is over and I will be leaving soon.

'I'm so sorry,' I weep into his chest, not sure for what exactly. For all of it, I guess.

Banner's hold never wavers. 'Thank you, Gilly.' It is all he needs to say. He allows my tears to end before he pulls back and wipes at my face. Without the curtain over his emotions and scent, I pick up the strains of eucalyptus and ice. It smells like safety. Like a net that will always be under me to catch me if I fall.

Lost in those black eyes, I blink up at him and hope he can scent my affection too. 'Stay in Coltonline. You will always have a place in my pack, Gilly Sommers. We would be honoured to have a tracker like you.'

Smiling, images flash in my mind, until they stop on the one that came to me in that clearing. The one that confused and shocked me in a moment when I thought I was going to die. 'I have to go home, Banner.' I rise up on the tips of my toes and plant a kiss on his cheek. Lost in his dark gaze, I speak my truth. 'My heart belongs in Farrowline.'

Banner nods in understanding. While I find myself able to openly say that I love Banner St Cloud, that he is one of mine, and my wolf and I will always be there for him, like I know he will be for me, I have to go home.

I belong in Farrowline.

Pack is Pack.

'Besides, you already have a tracker,' I tease and lean into his side when he pulls me against him and we start walking back to the den.

I feel the emotions leaking off him at the sight of the St Cloud siblings lined up on the porch and am unable to back away and give them space when Maddy, Gracie, Logan and the twins rush down the stairs to their big brother. Banner keeps me locked against him and I find myself in the middle of the embrace and know that I will leave a piece of myself here with Coltonline.

The next three days are a whirlwind of activity. There is a ceremony at the creek for the Alpha, his daughter and for the adolescents who were killed because of greed. Banner and the others found out what happened to the young female that was still missing. The group of young adolescents that were killed came across the traitors planning the attack a few months back and were murdered. The female's body was the only one they disposed of into the creek. The other two bodies were found before they could cover up the evidence. It's disgusting.

It broke my heart watching the members of Coltonline grieve not only their loss but come to terms with the horror of what happened. It will deeply affect this pack for a long time but with Banner now officially the Alpha, I know that they will rebuild and heal together.

With a change in Alpha status, the Beta has committed to stay in his position until a new Beta is chosen. Banner asked if I scented anyone that would have the energy of a Beta and I could only tell him that with guidance and help Maddy could potentially be one. It shocked him and his parents but it's the truth.

George decided to come back to Pack and only because Logan, Gracie and I ganged up on him. The poor male didn't stand a chance.

'Do you have to go?'

'Yes, Maddy, I have to go. But you can come to Farrowline whenever you want. Banner already said that if you keep up your grades you could spend the summer with me,' I reassure her for the tenth time today. I leave in the morning and while I told Banner over and over that I was fine to head back to Farrowline on my own, he and Logan will be travelling with me. In a car this time, thank the heavens.

'Look,' I point to the pile of clothes and shoes on the bed. 'You and Gracie can share these. I don't need all this snow gear anymore.'

Maddy perks up and dives into the mess of clothing. She squeals when she sees the boots.

I turn when a small voice at my bedroom door says, 'We will keep them in the cupboard for when you come and visit.'

'Deal,' I promise. Gracie is sad and it break my heart but she has so much good in the future for her. Once Coltonline calms, Banner promised to have Evan over for his first meal with the family and have the mating discussion with him.

'I will miss you.'

'Oh sweetheart, I will miss you too.' Throwing my arms around her, I hold her close and make room when Maddy jumps off the bed and joins. She throws herself into the hug, and before I know it, Jesse and Mason and there, adding more bodies. Logan heads in next and hugs me from behind.

'What is going on here?' Banner grumbles, his annoyance makes us all laugh.

Under all the bodies, I tell him to shut up and get in.

He does.

Chapter Fifty Five

I've never been so grateful for a car in all my life and while there is a note of sadness and loss as we make our way to Farrowline. We make it back in half the time it would take us on four legs. I couldn't believe that the only reason why they didn't come to Farrowline in the first place in a car was because it was broken down and needed repairs.

The two days I spend with the St Cloud brothers are some of the best I've had and sitting in the passenger seat, teasing Banner, I practically plant my face on the windscreen when we get close to my pack lands.

I can feel the pull of territory in my bones. A beacon calling me home. And I wind down my window and draw in the colours of the forest. We are close and coming up through the small road within the thick trees.

Darkness fell about an hour ago and I have my head out the window like Atticus, Adalee's pet dog, who likes to do that when he's in the car.

Everything is so familiar and yet new and exciting. I decided not to ring anyone and tell them I was coming back. I want to surprise my mum. I'm also deeply confused by the feelings I felt back in the battle with Elliot. I have no idea what it meant seeing that male's face when I thought I was in danger of losing my life but I definitely need time to think.

'Your scent has changed, Gilly. Can't wait to leave us hey?' Banner is teasing me and I hold out my hand, refusing to pull my head back in the car and smile when he grips my fingers. I owe Banner St Cloud so much more than he can ever imagine.

About to reply with some fantastic smartass comment, I turn my head just as I catch a strand of colourful scent in the air. Banner and Logan growl deeply when my eyes widen and I flick my head back to the window. I let the leash go on my wolf, allowing her to help as I pull in the information now bombarding my senses.

'What is it?' Banner demands, all alpha voice on full display.

'Loners,' I snarl. 'They're attacking Farrowline.'

The car screeches to a stop and all three of us are out of the car in a heartbeat. Logan waits beside me as Banner comes around the front of the vehicle. I swear the male has grown two more feet just from acknowledging that he is an alpha.

'Tell me,' he states.

'I can pick up on multiple battles.' I point to the different directions. 'We need to head, that way...' I know where I need to go. It's where I can scent the most blood. Pack blood. It makes the hairs on my body stand on end and my voice sounds more animal than human.

Banner begins to tell us what we need to do and informs Logan that they have to let me take the lead. I understand why. This is my territory.

Unable to hold her back anymore, I drop the final barrier between my wolf and I throw my head back and howl into the darkness.

I fly through the night, my feet barely hitting the ground as I make my way to the border of Farrowline. The two forces of pure nature run beside me, keeping me slightly in the lead but between them non the less. Here I might hold more power but Banner and Logan will always protect me.

I'm focused on getting to my pack. I know Gregor and Molly and Jay are at this battle. I know that Jax is a good distance away with Easton fighting their own loners and I can feel the Alpha far from here, protecting an entire section on his own. All I can think is that my packmates need me so that when I get the scent of two loners coming from the left, I bark a warning to the males, flop to my stomach, ignore the sticks that cut my underbelly, roll and lash out at the cheetah who flew at me, trying to get the better of me. My claws rip up his stomach, sending blood to rain down over me. Logan dives in and collides with the loner, sending it away from me. He falls in an unmoving heap.

I don't have to look to know that the second attacker was easily taken care of by the alpha beside me.

We spring back into action. Not allowing this to slow us down.

We come upon the fight my fellow Farrowline shifters are in from behind. Banner indicates for us to slow down and we assess the situation. Molly, Gregor and Jay are on territory line. A long row of loners are just ahead of us, with two or three shifters testing the three clearly injured wolves before they spring back and form a new line. They are trying to wear the dominant Farrowline members down which seems fruitless. Molly and Gregor are two of our most senior packmates. Jay on the other hand is bleeding from a deep wound and I know that he's losing too much blood.

Turning my head slightly, my gaze collides with Banner's and as if knowing what I want him to do, he nods that massive head and Logan and he disappear into the night.

This is my fight. This is my Pack.

Chapter Fifty Six

My wolf howls into the night, declaring her arrival and I run and jump and take out a small panther just as she thought that she could leave her line of arsehole loners to attack Jay again. I saw every move that she intended to do before she did it and I land easily within Farrowline territory, mouth and fur dripping with thick, metallic liquid of my kills.

Gregor and Molly don't react at first, they seem stunned at my appearance. I'm fully facing them, my back to the line of loners, but I don't need to look to know what each and every one of the intruders are doing. I can smell every breath they take. I can see with the colours of the forest the movement of their feet. The emotions they are feeling and their intention to do us harm.

Jay falls to his belly as if he can finally give in to the pain now that I am here. His weary eyes are full of confusion and shock to see me in what I can imagine is a very different light. Making sure to run my gaze over the two dominants who stand together, assessing my presence, I have to push back my wolf's anger that they are two shifters who challenged me at every possible step before I left for Coltonline. I'm not that female anymore though.

I have stared evil in the eye and I laughed in its face.

Turning slowly, I make sure to not drop the eye contact of Molly and Gregor until I'm fully facing the line of loners.

Blood drips from my lips, and I snarl, baring my teeth. Each one has only eyes for me. Two step back, recognising my dominance and power and if I was human, I'd grin. Instead, my wolf snarls viciously and swings her head around and barks a warning to the male who tries to step ahead of me. Gregor stares for too long and I growl for him to get back in line. I smell the shock and uncertainty before he does what I have instructed.

I'm not doing this anymore and my wolf and I are in full agreeance. I am a Circle wolf of Farrowline. He will listen to me.

My wolf is loving this new power, maybe a little too much. Yes, Molly and Gregor are stronger in terms of strength and sheer force of their beast but I am a tracker. My skills go beyond that and with the colours of Farrowline swirling around me, welcoming me home, I ready myself for the dance.

I move before they do. I stand in the right position to dodge claws and I fight with a grace I never had before going to Coltonline. Loners are taken care of quickly and I only let the other ones past when I feel Gregor and Molly are ready for them. It helps that Banner and Logan sprang from behind the line of loners and have taken out half the line. They never step onto territory line.

I'm a blur of movement. I could close my eyes and do this all day which is what I do so that when I rip the last throat out. I heave and slowly open them when a male appears in the trees.

Crystal blue eyes study me from a distance and I spit the chunk of flesh out of my mouth and hold his gaze. The air sizzles between us and I don't know what to feel.

I shift when I feel him go to do the same thing and I return Oliver's smile. It's hesitant but it is like Oliver is seeing me for the first time and I feel all self-conscious under his piercing gaze. I already know what he's looking at over my shoulder. Banner and Logan are behind me. Logan is helping Molly and Gregor with Jay. He's hurt but I know he'll live to see his pup be born and I find myself happy for the male I used to call my best friend.

Oliver focuses back on me and says, 'you're back.'

'Yep,' I reply, arms stretched as if to prove that I'm here.

'You're different,' Oliver states, his features haven't changed. He is studying me and I can only imagine what he sees. I know physically I've changed. I wonder if he can see the deeper stuff though. The changes in my soul.

'Am I?' I question, head titling to understand his tone.

'You...' he stops and frowns as if shocked by something. Looking at his feet, he draws those blue eyes back up to meet mine and makes a deep noise as if not sure what else to say. 'You look good, Gil.'

I don't know how to respond. We just stand like that for a few heartbeats.

I stare at the male doing the same thing back at me, his eyes widening a little as the air around us dances in colours that he can't see. He is trying to block off his emotions. There is nowhere to hide from someone like me though. Not this new version any way.

'Gilly, I—'

'I know,' I interrupt. 'I just—'

'I know,' he stops me from saying anything more and I hate how confused I am right now.

'Gilly!'

Oliver breaks the eye contact reluctantly at the sound of Tobias's voice. I don't think about what I'm doing, I just run into my Alpha's waiting arms.

Cedar. Wind. Earth.

Tobias's emotions bombard my senses. I see the colours that inform me of the pain an alpha feels when one of their own isn't around for them to protect. The intensity of the relief he feels is hard to breathe through.

Chapter Fifty Seven

There are so many people waiting for me at Mama's den despite the late hour and I hug them all. Ridley is a foul-mouthed mess who demands to know why I didn't ring ahead to tell her I was coming and that I look fucking hot. She demands to know what I've been doing because my arse is like a firm melon and she wants one. My mum hasn't let go of my hand and keeps throwing me odd looks that she isn't subtle about. Mama bear-hugs me and I love every minute of it.

Delfina pulls me into her lean body and then whispers in my ear that she likes the new scent on my skin, which is hilarious and confronting at the same time. 'You smell like power,' she murmurs. I'm a tracker but I can't smell myself and out of everyone, she is the wolf shifter who could pick up on the fact that I am a very different female to the one that left here. 'I can't wait to go on a hunt with you,' she continues wickedly in my ear and is pulled away by Dominic who informs us that we are *not* going hunting together.

'Farrowline doesn't have the energy right now to clean up the mess you two could make on a hunt,' the big, sexy Beta tells us. I laugh in agreement when Liam seconds that and kisses my cheek in greeting. Sara is all sweet and beautiful as she tells me how much I was missed.

Gene and Kurt know that something is off about me and only embrace me for a few seconds before letting me go. Adalee and Easton are so attached to each other that they hug me at the same time.

Nicolette is the last to welcome me back to pack and she does so with a small nod of her head and a quick knowing smile before she goes back to typing on her device.

Banner and Logan are standing with the alpha just outside the den and when I can finally detach myself from the rest of the pack, I head straight for them, my eyes searching for Oliver and finding him missing. Something happened in the forest. Something that we need to discuss.

'We need to talk,' Tobias says, resting a hand on my lower back and indicating for the Coltonline males to follow.

The Alpha leads us away from the rest of the Pack and we discuss everything that happened to the old Alpha of Coltonline and how I uncovered the plot to change the way the pack worked. Hearing of the death of the Alpha of Coltonline had all the males of Farrowline extremely upset. Tobias had to take a moment and I'm sure it's because the memories of his father were stirred hearing our story. It was really hard. I left out the details of George and my training and the way I was falling for Elliot, the evil son of a bitch. They know the basics of the hunt and the outcome. By the end of it, I was tired and sad.

Sitting around Mama's backyard, I laugh at the way Jax explains over breakfast all the issues they've had since I left. I spent last night in my bed at my parents den and while I wanted to feel the emotions of being back in my old room under their roof, I felt odd. Like I didn't fit there anymore.

Jax starts telling me all the times that they needed to track loners or that he lost his favourite watch in the forest somewhere and no one can find it. He is adamant that he was going to come and get me from down south so that I could come and help him look.

'No one seemed to care that I lost the watch,' he states, all offended and serious.

'Fucking hell, this damn watch! I will buy you a new one!' Dominic grumbles and pulls out his wallet dramatically.

'Well, if you didn't insist that we do that damn training exercise in our human form, I wouldn't have lost it.'

'No one told you to wear the watch.' Dom throws a stack of bills across the table at him.

The argument goes on and on, until I say, between mouthfuls of Adalee's delicious pancakes, 'I will find your watch Jax.'

That has him smile broadly at me. 'Have I told you how happy I am that you are back?'

I just roll my eyes and let the next conversation start.

Everyone is happy, well mostly everyone. The feeling is infectious and I try desperately to stop staring at the crystal eyed male down the table who doesn't participate.

Oliver is quiet. His gaze keeps flicking to mine and if I didn't know any better, which I do, because I'm a fucking tracker, I'd say that he's growing more and more agitated. He monitors the way Banner filled mine and Logan's plates or how he continues to refill our drinks. When I couldn't get the cap off the syrup bottle and I handed it to Banner, I swear I tasted rage from Oliver. It was slowly pulled back though and contained by the powerful Farrowline male.

To be honest, all the Farrowline males have been watching the way I am with the new wolf shifters. They don't miss how close they stay to my side or how anxious I'm becoming knowing that they will be leaving after breakfast.

Alpha Tobias welcomed the Coltonline males with open arms and he and Banner spent last night and this morning chatting away about alpha business.

'Let me know how it goes with Gracie and Evan. I want all the details of the dinner. She told me that she'd ring after she had her next date with him and she explained the mating bond,' I tell Logan's shoulder as I hug him close.

'I'll have her video chat you the moment it finishes,' he promises. Sighing into my hair, the male I feel a deep connection with, holds me close, uncaring of the others watching us. 'Don't forget who you are, Gilly Sommers. You're incredible and I'll speak to you soon.'

'I'll speak to you soon,' I state, knowing that Logan and I will always keep in contact.

Pulling back, when all I want to do is hold him forever, I take his cheek kiss it and watch him head to the car.

Banner claps hands with Tobias before saying goodbye to our Beta in respect. He doesn't look at me until he is basically standing before me. 'I can never repay you for what you did for my pack.'

'You helped me too, Banner. There is nothing to repay.'

He makes a deep sound like he doesn't agree. 'You need to continue your training. George gave you a list of instructions on what you need to work on.'

Rolling my eyes, I nod. George hand-wrote me a note and gave it to me before I left Coltonline. In it was a list of my downfalls and what I must do to better my tracker abilities. It was super rude and a little insulting but that is George so I just thanked the male and gave him a kiss which he complained about because I smelt like sadness. Sadness tastes like salt. I agreed, it isn't nice.

'Get one of these males to help you, I think you know which one you should pick,' Banner finishes before throwing his arms around me. I know who he is taking about.

'I promise.'

He hugs me close and I kiss his cheek. 'I'll miss you, Banner St Cloud. Alpha of Coltonline.'

'And I will miss you, Tracker of Farrowline.'

That's it. When I hug myself around the middle and step back so that he can jump in the driver's seat, I hold myself together watching the males pull away. I know that I will see them soon enough. That Gracie will have a mating ceremony that I refuse to miss and that Maddy will come up in the summer for a break from her brothers, but I hate watching them go.

Tobias steps beside me and pulls me against his monstrous frame.

Resting my head against his solid side, I reassure him that I'm fine and know he can scent the lie as much as I can.

Chapter Fifty Eight

'Tobias,' I knock on the door and wait for him to wave me inside. It's only early morning but the Alpha is in full work mode. I take a seat on one of the comfy chairs across from his massive desk. The view from his office always takes my breath away. The space is large with a whole sitting area and a private bathroom. Tobias indicates that he will be right with me with a small gesture as he gets up and heads to the mini fridge in the back corner. He grabs a juice and a soda and while he talks business to whomever is on the phone he is holding between his face and shoulder, he comes over to offer me the two options. Both are my favourite.

I can't help but smile and take the soda. I watch Tobias head back to the fridge, replace the juice with a water and place it down on the desk. He comes back over to me, opens my drink and hands it back. Never missing a beat with his client. Tobias's voice fills the space while I find the nerve to discuss what I came here to talk about.

It's been a hard week.

For days, I sat at pack barbecues and tried to stay within the conversations. I went on patrol and barely leashed my wolf, who refuses to allow anyone to treat me anything other than a leader. Which has stunned a number of dominants. I walked around at work and attempted to speak to clients and have lunches with my packmates like I used to.

I sat in Circle meetings and agreed when decisions are made. I helped Mama and my mum and assisted Ridley with Luna business when all I wanted to do was sit in the woods and practice my tracker abilities.

Tobias gets off his call and sits across from me in his large, CEO, Alpha, chair.

'It's nice to see you, Gilly. You've been a bit absent this week.' It's not an accusation, more like an observation. His green eyes study me and I realise that in this meeting there will be nowhere to hide.

'Yes, sorry Tobias, I've had a lot on my mind.'

Tobias nods as if in understanding. 'I know you do. Adjusting back to normal must be hard, especially after what you had to do in Coltonline.' He waits as if expecting me to add something. I don't and I watch as understanding flicks across his face. 'You learnt a great deal in the south, didn't you?' I'm very aware that he is trying to use his Alpha senses to work out my energy and my emotions and has found me not so easily readable.

'I learnt more than I could've ever expected,' I confess, a little ashamed that I had to leave my pack to understands myself. I feel his salty sadness on my tongue. 'I'm sorry.'

Green, piercing eyes flash to my face. 'You never have to be sorry to me, Gilly. You left Farrowline when you needed space to learn who you are and you did that. Now, you need to work out how we move forward.'

I love that he understands what I came here today to speak about. 'That's why I'm here. Tobias, I have appreciated everything that you do for me. Ridley and you are my lifelines but I need some time and space to allow myself to continue to grow.' Tobias sits back in his seat. His tree-trunk arms around his middle. 'I would like permission to live in the cabin at the edge of territory that Delfina and Dom sometimes use and…I'd like to take some time away from Farrow Group.'

Tobias sighs as if he was worried I'd ask things like this. 'Gil, I don't want you to isolate yourself from Pack—'

'I'm not,' I cut him off. 'Truly.'

'Is this about Jay and Katrina still?' I shake my head, deeply embarrassed that he'd ask me that.

'No,' I say simply. 'You can be assured that I'm definitely over that.' I saw Jay in the pack's makeshift hospital in Kieran's den. The healer of Farrowline gave me a few minutes to speak to my old partner and his new mate. They were hesitant at first by my appearance but after they heard what I had to say, they were a great deal warmer towards me. We won't be having dinner together anytime soon, but there is no more animosity and tension between us anymore. I made sure they understood that.

'I just need my own space at the moment. I'll still do my duties and patrols.' I wait patiently, emotions locked behind the wall I've learnt to create in my mind. Tobias doesn't need my rolling emotions interfering with his permission to go to the cabin for a while. If he could feel how hard it is for me at the moment, he would say no and try to fix everything for me. Which I love him for but I need to do this on my own.

Banner was right, I don't think I can move forward with anything until I learn who I am. The wise bastard's voice is still haunting me.

'Okay Gilly. Do what you need to do. However, if you start to withdraw and isolate yourself, I'll send Jax and Dominic to come and get you.'

I laugh and thank him with a smile, knowing that he is telling the truth.

Chapter Fifty Nine

'I saw something!'

Hunting, I block out the noise of the argument happening behind me right now as best as I can. There is something odd here.

'You can't call for help if you think you see something strange, Jenny. What does strange even mean?' Gregor barks at the younger female. The male is getting on my nerves.

I was sitting with Delfina in the section of the forest used for the dominants to rest and relax when we heard Jenny's howl for help. To say that the majority of wolf shifters relaxing around the clearing jumped up and responded is not an understatement.

'She isn't lying,' Darrow defends his packmate while Chase nods profusely. The trio are always up to something, however, they've done the right thing. Darrow is Dominic's cousin, Chase is his best friend and are now defending the female they both love. Darrow and Jenny fight constantly but they are fated. Not that anyone knows that. Maybe Tobias does and is why he never really steps in when the pair get into one of their moments.

I have no idea why I didn't wake up and see that what Jay and I had a different kind of love. Love, yes. But not mating love. Jenny and Darrow smell connected and I can see the colour strain that runs between them. It's faint and new and I wonder if they realise that they're already in their mating dance. This is the most time I've spent with my packmates in days and it's all getting a bit much. I've been working at the cabin, making it liveable. My mum and Ridley helped, despite my attempts to get them to let me do it alone. I appreciated them though. Ridley went a bit crazy with the new furniture and had half the pack assemble everything for me. She even had someone come in and fix the pipes so that I could have a fancy fridge with a water dispenser. Rid has been itching to get her hands on the cabin for months, in her eyes it was creepy and outdated.

I felt bad taking away Delfina and Dom's "sex cabin" but they were cool about me making it my own. Delfina was a little too forthcoming with how they don't need the cabin anyways, that their sex life was beyond healthy. It was too much information.

'Enough,' I say, very calmly and am ignored. Delfina left to investigate further in territory where I asked her to follow my instincts. Meaning, I'm the most senior dominant here right now. An argument explodes and Darrow starts telling Gregor that he's not allowed to speak to Jenny so poorly and then starts getting into trouble by Molly and Gregor about showing respect.

'I said enough!' I bark, very aware of Oliver and Jax coming between the trees. It doesn't stop me from acting on this issue. Maybe a few months ago, I would've waited for them to come and sort this shit out, but not anymore.

The fight stops and I'm now the centre of attention. Males and females that have known me my entire life look at me like they are seeing me for the first time. And you know…maybe they are.

Standing tall, making sure that my emotions are in check, I growl. 'When I say enough, I mean, enough! Gregor, Jenny did nothing wrong by calling for help.' I watch as his brow furrows and he goes to respond, '*and,*' I emphasise the word, making sure he knows that I haven't stopped speaking, 'there is something out here.'

That has everyone hesitate. There is a moment of silence as everyone comes to terms with the deeper power play that is happening right now. We can all feel it. Our wolves are close to the surface, scenting the air. Assessing me and my ability to lead their pack and families through good times and bad.

'What do we need to do, Gilly?' Molly asks, stepping away from Gregor. Her question has me almost sigh in relief. She accepts my word and has shown everyone that she will listen to me.

'We scout the area. There isn't an intruder, however, there's something out here. Something I don't like.' I begin to give directions of where I want everyone to go and then begin to head to the edge of territory lines.

'You can't,' Gregor starts, stepping forward like he's going to stop me from exiting territory. The group goes quiet to watch the exchange.

My focus slowly moves to the larger male. There was a point in my life that everything Gregor said, I'd do. The male has my respect but I clearly don't have his. 'I can do whatever I think is necessary for the protection and safety of Farrowline. I am a Circle wolf and your leader, Gregor. It's about time you remind yourself of that because the next time you question me, we will have an issue.'

He doesn't like what I've just said but he doesn't need to. 'I apologise, Gilly. We aren't allowed to step outside of territory lines.'

I take a breath and scent his protectiveness. I'm not angry about that, it is who is he. 'Yes, all of you are not allowed to step from territory lines as the Alpha has said, however, I'm not the young female you all see me as. I am blood bound to our Luna and our Alpha and am a leader of this Pack despite my age and my history with you all. My wolf and I have earnt this position through hard work and a hunt that saw me look into the eyes of pure evil.' I'm grandstanding, I know I am. However, this needs to be said. Everyone is staring wide eyed at me. Most of them are concerned. All of them are listening though.

'We can see that you are different,' Molly adds kindly. 'It's hard for us though, Gilly. I held you as a pup.'

Nodding, I understand that. 'I get it. I just would like you all to accept that I am not that female anymore. That I am a tracker and a leader. I have seen what happens when a pack is disjointed. I have seen the horror of betrayal. That is not Farrowline. And I will have your respect or you can take your concerns to Alpha Tobias and the Circle and raise your issues to them.' My gaze flicks to the two males standing in the trees watching me. Oliver's piercing gaze holds mine before I look away slowly. He has been distant lately. Barely speaking to me. Barely acknowledging my presence despite the weird moment we had in the forest when I arrived home. 'I have given instructions,' I say. 'Go and search the area, look low and high.'

Gregor is the last to leave but nods as he goes while I head to the edge of territory and step over.

Chapter Sixty

'That was interesting,' Oliver states and I fight the need to roll my eyes. My focus is on the weird scent that is drawing me into some thick shrubs. Jax is keeping his distance as he always does when I'm on a hunt. He's totally oblivious to the fact that he could never go far enough away from me so that I can't smell him.

'It's what I've had to deal with from the moment I became a Circle wolf,' I say tiredly. I thought things would change when I got back to pack. It seems I was wrong.

'What?' Oliver's rage takes up the entire forest and I stop walking to understand what's wrong. I look around, drawing on the colours of every scent signature. 'Gilly!'

Swinging around, I'm so lost. There is no danger and then I see the look on his face. The outrage that is staring back at me. 'What's wrong?'

Oliver looks like he is going to explode. 'You never told us that! If I had known that this is how the dominants were treating you, then I would've fixed it.'

Shaking my head in exasperation, I have no power over my own anger. 'That's the problem!' I shout, completely over it. Oliver's face hardens.

'You can't fix it. Having you all come to my rescue doesn't make anyone respect me or make them take me seriously as a dominant female with a wolf that has value in this pack. I need to prove my worth to you all and that is the only way I am going to get their loyalty and respect!' I want to pull my hair out, I'm so furious. Jax hasn't moved and keeps watching me closely.

'What else has happened that we don't know about?' Oliver demands to know.

'I don't know!' I try to stomp away and then swing around when a large hand grips mine. The heat of it is shocking and while I have held Oliver's hand many times, the spark that sizzles along my skin has me pull away quickly. Oliver doesn't seem to notice. He is waiting impatiently for me to tell him.

'Is that why you went to Coltonline?'

'What do you want me to say, Oliver? That I went to Coltonline because my wolf wanted to hunt or that I left to run away from the suffocating hole that I had placed myself in by trying to drown my heartache and confusion under a mountain of alcohol and poor choices?' I snap. The tears stream down my face. Each one tracked by the male standing before me. His expression grim. 'Do you all want to know that before I went to Coltonline, I was drowning under these tracker abilities that have only been getting worse each and every day since I gave my blood oath to Ridley and that I needed to leave to try and find myself?' I'm panting, I'm so worked up.

'Yes,' Oliver states so simply that I frown in confusion. *Is that all he has to say to me?* That is exactly what we, that I, want to hear. You see, you seem to have forgotten that just because you are a leader in Farrowline that you are somehow on your own in all this.' He waves his arms around, indicating to territory. 'If you had opened up, Gil, you would've learnt that I was a fucking terrible leader in my first three years.'

Jax laughs in the distance while my jaw hits the floor at what I'm hearing. 'You were?'

'Yes, he really was,' Jax pipes in and I look to the big, bulky beast of a male. His yellow eyes are kind and reassuring. I love Jax so much. He makes me feel like I am the only one in the world. 'And so was I,' he confesses honestly. 'You have to remember that Tobias, Dom, Oliver and I were young too when we became leaders. We lost so many of our senior dominants in the Vestraline attack that we had no choice but to stand up and lead. Nicolette too. To be honest, we weren't ready for the responsibility. We were young. I was making dumb choices and partying hard, until I become Gamma. Long before I was ready.'

His words have me cry a fresh wave of tears. 'I really needed to hear that.' I want to scream and shout and hug them both.

'And we should have told you and seen the problems.' Oliver sounds dejected and I step into his warmth for a moment, despite how he tenses and wrap my arms around his middle.

'Thank you, for telling me now.'

Jax's oversized hand come to rest on the top of my head. 'You will carve out your place in Farrowline, Gil. No one here questions your ability and worth as a Tracker and a leader. It might take time, but you are a Circle wolf for a reason. Don't let it change you though. We still want and need our kind-hearted Gilly who would do anything for the pack. We still want *you*.'

Pulling away from Oliver, I feel a little self-conscious as those crystal eyes take me in and I turn back to why I'm out here, outside of territory lines. Walking into the scrubs with two forces of nature behind me, protecting me and keeping me safe, I bend down and wipe away the leaves that have been touched by scents that hint to intruders. Hitting the device that has been staked into the ground, I jump up and am pulled to Oliver's side like I've just uncovered a poisonous snake that might bite me.

Jax crouches down and growls. 'It's a camera. They are watching our territory lines.'

Oliver swears and pulls out his phone.

'Why?' I ask, thinking I know the answer.

'Intel, I imagine. They are tracking us.'

That has me baring my teeth. 'Loners are tracking our lines. It's Cade. I know it is.' I can't smell him, but there is a stench in the air.

'How did we miss this? How long has it been here?' Jax asks me and I shrug. They aren't new. The scents are a few weeks old. Maybe a month and a half.

'Can you find the rest?' Oliver asks, hanging up the phone from a very grumpy Alpha and Beta.

'Of course I can,' I tsk and then smile wickedly when the blue eyed, beautiful male tells me to hunt.

Chapter Sixty One

The tension is thick against my tongue and I shuffle in my seat at the table, torn between running outside to escape it and finding a strong drink to wash away the taste. Tobias is furious. He is pacing back and forth at the closed doors that lead to the outside area of his den and I kinda wish someone would open them. I didn't think I'd miss Coltonline so much but those wolf shifters understood the issues I faced because of their uncle.

I found countless recording devices along the border of our territory. They were far enough away from the line that we couldn't see them but still close enough that whoever is watching could see our patrols.

'I can't believe that we missed this. How did we miss this!' Dominic demands to no one in particular. Everyone is on edge. The entire pack is on lockdown with many of our dominants on patrol. We in the Circle have only just come in from territory lines. Liam and Easton are still out there, keeping everyone on high alert. We're worried that disabling the devices might send more loners out here to investigate. And on top of that, we have just been notified of a massive storm that will hit Sylo at the end of the week, with concerns of flooding and damages.

I can't care though. All I can think about is how bad it smells here and how I really need to leave. 'Excuse me,' I say quietly, jumping up and rushing down the hall towards one of the many bathrooms in this den.

Opening the door, I hurry into the space, not fully closing the door behind me and try to get the damn window open to let in some fresh air. Ridley has some kind of scented candle in the space and I don't want to throw up but there is bile rising in the back of my throat. Too preoccupied and sensory overloaded, I don't sense Oliver until he is standing right behind me, his body trapping mine against the side wall. His hands beside my head opening the window for me so that I can stick my face out into the night. Sucking in lungful's of air, I close my eyes and control my breathing.

'Better?'

'Yes,' I croak out becoming very aware of the heat pressed in behind me. Of the way his sandalwood and citrus scent reminds me of home and safety. I hear the top draw of the vanity being opened and closed.

I expect Oliver to back away but he doesn't, he just starts collecting my hair and begins to tie it back with a hairband he must have found. I hate having my hair out when I'm not feeling the best and it warms me to know that Oliver understands that. This males knows me.

'You good?'

I nod, not wanting to answer because I fear my voice will be too husky. He smells amazing and even though he is my friend, I'm beginning to think about things I'm not sure if I should be thinking about. Things have changed between us though. He and I both feel it.

'Good.'

Turning slowly, I lean against the wall and window frame and watch as the large male picks up the burning candle beside the sink and blows it out just before he flicks the switch on the wall to start the vents.

'Thanks.'

He shrugs, mimicking the way I'm resting against the wall by doing the same to the vanity. Our feet are almost touching. 'It reeked enough to give me a headache, I can't imagine how that was for you.'

'Really fucking smelly,' I confess and giggle when he laughs loudly.

'I bet.' He throws me a genuine smile that has my heart sing and pound at the same time. I spoke badly to him in the forest and regret how I shouted. He seems to pick up on my regret because he says, 'Gilly, you don't need to apologise or say anything. What happened today was needed. We both needed it. I'm just sorry I didn't see what the problems were or that you felt you couldn't come to me for help. Now, why did being out there make you feel so sick? I want to understand better.'

I open and close my mouth, unsure how to respond and so used to keeping my overbearing tracker abilities to myself. In that moment, I find myself confused by my own behaviour. *Why did I cut them out of this?*

'You don't want to tell me?' I watch as his eyebrow rises in accusation.

'I guess I'm just so used to hiding the struggle to keep myself together,' I confess, unable to not open up to him. This is a male who has held my hair back when I was drunk and vomited everywhere. He's a male I've run to on multiple occasions to help me. I've shared meals with him. A bed with him. Have watched in secret awe of how amazing a leader he has become around Farrowline.

'Why do you think you need to hide?' There is no accusation in his tone. Oliver wraps those tree trunk arms around his body and waits patiently for me to respond. He is blocking the door and I know from past experience that he can stand there all night until I respond.

'I don't want others to judge me. I feel like no one will understand and I don't feel like everyone should change their behaviour or stop burning smelly candles just because of me,' I blurt out, feeling like a fool.

Oliver tsks me...like a good old fashion Mama tsk, and I can't help but chuckle. 'You think that we want you to be in pain or struggle through a Circle meeting or a barbecue or any other event? No one wants that and if we have to stop the candles and make sure windows are open or control our emotions a bit better then it isn't a hard ask. We would do anything for you, Gil. I would do anything for you.' His words hang in the small space between us. The colours around us dance and shimmer and I follow the one that leads from my chest to his. It is dim, a light that confuses me greatly because I can't remember if it's new or not. I can't remember when it formed or if it was there yesterday.

'You still okay staying at the cabin or are you ready to come back to Pack?' Oliver's voice is different and I look up from the strand linking him to me and frown at the confusing expression on his face. I can't shake the feeling that what he's asking has a deeper meaning. Like he's enquiring if I need more time before we speak about this energy between us.

'I need more time,' I whisper and watch as he nods.

'Then that is what you will have.'

Chapter Sixty Two

Walking silently through territory, I draw on the colour in the wind and find peace here in Farrowline.

'What are you doing?'

'Getting Jax's watch before the storm starts,' I tell the male who comes from the trees. I don't look up, I knew he was coming. 'I meant to do it a few days ago but the extra patrols have kept me busy.' They've kept all of us busy. I haven't seen Oliver since the last Circle meeting and I'm kinda regretting not working at Farrow Group anymore. I miss the lunches I'd have with him or the casual conversations in the staff room.

'You know the storm is about to hit soon?'

'Not for another half hour or so,' I reply absently.

'You know exactly when the storm is going to hit?' Oliver asks like he doesn't believe me.

I throw him a 'don't insult me' kind of look which makes him put his hands up in submission dramatically. I can't help but chuckle.

'I think there's a great deal that you don't know about me.' I'm half teasing, half serious.

'We had this conversation on the phone already, didn't we?' He smiles that grin that allows him to get away with anything.

'Why are you out here?'

'I came to check that you were safe out here on your own in the cabin. Your mum said that you hadn't been to the dens to pick up any of the prepared food so I wanted to make sure you were okay.'

'I didn't know there was food waiting for me. I've been so focused on the cabin and patrols and my tracker training.' I would never have willingly missed food.

'Tracker training?' Oliver questions and I look up to see him frowning at me.

'Um, yeah. I met a tracker in Coltonline and he gave some exercises that help me to stay focused on my abilities.'

I can tell that I've stunned him. 'Coltonline had a tacker?'

Damn. 'Uhhh, not technically.'

Oliver makes a deep sound that tells me I've been busted. 'What does that mean?'

'It's a long story,' I offer and walk a little faster.

Oliver falls into step beside me. We walk in silence but I know he will question me later. The rain is going to start soon, I can taste it in the air. Jax sent out a detailed message to us all to brace ourselves. I head straight for the place his watch is buried under some leaves. In all fairness, he wouldn't have been able to find it without someone like me helping. We are deep in territory, in a section not used much by others. It's patrolled, but its far enough away from territory lines to never be much of a problem area. Good for training purposes and I guess that's why Jax and Dom were out here in the first place training some of the younger dominants.

Bending down, I brush away the dirt and sticks burying the watch and pick it up. It's an expensive piece but I also know it's a watch that his uncle gave him when he was younger and means a great deal to Jax. I hold it out for Oliver and look away quickly when I see the admiration in his eyes. It makes me feel all hot and bothered, which is confusing. Oliver is...well, Oliver. Since the battle with Elliot in that clearing and his face flashed through my mind when I thought I was going to die, my mind and body have been thinking and feeling some strange things.

The wind picks up pretty quickly and I grab the hand Oliver offers, the male is powerless to his instinct to protect and get me out of this storm.

It's a big one.

A monster storm.

I step back from the window as it begins to rattle with the force of the wind and rain. It's pitch black and I look over my shoulder at the male whistling in the kitchen as he stirs the food he's preparing on the small electric stove. When we got back to the cabin nestled in deep forest, I saw the pile of bags that he had brought over for me. It was full of food and supplies to bunker down for the next few days. The information Jax sent said that we can expect this kind of weather system for three days before it passes Sylo. One of those once in a lifetime storms.

'Come eat, Gil.'

Loving the excuse to get away from the window, I sit at the small four seater table that was originally in the cabin. Despite the new furniture like the king sized bed against the wall and the new television and cosy four seater lounge across from it, I haven't replaced it yet. The cabin is a small studio space with a kitchenette against the back wall and the bathroom to the left. The fireplace has been cleaned and fixed up so that a healthy fire is crackling, warming the space and adding to the relaxing vibe that I needed by moving out here.

'You got a new rug,' Oliver states, placing a bowl of steaming hot curry before me. It's one of my favourite Adalee recipes. I look around for the bread and do a little happy dance when the male comes back from the counter with a plate. He chuckles at my moving body and finds me something to drink from all the supplies we were given.

'I thought it was time to get rid of the dusty rug that is older than Mama,' I say between mouthfuls. It's so hot but I keep shovelling it into my mouth, barely chewing. I haven't eaten since breakfast.

The floors of the cabin are solid timber. There are only two windows in the space, one next to the door and one behind the kitchen sink. Both giving me a show of the storm.

Oliver sits down beside me with more plates to lay out between us. His hand comes over to grip the one I have clutched around my fork and I finally realise that I was staring at the lightning illuminating the sky.

'This is an old cabin but it's strong. We are safe in here. You are safe with me.'

I find myself instantly calming under his touch.

CHAPTER SIXTY THREE

'Come on, lets watch a movie on this massive new television.' Oliver laughs at the flatscreen that was delivered the second day I moved out here. It's so fancy that I have no idea what any of the buttons do. I just know on and off and the streaming icons to press. 'Did Jax pick this one?'

'Yep, best in the store.' I chuckle and pull the bowl of popcorn into my lap. I lay my back against a cushion and throw my legs on the lounge so that my feet are pressed just under his thigh. He just laughs, knowing exactly the kind of fuss Jax would've made in the tech shop to buy me a television. It didn't matter that I gave him a budget and that he didn't listen to the zero's I had instructed was my limit. Jax purchased me the device and growled at me when I asked how much it was. The sweet, oversized idiot.

We flick on a silly action film that starts weirdly on a docked boat and then both sit a little awkward as the first scene morphs into a very explicit sex scene. The air around us sizzles and brightens and I clear my throat and try to remember how to eat when everything on the screen gets hotter and hotter. There is a lot of panting and moaning and honestly, I worry for a moment that I've pressed some kind of button and turned on the porn channel.

Oliver throws me the side eye when I shuffle, completely involuntarily I might add, and then tries to stay focused on the film. He sits in all his hotness at the other end of the couch. His massive frame taking up most of the space so that my knees are bent.

The cabin is dark. The fire is crackling and I swear, the entire scenario is not helping me to get control over my emotions. The wall I have learnt to cover my scent is slowly crumbling and while Oliver is strong and powerful, I can still pick up on the fact that he's struggling too. We are friends though and I refuse to jeopardise that. Also I said I wouldn't do this without a mating bond. Yes, I feel a connection to Oliver and yes, I want to forget that I've known him my entire life, but I...I...

Those crystal blue eyes flow slowly to me and I look up at the male whose wolf is staring back at me. Everything between us is charged, like in the forest when I returned. I watch as the thread leading to my chest to his flickers and flashes before growing just a little darker and I gasp at the realisation of what it could be. Testing it, knowing he is watching me, I sniff the air and stare wide eyed at the male studying me patiently as if waiting for me to work it out. The bowl of popcorn slips from my useless, heavy arms and collides with the floor in a dramatic heap. The plastic bounces on the wood and litters the ground.

'Wha...Oliver?' I'm afraid to move. Afraid that this is wrong. In a single moment, I feel my world teetering on a cliff and fear that in one puff of wind, I'll fall harder than I've ever before. This is not a game and Oliver knows it, he most definitely has known it longer than me. All males hear it before the females.

It all makes perfect sense now. The battle and seeing his face. The need to call him all the time. The way I've followed him around my entire life, wanting and needing his attention. The way, I'd rip out my heart in order to keep him safe. The strand that flows now brightly between us. I crave his scent and I have been so dumb.

Oliver nods grimly, like he is unsure how I'm going to react. 'I've known since the moment you got back to Farrowline. I felt the bond. I can't believe that after all these years you were right there.' He offers his story of how he realised what we were. 'I had to keep my distance at first. It's been a bit hard to wrap my head around it.'

My heart sinks. He doesn't sound too impressed at the idea that I am his mate and it stings a little.

'When you were gone, Gil. I felt like someone had torn me in two. I couldn't eat. I couldn't sleep. I had no idea why I was acting so strangely until I saw you with that damn loner's throat in your mouth, standing like the powerful and amazing female that you are.'

Words fail me. I know Oliver is waiting for me to respond, but I've lost the ability. I've been through hell. I've made such dumb fucking choices and I have been broken down pretty hard. Banner's words come filtering through my mind and I reminisce on what he said to me. He told me that a mating bond wouldn't come until I discovered who I am.

'I have worked so hard,' I begin, not able to hide the tremor in my voice. 'These last few months, I have tried to discover who I am. To find harmony and balance within my own body. Between my wolf and my human again.'

Oliver frowns. 'I know that this is not an ideal time. We can wait, Gil. I know you are taking steps to find yourself. This cabin and leaving Farrow Group. I don't want to get in the way of all that,' he states firmly. 'I won't get in the way of that.'

His words rest comfortably against my chest, reminding me who he is. Oliver Tyler with his long, mousey hair and his beard and stunning eyes has always been behind me, guiding me or providing space. In that moment, staring into his eyes, seeing his wolf, I know that isolating myself is not the answer to my problems. I don't want to be George. I don't want to hide behind a wall so that my emotions and scent can't be picked up.

So I drop it completely and watch as Oliver's eyes widen at the scent in the air. At the energy I am projecting. I see a single tear drop from the corner of his eyes and I feel it in my soul.

He has been a solid rock for me my entire life. A male who knows me inside and out. It just took me finding out who I was and accepting myself for me to open enough to find my mate. To realise that Oliver is the other half of my soul.

'Oliver,' I whisper, the space between us is alive with so much information that I fear I might pass-out. It's so much to process. 'You are my mate,' I finish and react when he does.

CHAPTER SIXTY FOUR

Oliver lunges for me as I push myself from my half lying position and we collide with teeth and hands and words of love and affection. He is everywhere. Completely surrounding me. My nervousness from before has evaporated to be replaced by the bond that now vibrates with life between us. A bond so secure and strong that even death couldn't break it.

We're a storm of emotions and lust, matching the intensity of the wind and rain beating against the walls and roof of the cabin.

I can't get enough. His scent and tongue has lit a match inside me and the fire burning between us is ferocious.

Arms and legs wrapped around his body, I hold on, knowing that he has me safe and secure. We move around the cabin, bumping into tables and walls. Panting and moaning, I become the human girl from the movie as things smash onto the floor and we knock over breakable shit that crashes to the hard wood. I frantically pull at his shirt, needing to get to his skin. My wolf needing to feel that heat and maleness. Right. This. Minute.

Oliver doesn't disappoint. He dumps my arse on the kitchen table, pushing all the contents onto the floor and moves back a little so he can pull his shirt over his head. My mouth waters at the sight, my legs are locked around his waist, refusing to let him go and I lick my lips. He is solid muscle. An eight-pack glistens before me and I don't care that I'm practically drooling everywhere.

He is my mate. A male who completes my soul and I finally look up and see the emotions on his face as he stares down at me. Hand coming up to cup my cheek, I lean into the caress.

'You are mine Gilly Sommers.' I feel the tears slip down my cheeks and grab at my shirt to peel it off. Oliver helps and then steps back so that he can look at me. I'm half naked, my breasts on display and I don't feel at all self-conscious. He is my mate.

The look in his eye does help. Like he is the luckiest male alive, he stands, jaw slack as he takes me all in.

'I will love and protect you for the rest of my days and in every life after this one.' His voice never wavers, even when I lean forward, legs dangling as I stay seated on the table and start to open his belt. His eyes stay fixed on mine as he helps to remove his pants. I don't know when he turned the television off but the only light in the cabin is the roaring fire. I don't need light though and when he stands tall and I get a full glimpse of his body I nearly come apart at the seams.

I am the luckiest fucking female in the world. He is perfection. Totally and utterly perfect. Not just because of the washboard abs and the muscular thighs and arms or the fact that his entire shoulder spans two of my own. Or the fact that his hair is shinier and falls around his body better than mine does or that the stylish long beard makes me all wet and ready for him. It isn't fully about the monstrous, mouth-watering sight of his thick dick jutting out between us.

It's the way he makes me feel like I am the centre of his existence. I have never had anyone look at me with such...devotion, as the way he is looking at me now. Like I am a gift that he will forever be grateful for. He is the kindest, fiercest males I know. He is protective and a little bossy but he is always there when I need someone to lift me up or listen when I need an ear.

'Everything I have is yours,' he continues, bridging the gap between us. Our eyes are locked and I'm unable to look away. I don't want to as he binds us together forever. 'Gilly, will you stand by my side and protect my back like I will forever protect yours? Will you take my name and build a family and den with me? Will you continue to make me a better male and teach me what it means to be mated to a tracker so that I can always support you and take care of you like I hope you will take care of me.'

His words are too much, too sweet, and I hurry off the table and remove my own pants under his watchful eyes. They burn with an intensity that has me dripping for him. Without a word, he grips my hips and lifts me back when I am fully nude and sits me on the table. I spread my legs, making room for him and he places himself between them. His erection teasing my entrance.

Oliver waits, his right hand on my face leaning my head back to that he can look me in the eye. We just stare, mouths closed, panting each other's air. My tracker nose is going ballistic and is heightening this experience as it feeds off our arousal, my mates love for me. I have never experienced anything like this before.

'Oliver,' I say, unsure how I'm able to speak right now. 'I am honoured to be your mate.' His hand moves from my face and before I know it, his scorching hands grip my hips and he pushes into me in a single thrust that has my back arching into his chest and my head flies back as I scream out his name. He doesn't move though and his firm grip keeps me in place.

Opening my eyes, I stare into those blue depths and smile at what I see. 'Everything I have is yours. I will protect your back and always find you when you need me,' I add, my wolf needing him to know that there is nowhere he can run now, that he is mated to a Tracker. Oliver grins the smuggest male grin I have ever seen and gifts me by pulling out and slamming back in. I swear loudly. He feels so good. I groan.

'I will take your name.' Thrust. 'And build a family and den with you.' Thrust. Thrust.

I cry out under the intensity of him inside me. My wolf is going crazy and I claw at his large shoulders. The mighty male doesn't care. He just keeps torturing me.

'You're already the most perfect of males and I couldn't ask for a better mate than you. You are mine.' He begins to move faster. Giving me what I want. And fucking hell, it is everything I want. 'And I am yours.'

Oliver offers me his wrist as he pounds into me and I do the same. My canines nip the flesh and we complete the mating bond. That seems to snap the leash he was trying to control himself with because he pulls me off the table and with our bodies still locked, we fall onto the bed.

We don't leave it for two days.

Chapter Sixty Five

I think we broke the pack. Everyone was completely stunned and for the first time in my entire life, no one spoke. I have never experienced it before.

We came from the cabin after four days of learning everything about each other. I told him every detail from my trip to Coltonline and he opened up about details of himself that I didn't know. We barely got out of bed and thanks to the storm that lasted three days, we weren't really questioned.

Now, we stand, hand in hand in the Alpha's den for a Circle meeting and wait for everyone to absorb this information. Jax's jaw is in his lap. Easton and Delfina have the same shocked expression on their face. Dominic is wiping the water he spat everywhere when we first walked in. Nicolette is typing away at her laptop, while she stares at us over the top of her screen. I can't read her expression.

Ridley is dabbing at her eyes to hide the fact that she's so happy she is crying and Tobias just nods like he expected this all along which he probably did, *damn alphas and their power.*

Tobias stands up from his seat and we all watch as he makes his way over to us. His focus is on Oliver and then moves slowly to me. The love in his energy is enough to have me turn into a blubbering mess and when Oliver's arm comes over to pull me into his side, I'm powerless to the emotions of the moment.

'Someone needs to crack a window, the happiness in this den is overwhelming,' I joke and laugh when Jax hops up to do what I've said. Everyone starts cheering when Tobias pulls me from my mate and wraps me into his comforting embrace. 'I can't tell you how relieved I am that you have found your happiness, Gilly. There aren't many wolves that would leave everything they've ever known to help others. You are selfless and courageous and I am so immensely proud of you.'

That's all that is left to say. The Circle gets up and hugs and laughs and kisses and I find myself no longer worried about my place in Farrowline. That my self-doubt was based on a fear of myself which I don't have anymore. I know who I am. I know what my wolf can do and I know that no matter what I have the support of a group of dominant wolf shifters who would give their life for me.

Smiling up at the male staring down at me, I detach myself from Tobias and fall into his waiting arms.

'I'm bored, let's go back to the cabin,' Oliver purrs in my ear, his words have me shiver in need.

'You're not bored,' I tease, tilting my head so that his lips can find my neck.

'Yeah, I am.' Fuck, I'm in trouble. His voice alone is setting me on fire.

'You are mated to a tracker now, Oliver, I can scent your lie,' I moan. The rest of the den falls completely away. Oliver and I are so wrapped up in our own bubble of happiness and love that nothing else matters right now.

'Hmmm,' he growls against my face and I actually moan. 'I could never forget that my mate is Gilly Sommers-Tyler, the Tracker of Farrowline.' And with that, my mate whisks me up into his arms and carries me from the den, uncaring that Tobias is shouting at us that we haven't started the meeting yet.

A MONTH LATER...

'Gilly, wait!'

I don't and I can't believe that he thinks that I would. I push harder. My wolf howling into the night, drawing everyone's attention to the potential threat at the edge of the territory. I can feel the others running to meet me. My mate is close to my heels, keeping me safe despite not being impressed that I reacted so fast to the scent that tells me there are newcomers at our lines.

I push harder, my paws almost silent as they fly over the littered forest floor and I pull up short at the border to Farrowline and shift at the sight before me. Oliver is beside me in an instant, his arm out, keeping me behind him as he glares at the two males standing like demons in the night just outside territory lines. I have no intention of staying quiet and pull on every colour in the wind to inform me that these males are different somehow. Wolf shifters. Powerful. Gorgeous and leaking male dominance and arrogance. But still, different.

'Declare yourselves,' Oliver demands, his voice ringing out through the forest, not leaving any room for denial.

His body is close, ready to protect me if needed. My mate. The male who owns every part of me, always putting my needs first. My wolf and I know that we are in no danger. These males have no ill intentions and I watch, interested as they both look to the trees and at the wolves that storm through. Each one shifts and I throw my focus over my shoulder to the female who gasps.

The entire world stills. What the fuck? My focus flies from the female standing in shocked horror at the sight of the two, very attractive and very scary looking males and the two newcomers who are both glaring unhappily at Nicolette Farrow. I have never seen or felt so much emotion from the alpha's sister. Even when her entire family was torn apart by the actions of another pack.

Tobias steps over and demands to know what is going on. His tone is harsh and cuts through the shock.

Oliver moves closer to me, his body pressing into mine, clearly working out that I'm processing a great deal here.

One of the males steps forward, 'Alpha Tobias, we regret to have come unannounced. My name is Diego and this is Luis. We are currently staying with the pack of Rhiattline. We would like safe passage to visit your pack for a time. The Alpha of Rhiattline said he would contact you but it seems that he must have been held up. We mean no disrespect.'

Rhiattline. I look over to Nicolette in shock, needing to know more and loving my tracker nose right now. It's a gossipers best friend! Rhiattline is Mama's birth pack and the pack that she sent Nicolette to a few months ago. Nicolette and a group of females went on a trip and we all know that Mama sent her daughter there in hopes to help her find her mate and it seems...well, fuck!

I follow the dimmed, colourful strand that flows from the male speaking to Nicolette's chest and swallow my apprehension. Nicolette does not seem happy at all. Frankly, she looks like she is ready to kill someone.

But there is something else, something that has my attention and I make a small noise I didn't mean to make and step back into Oliver's chest and clap my hand over my mouth. Everyone is staring at me. The two newcomers are intense and Tobias frowns knowing something is going on.

Nicolette looks to me with a pleading expression that I don't think I can help her with because there isn't just one strand of colour binding her to Diego there is another one linking her and Luis together too.

Meaning...Nicolette's world is about to be shaken, and by the look on her face, I know she will not allow it.

TO BE CONTINUED

BOOK 5 OF
THE PACK OF FARROWLINE
SERIES

COMING SOON

ABOUT THE AUTHOR

A L Rojo is an author, educator, wife and mother who lives in Sydney, Australia. From a young age, she understood the power of getting lost in a good book. After giving herself permission to explore her creativity, she found that she loved writing novels that focus on strong female characters, love, spice, and the wonderful complexities of life. Her goal is to simply create worlds where anyone can escape into, for however long they may need. She says that along this journey she has left behind a piece of herself in every character she creates.

To get the latest updates, follow A L Rojo and The Pack of Farrowline below.

Website: www.alrojo.com.au
Facebook: A L Rojo
Instagram: alrojo_writer